"It was this wonderful time between magic and so-called rationality."

—Wally Feurzeig, co-creator of the Logo programming language, on the early days of Logo

First Second
New York

"Lost & Found" was previously published on Tor.com

Copyright © 2018 by Humble Comics LLC

Published by First Second
First Second is an imprint of Roaring Brook Press,
a division of Holtzbrinck Publishing Holdings Limited Partnership
175 Fifth Avenue, New York, NY 10010

All rights reserved

Library of Congress Control Number: 2017941170

Paperback ISBN: 978-1-62672-607-9
Hardcover ISBN: 978-1-62672-608-6

Our books may be purchased in bulk for promotional, educational,
or business use. Please contact your local bookseller or the Macmillan Corporate
and Premium Sales Department at (800) 221-7945 ext. 5442 or by e-mail at
MacmillanSpecialMarkets@macmillan.com.

FIRST
EDITION

First edition, 2018

Book design by Rob Steen

Printed in China by Toppan Leefung Printing Ltd., Dongguan City, Guangdong Province

Paperback: 10 9 8 7 6 5 4 3 2 1
Hardcover: 10 9 8 7 6 5 4 3 2 1

Chapter

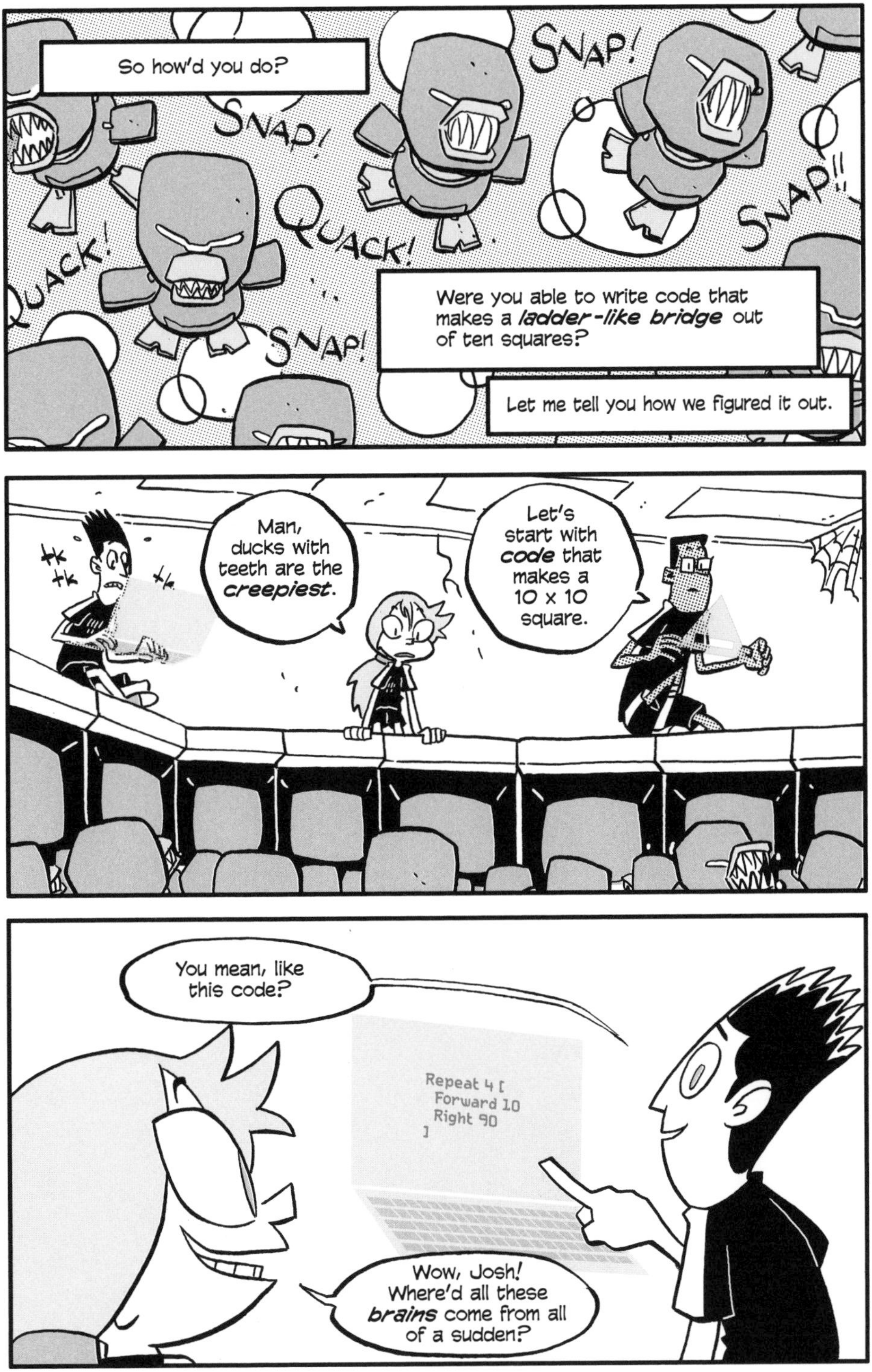
So how'd you do?
SNAP!
SNAP!
QUACK!
QUACK!
SNAP!
SNAP!!
SNAP!
Were you able to write code that makes a *ladder-like bridge* out of ten squares?
Let me tell you how we figured it out.
tk tk
tk
Man, ducks with teeth are the *creepiest*.
Let's start with *code* that makes a 10 x 10 square.
You mean, like this code?
Repeat 4 [
Forward 10
Right 90
]
Wow, Josh! Where'd all these *brains* come from all of a sudden?

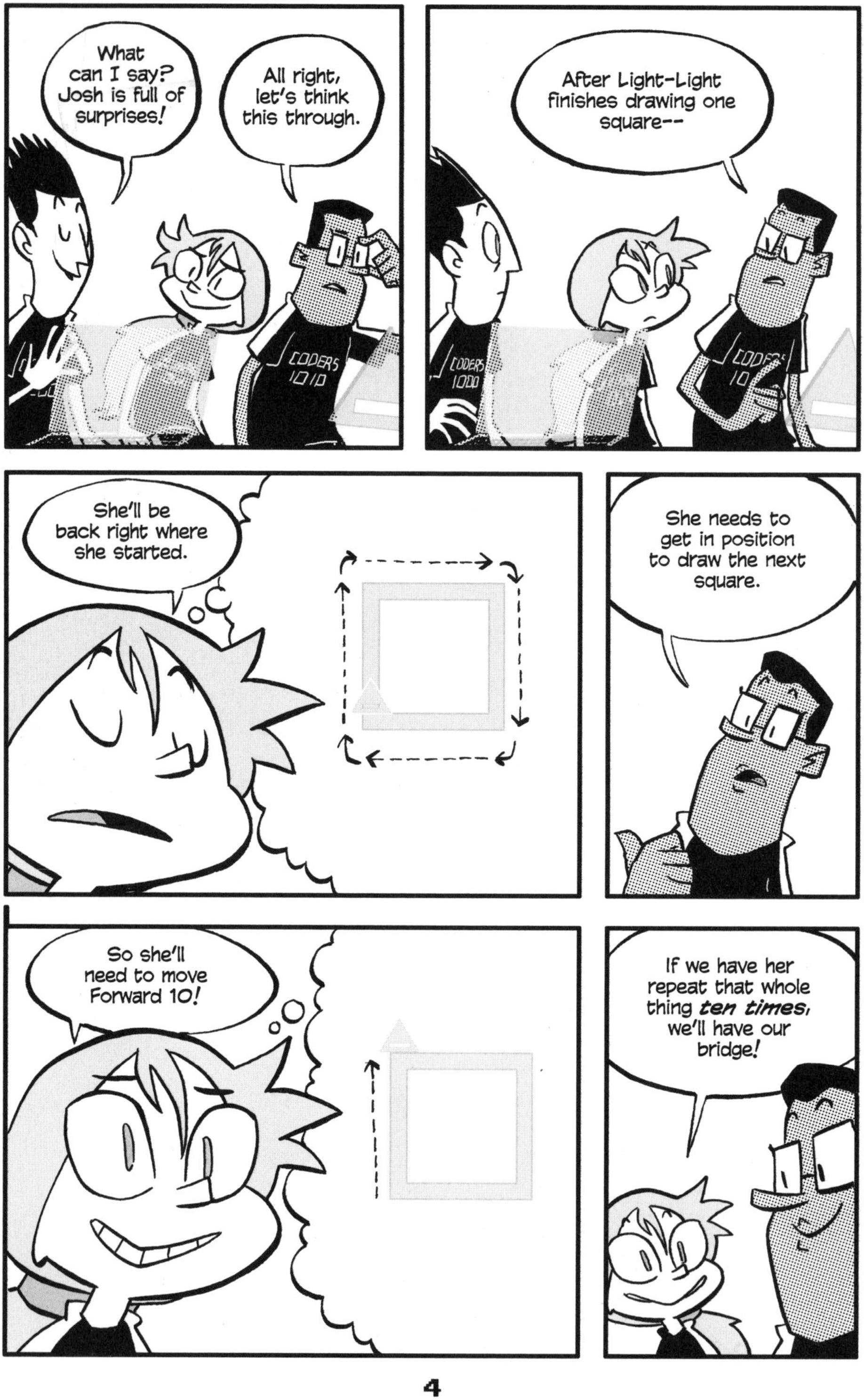
What can I say? Josh is full of surprises!
All right, let's think this through.
CODERS 1010
After Light-Light finishes drawing one square--
CODERS 1010
She'll be back right where she started.
She needs to get in position to draw the next square.
So she'll need to move Forward 10!
If we have her repeat that whole thing ***ten times***, we'll have our bridge!

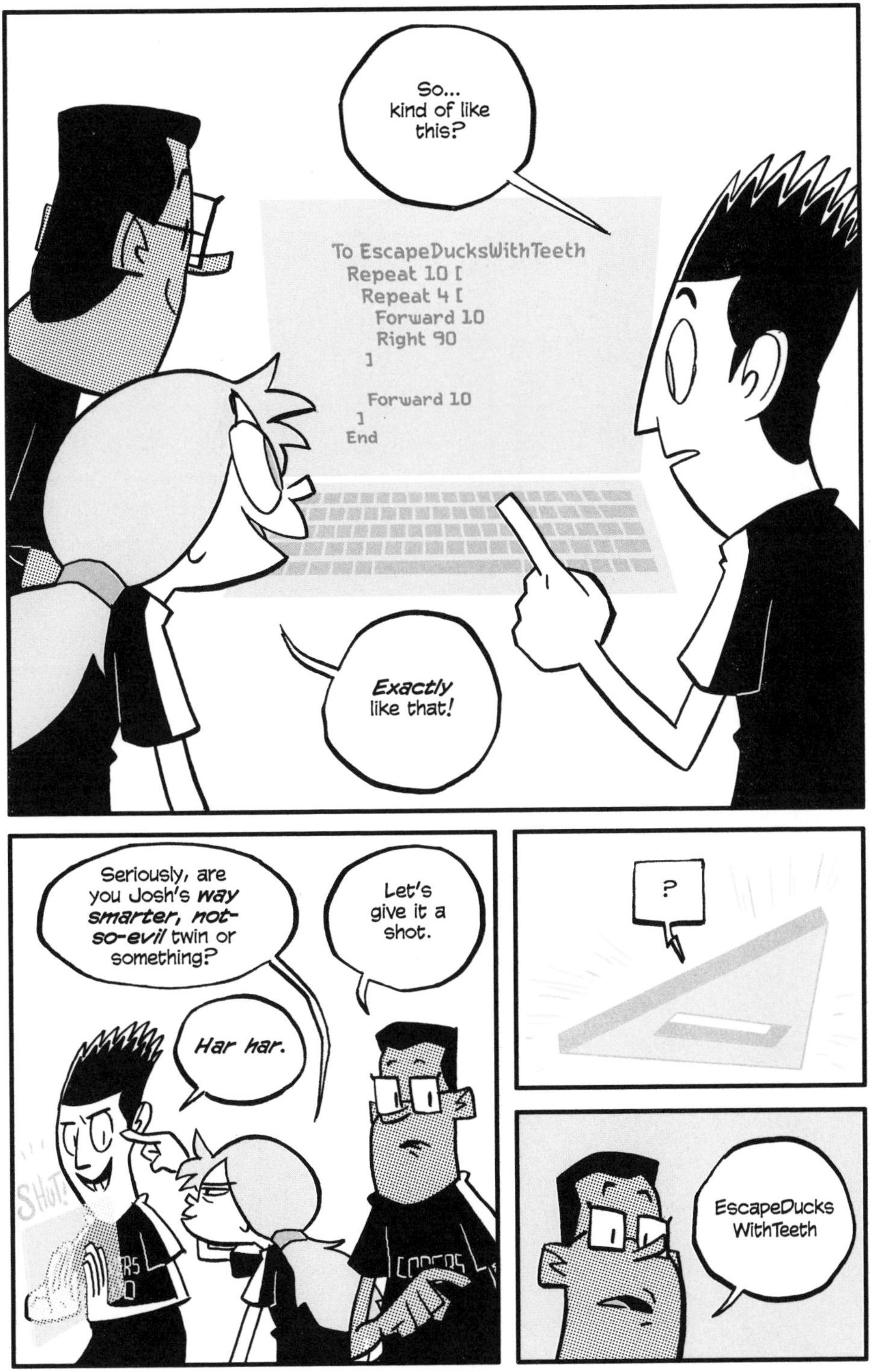
So... kind of like this?
To EscapeDucksWithTeeth
Repeat 10 [
Repeat 4 [
Forward 10
Right 90
]
Forward 10
]
End
Exactly like that!
Seriously, are you Josh's ***way smarter, not-so-evil*** twin or something?
Let's give it a shot.
Har har.
SHOT!
?
EscapeDucks WithTeeth

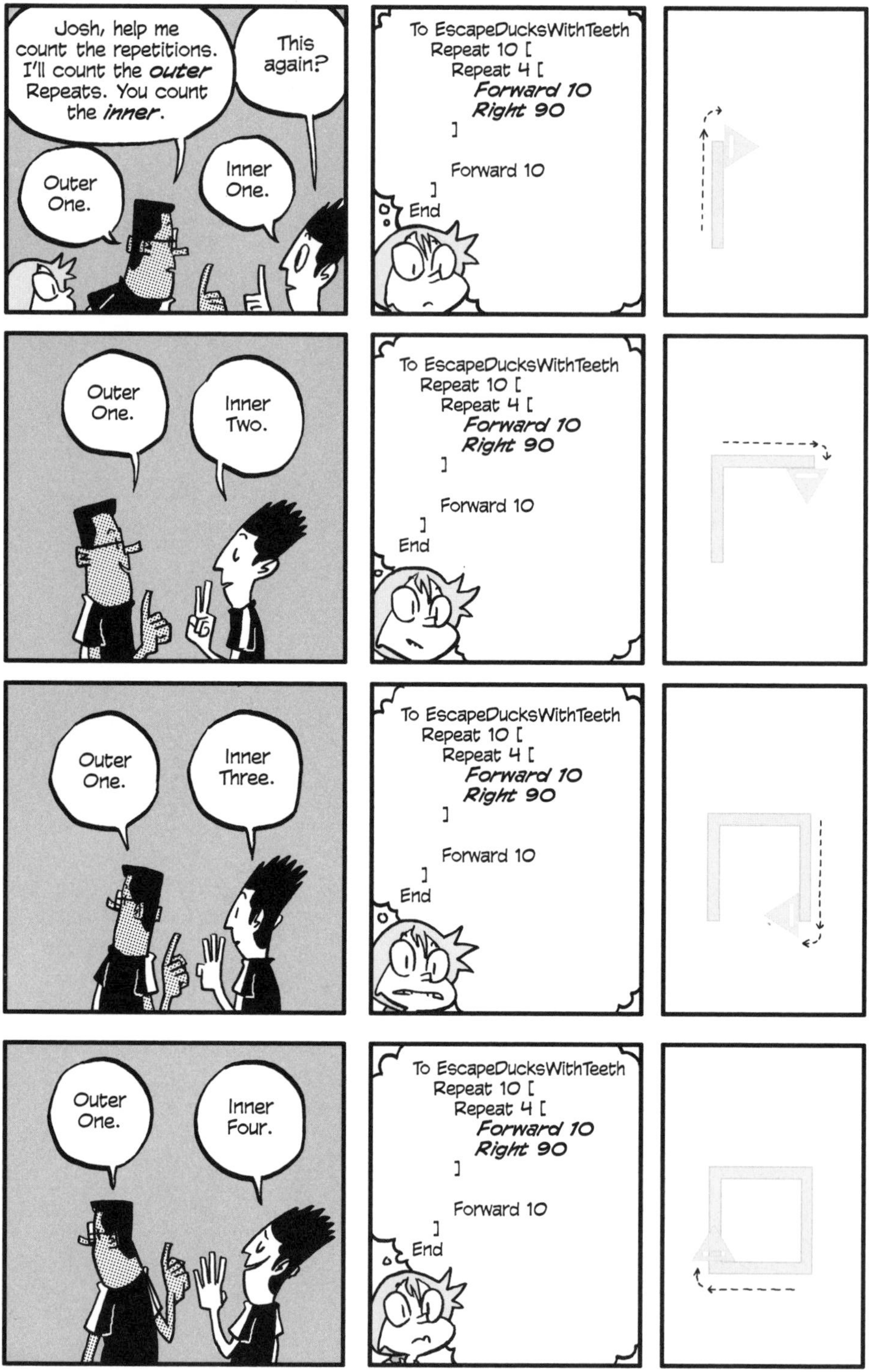

Josh, help me count the repetitions. I'll count the *outer* Repeats. You count the *inner*.
This again?
Outer One.
Inner One.
To EscapeDucksWithTeeth
Repeat 10 [
Repeat 4 [
Forward 10
Right 90
]
Forward 10
]
End
Outer One.
Inner Two.
To EscapeDucksWithTeeth
Repeat 10 [
Repeat 4 [
Forward 10
Right 90
]
Forward 10
]
End
Outer One.
Inner Three.
To EscapeDucksWithTeeth
Repeat 10 [
Repeat 4 [
Forward 10
Right 90
]
Forward 10
]
End
Outer One.
Inner Four.
To EscapeDucksWithTeeth
Repeat 10 [
Repeat 4 [
Forward 10
Right 90
]
Forward 10
]
End

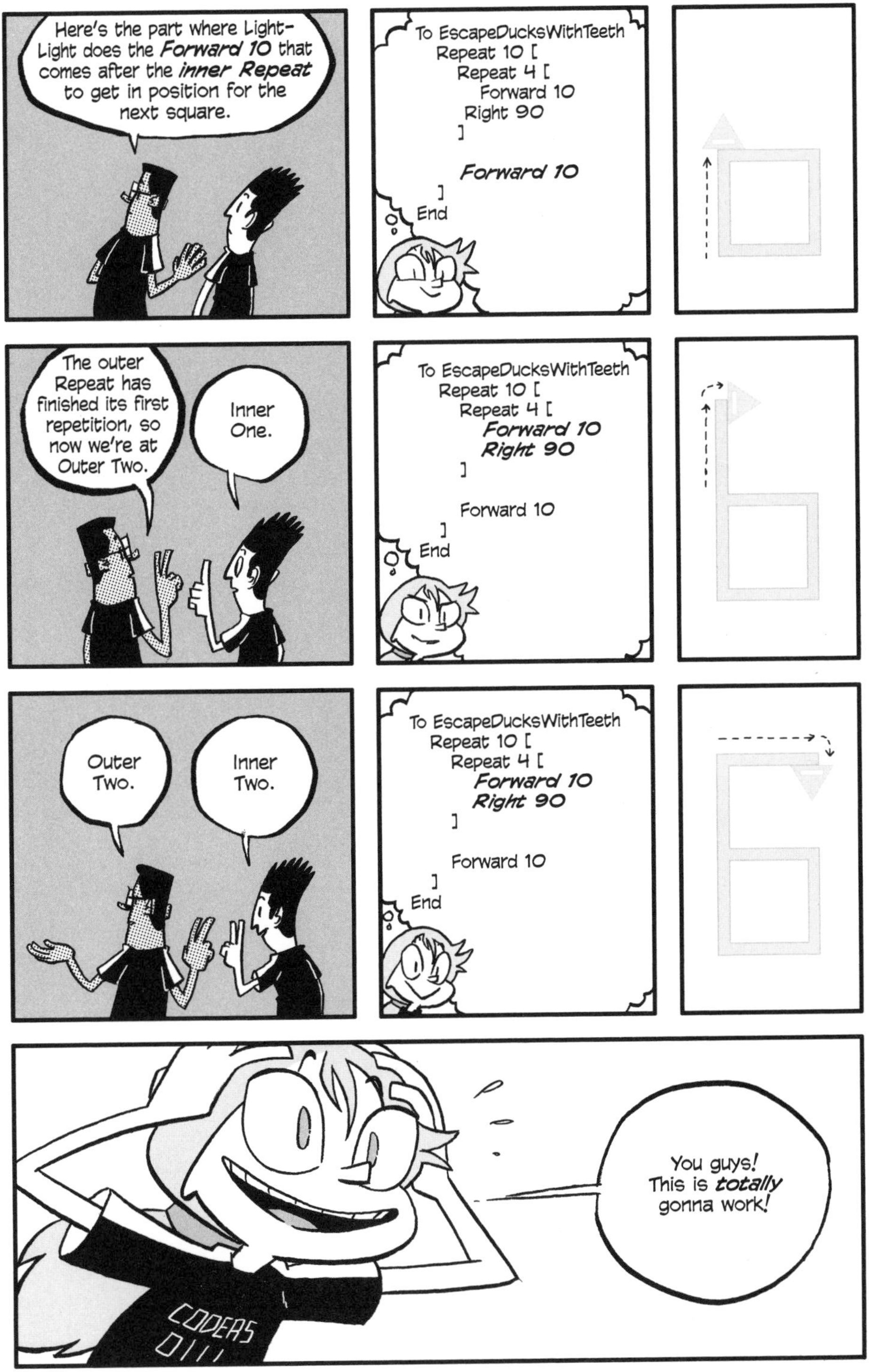
Here's the part where Light-Light does the *Forward 10* that comes after the *inner Repeat* to get in position for the next square.
To EscapeDucksWithTeeth
Repeat 10 [
Repeat 4 [
Forward 10
Right 90
]
Forward 10
]
End
The outer Repeat has finished its first repetition, so now we're at Outer Two.
Inner One.
To EscapeDucksWithTeeth
Repeat 10 [
Repeat 4 [
Forward 10
Right 90
]
Forward 10
]
End
Outer Two.
Inner Two.
To EscapeDucksWithTeeth
Repeat 10 [
Repeat 4 [
Forward 10
Right 90
]
Forward 10
]
End
You guys! This is *totally* gonna work!
CODERS 0111

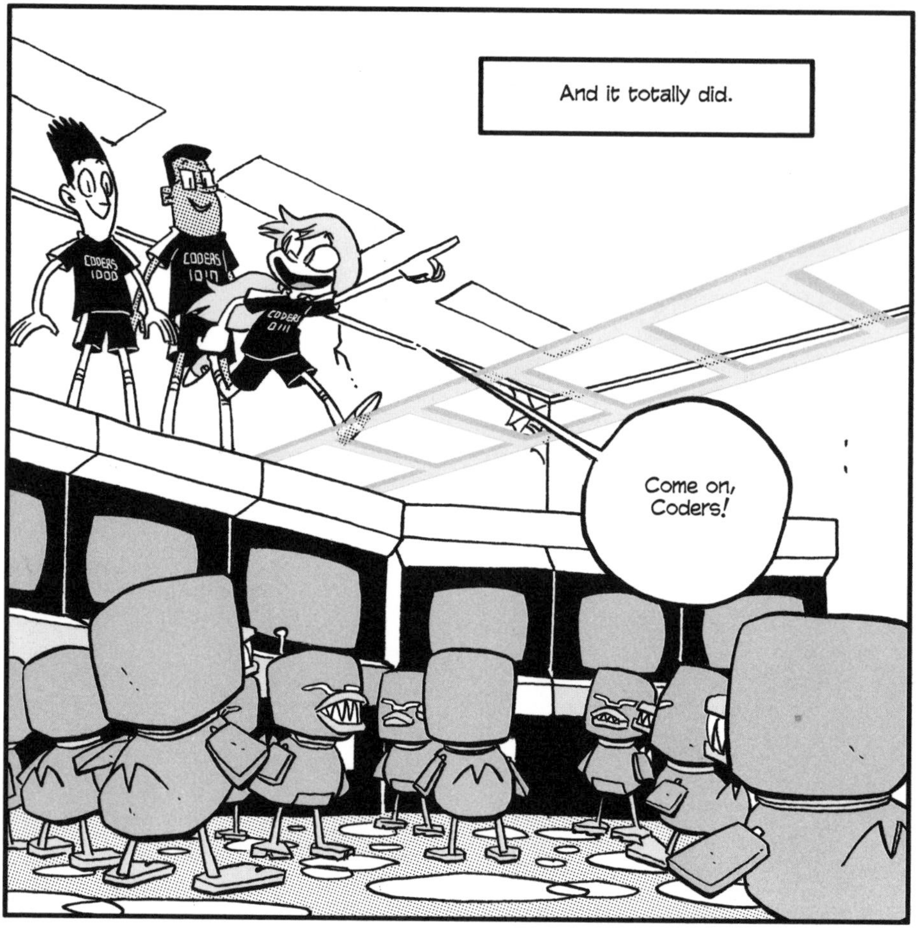
And it totally did.
CODERS 1000
CODERS 1010
CODERS 0111
Come on, Coders!

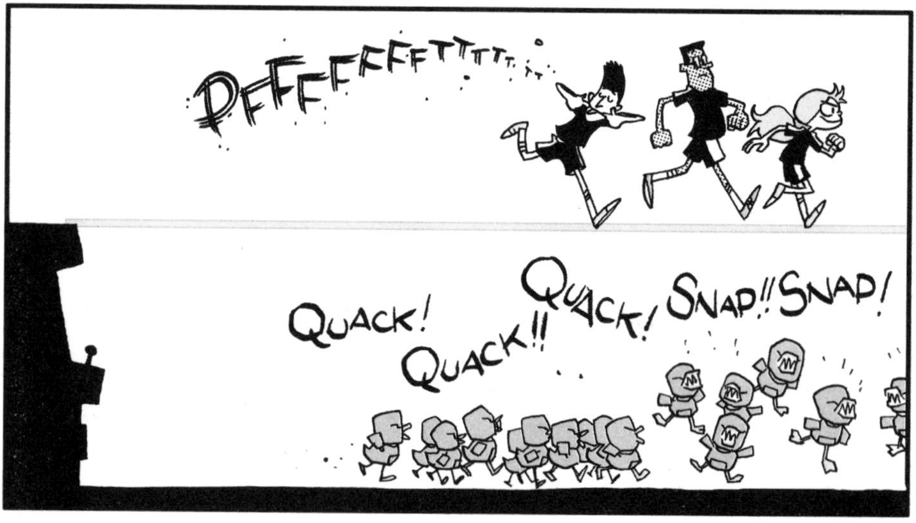
PFFFFFFFTTTTT...
QUACK!
QUACK!!
QUACK!
SNAP!!
SNAP!

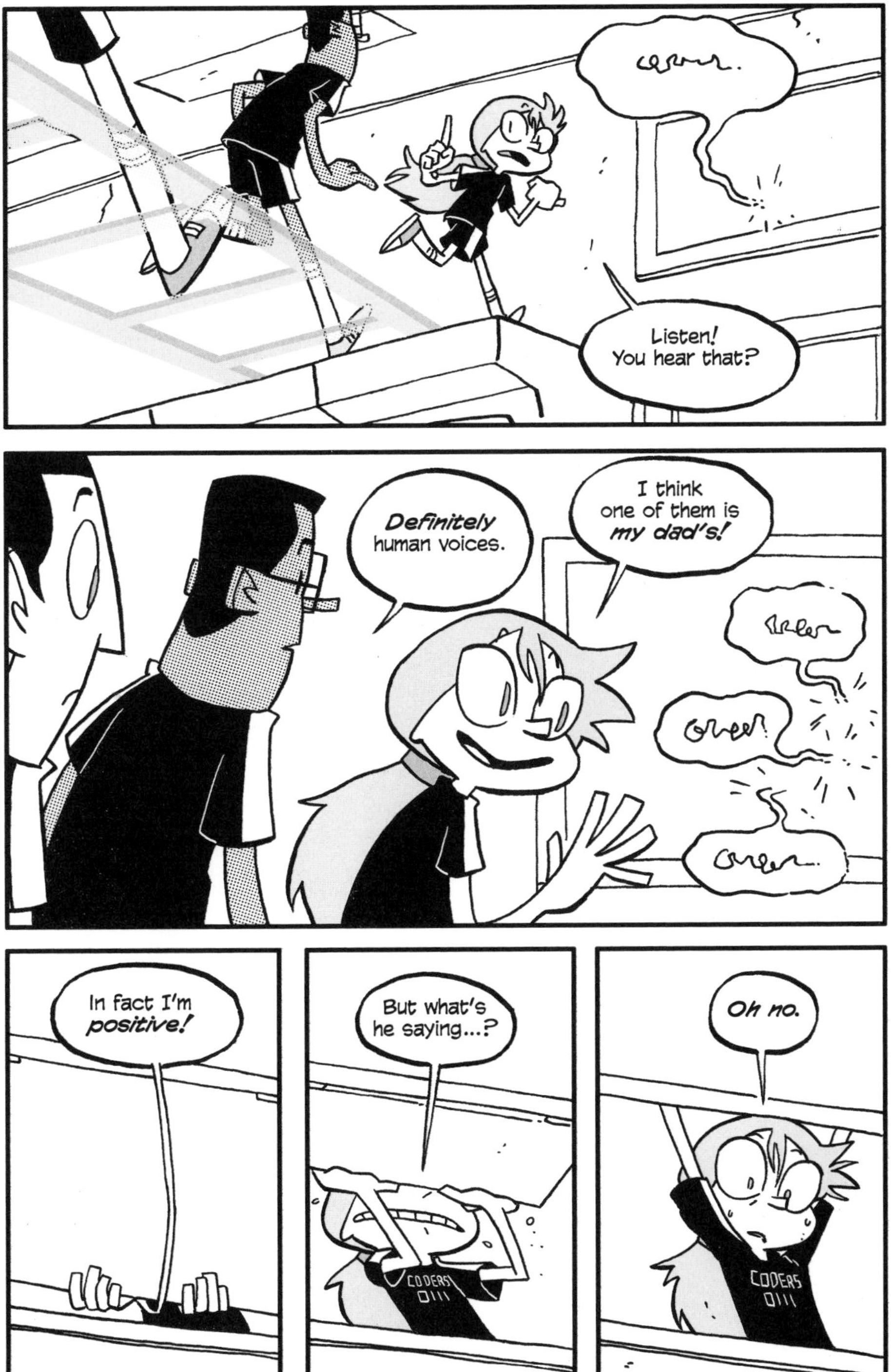
Listen!
You hear that?
Definitely human voices.
I think one of them is *my dad's!*
In fact I'm *positive!*
But what's he saying...?
Oh no.
CODERS 0111
CODERS 0111

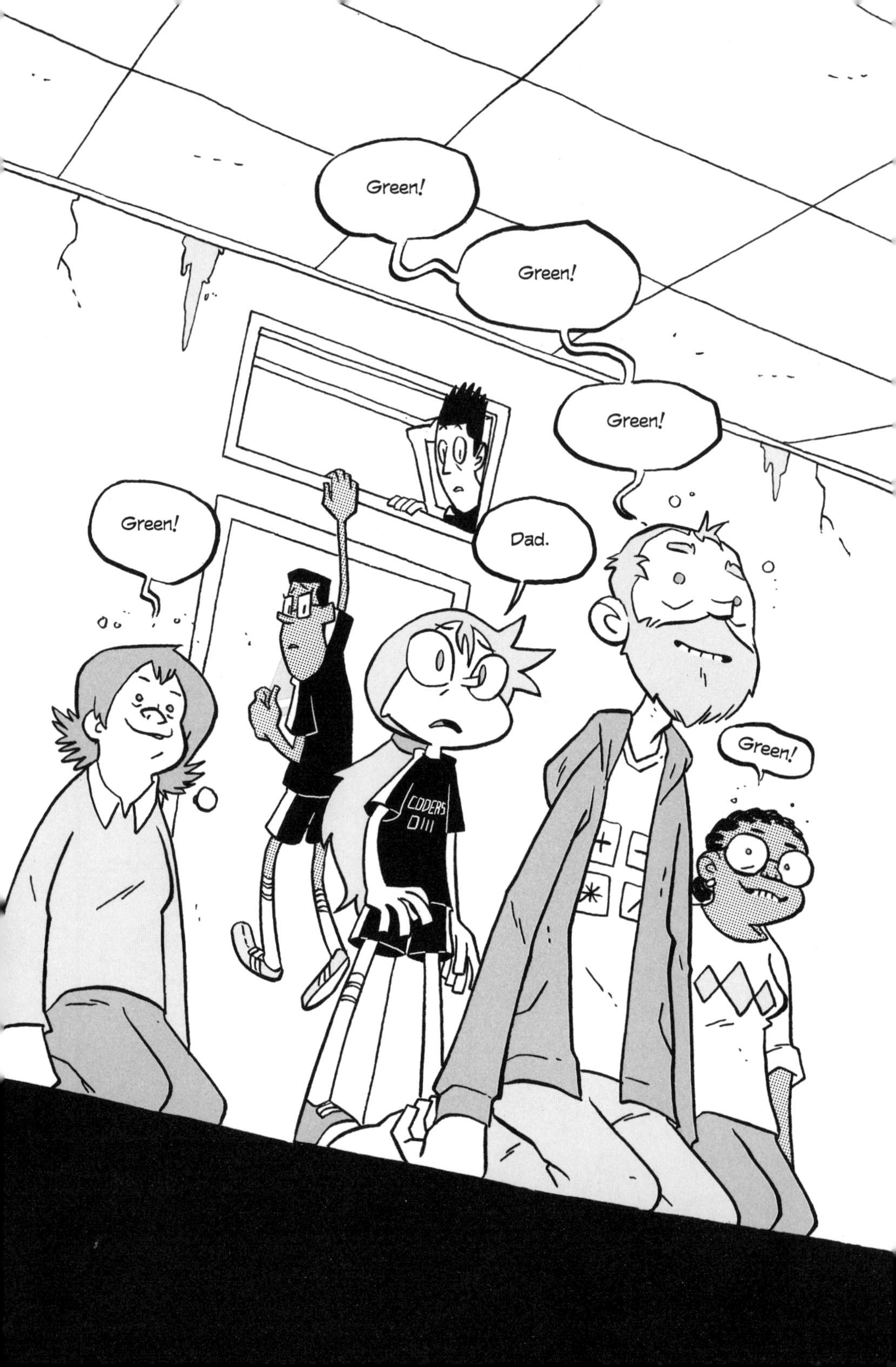
Green!
Green!
Green!
Green!
Dad.
Green!
CODERS
D111

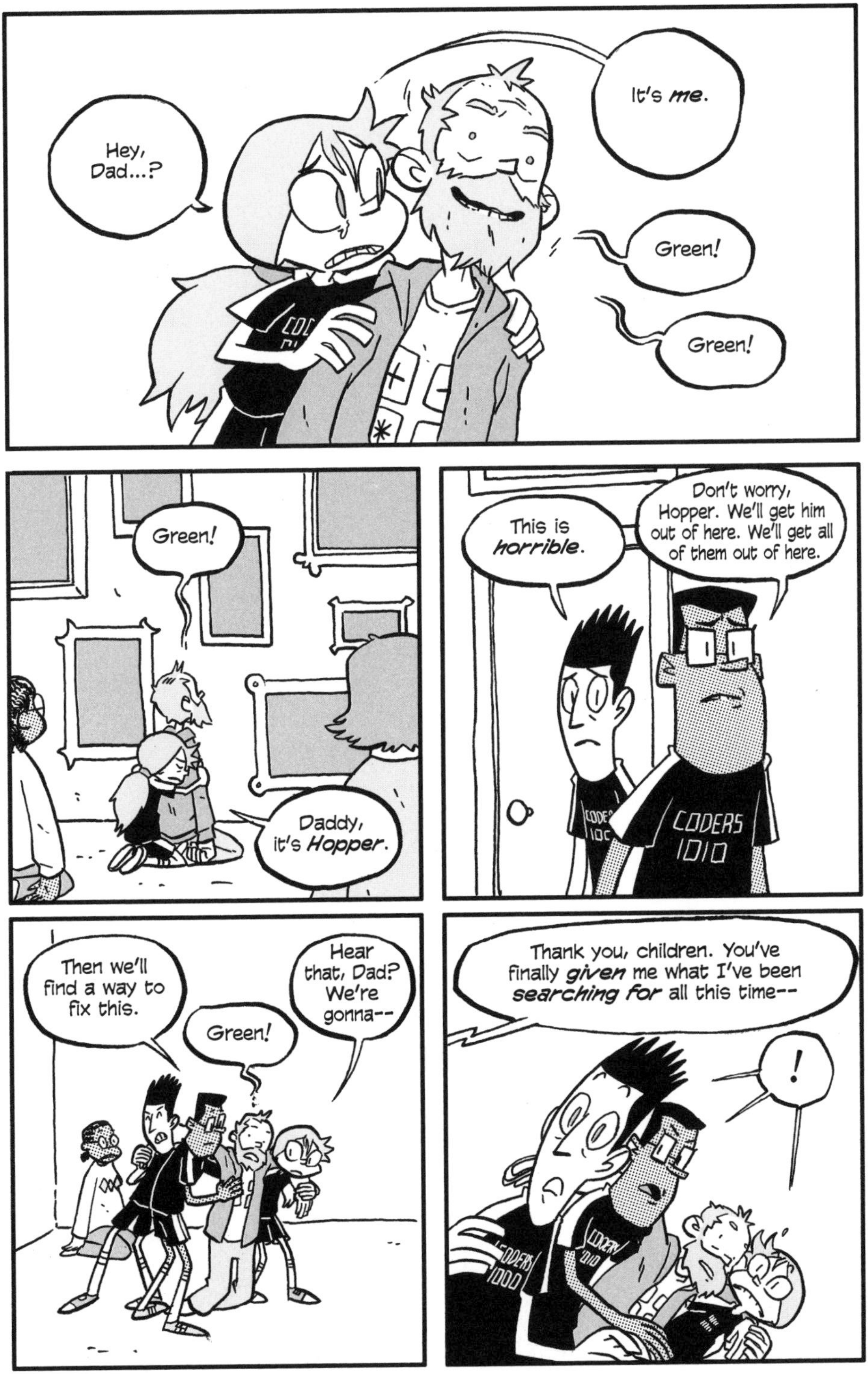
Hey, Dad...?
It's *me*.
Green!
Green!
Green!
Daddy, it's *Hopper*.
This is *horrible*.
Don't worry, Hopper. We'll get him out of here. We'll get all of them out of here.
CODERS 1010
Then we'll find a way to fix this.
Green!
Hear that, Dad? We're gonna--
Thank you, children. You've finally *given* me what I've been *searching for* all this time--
!

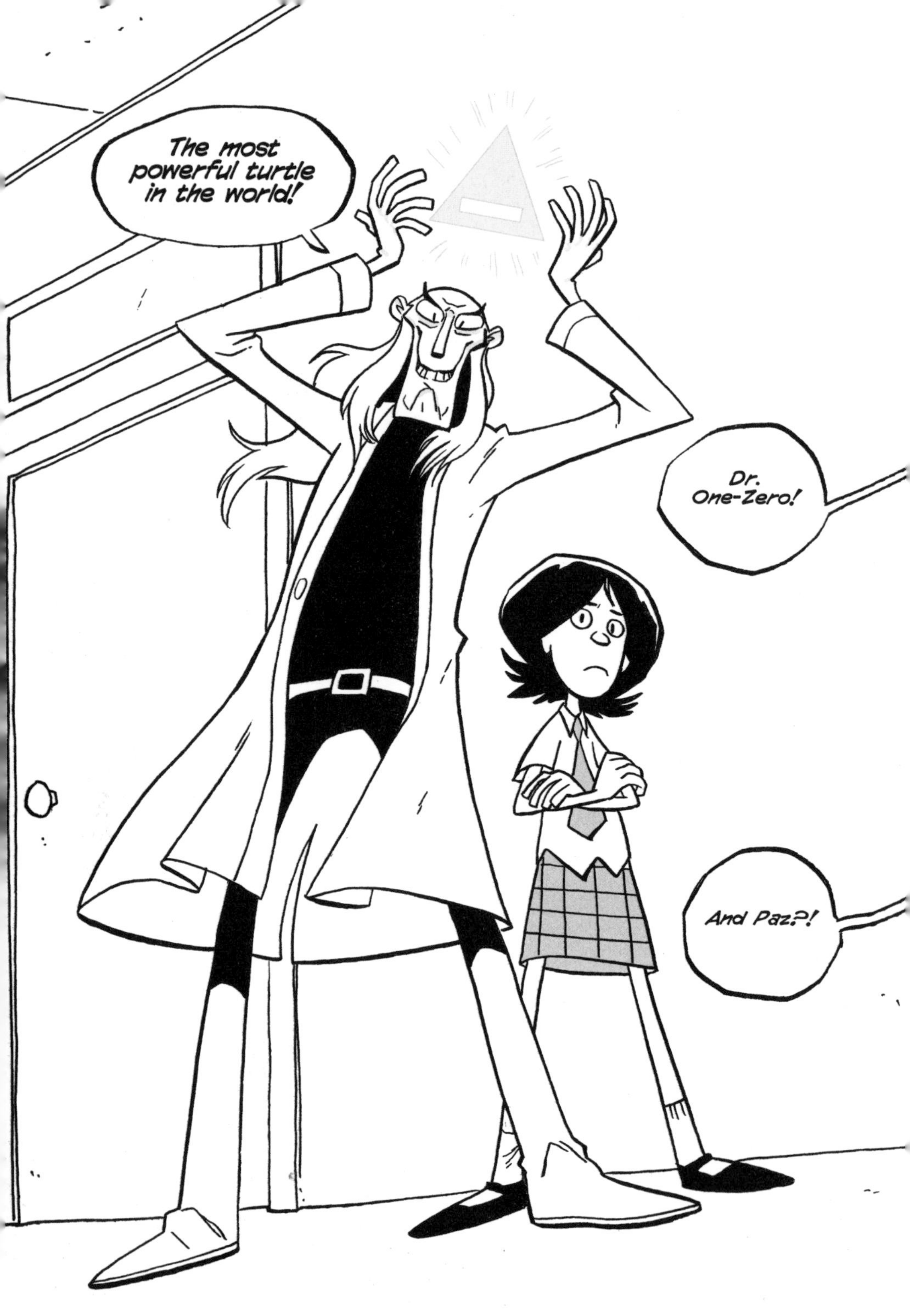
The most powerful turtle in the world!
Dr. One-Zero!
And Paz?!

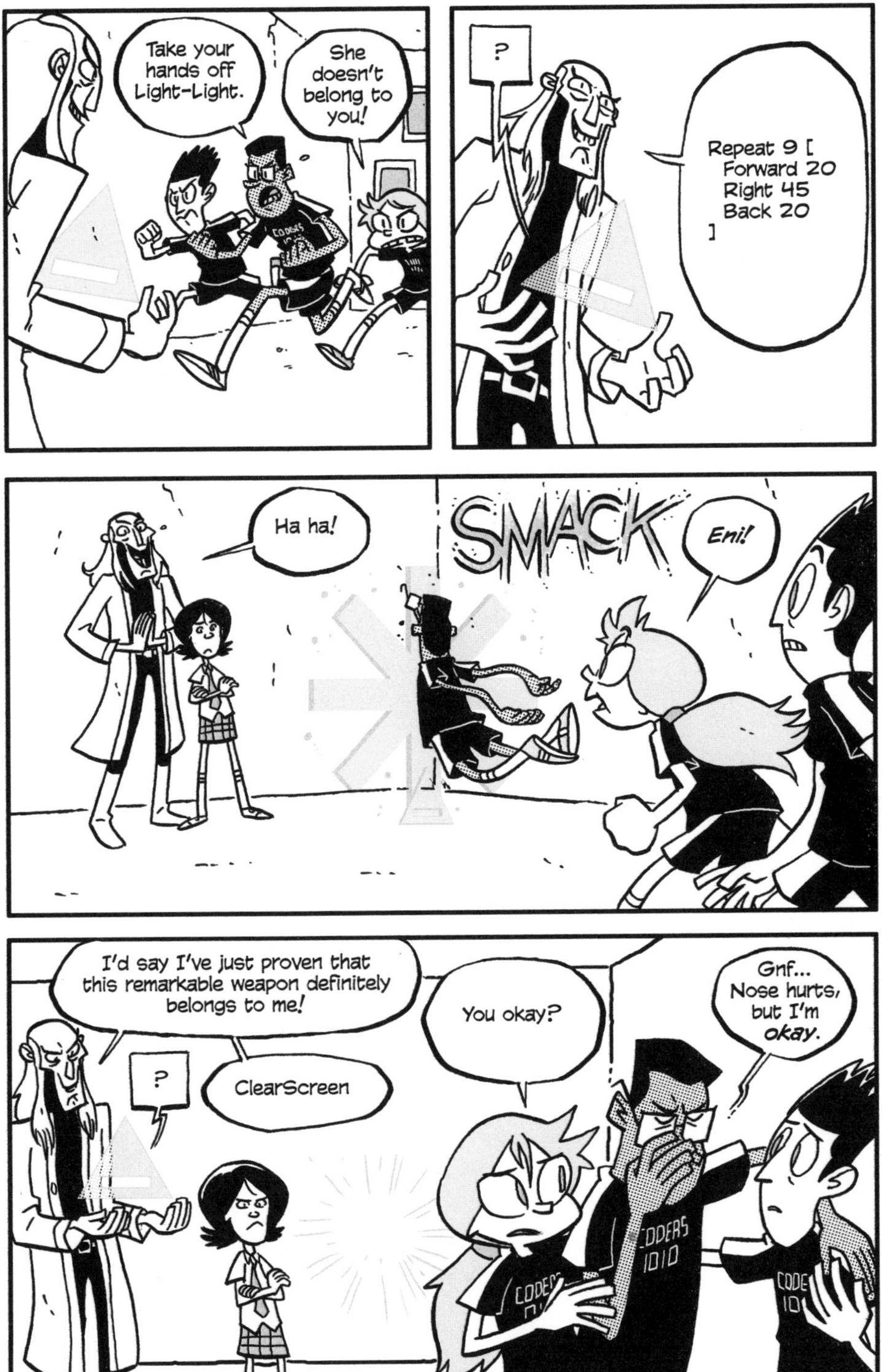
Take your hands off Light-Light.
She doesn't belong to you!
?
Repeat 9 [
Forward 20
Right 45
Back 20
]
Ha ha!
SMACK
Eni!
I'd say I've just proven that this remarkable weapon definitely belongs to me!
?
ClearScreen
You okay?
Gnf... Nose hurts, but I'm okay.

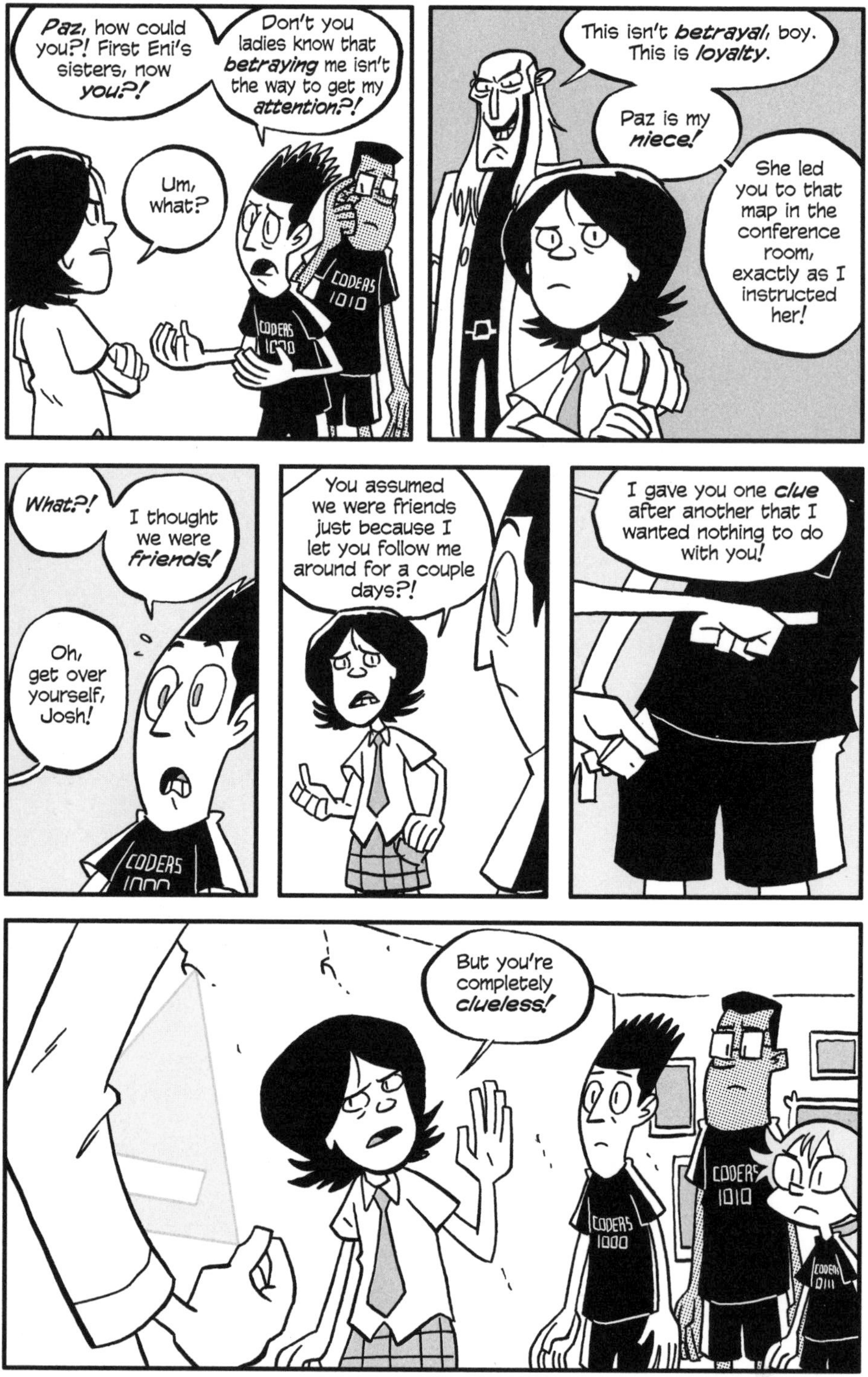
Paz, how could you?! First Eni's sisters, now you?!
Don't you ladies know that betraying me isn't the way to get my attention?!
Um, what?
This isn't betrayal, boy. This is loyalty.
Paz is my niece!
She led you to that map in the conference room, exactly as I instructed her!
What?!
I thought we were friends!
Oh, get over yourself, Josh!
You assumed we were friends just because I let you follow me around for a couple days?!
I gave you one clue after another that I wanted nothing to do with you!
But you're completely clueless!
CODERS 1000
CODERS 1010

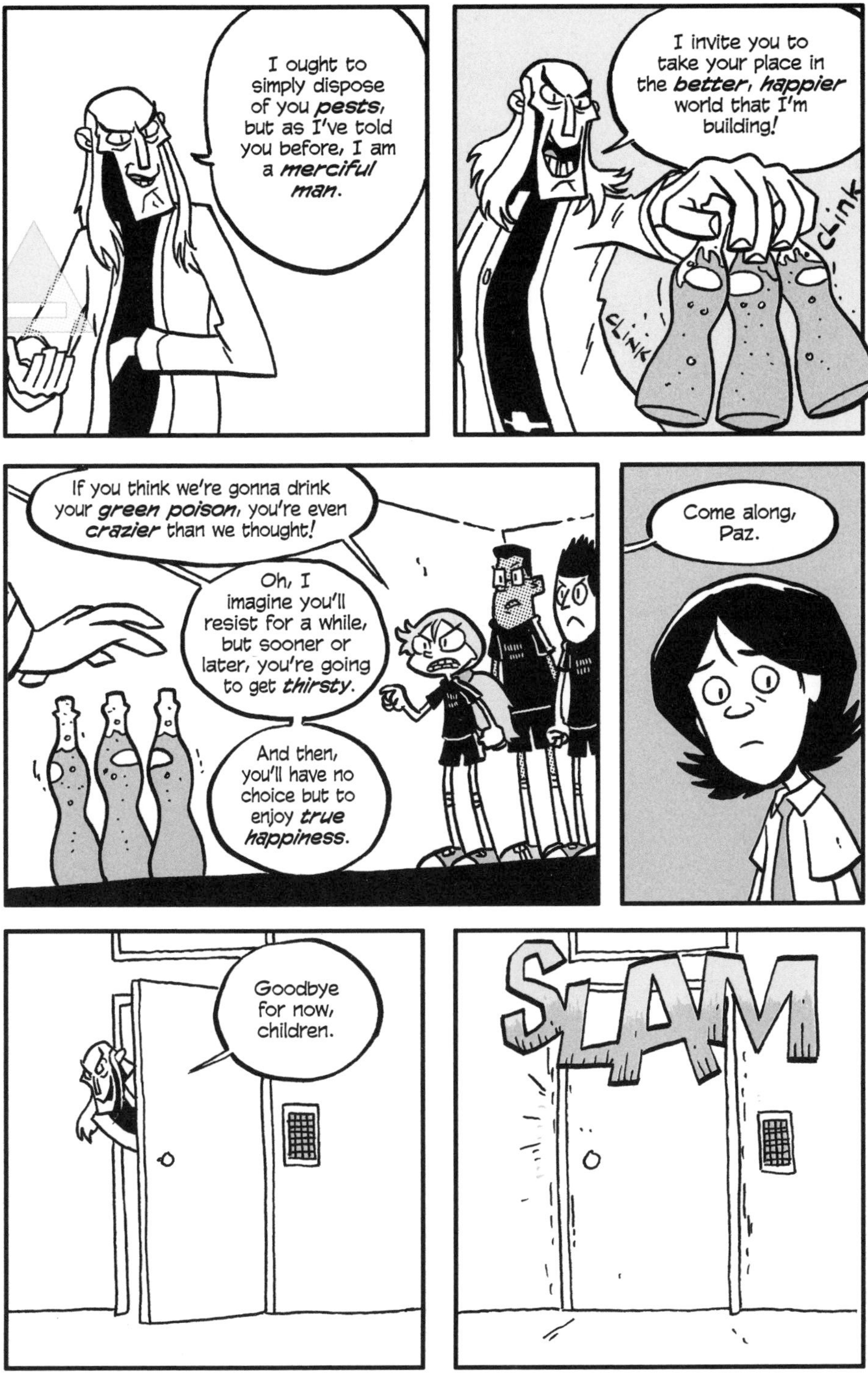
I ought to simply dispose of you pests, but as I've told you before, I am a merciful man.
I invite you to take your place in the better, happier world that I'm building!
CLINK
CLINK
If you think we're gonna drink your green poison, you're even crazier than we thought!
Oh, I imagine you'll resist for a while, but sooner or later, you're going to get thirsty.
And then, you'll have no choice but to enjoy true happiness.
Come along, Paz.
Goodbye for now, children.
SLAM

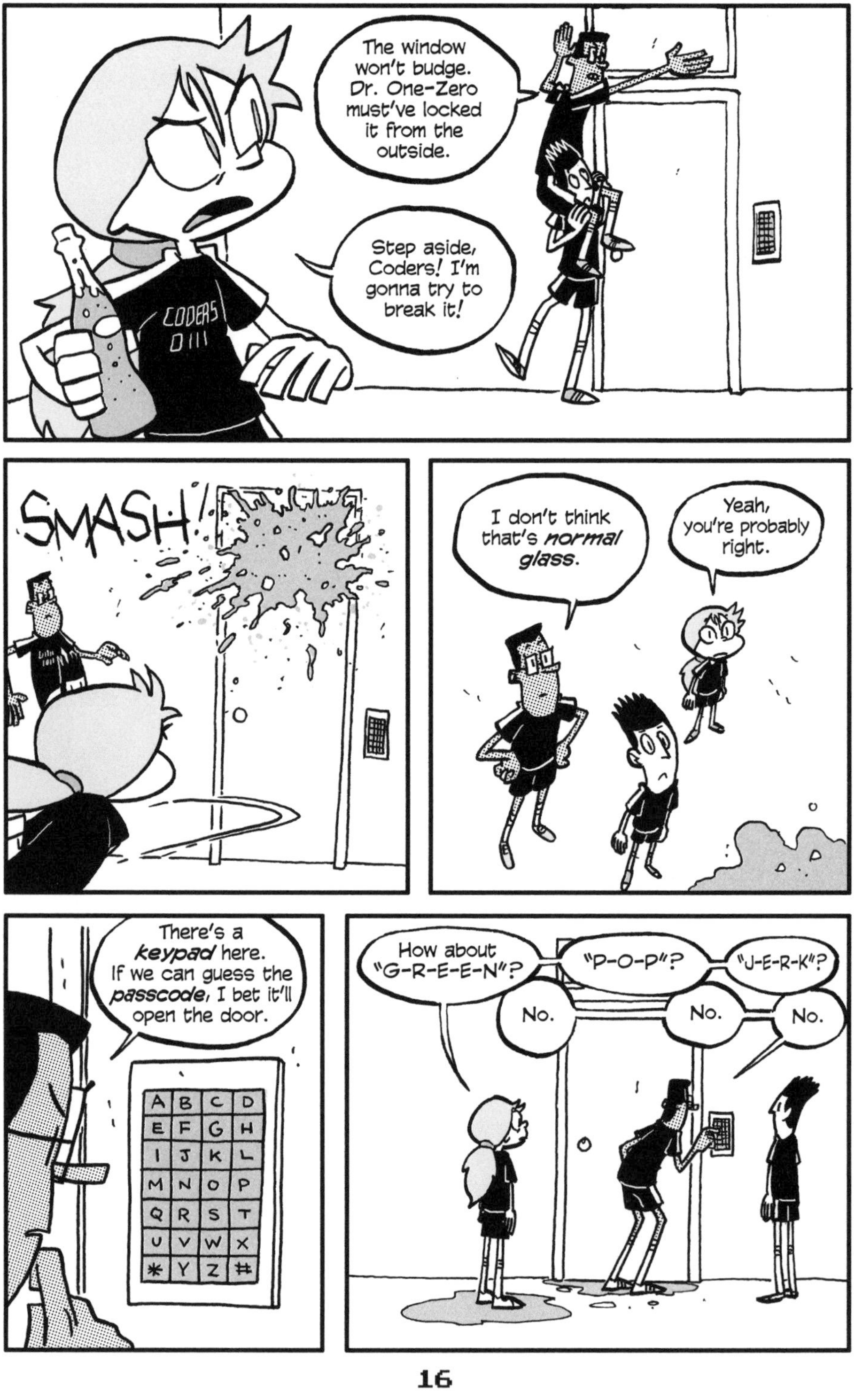
The window won't budge. Dr. One-Zero must've locked it from the outside.
Step aside, Coders! I'm gonna try to break it!
CODERS
SMASH!
I don't think that's *normal glass*.
Yeah, you're probably right.
There's a *keypad* here. If we can guess the *passcode*, I bet it'll open the door.
A B C D
E F G H
I J K L
M N O P
Q R S T
U V W X
* Y Z #
How about "G-R-E-E-N"?
No.
"P-O-P"?
No.
"J-E-R-K"?
No.

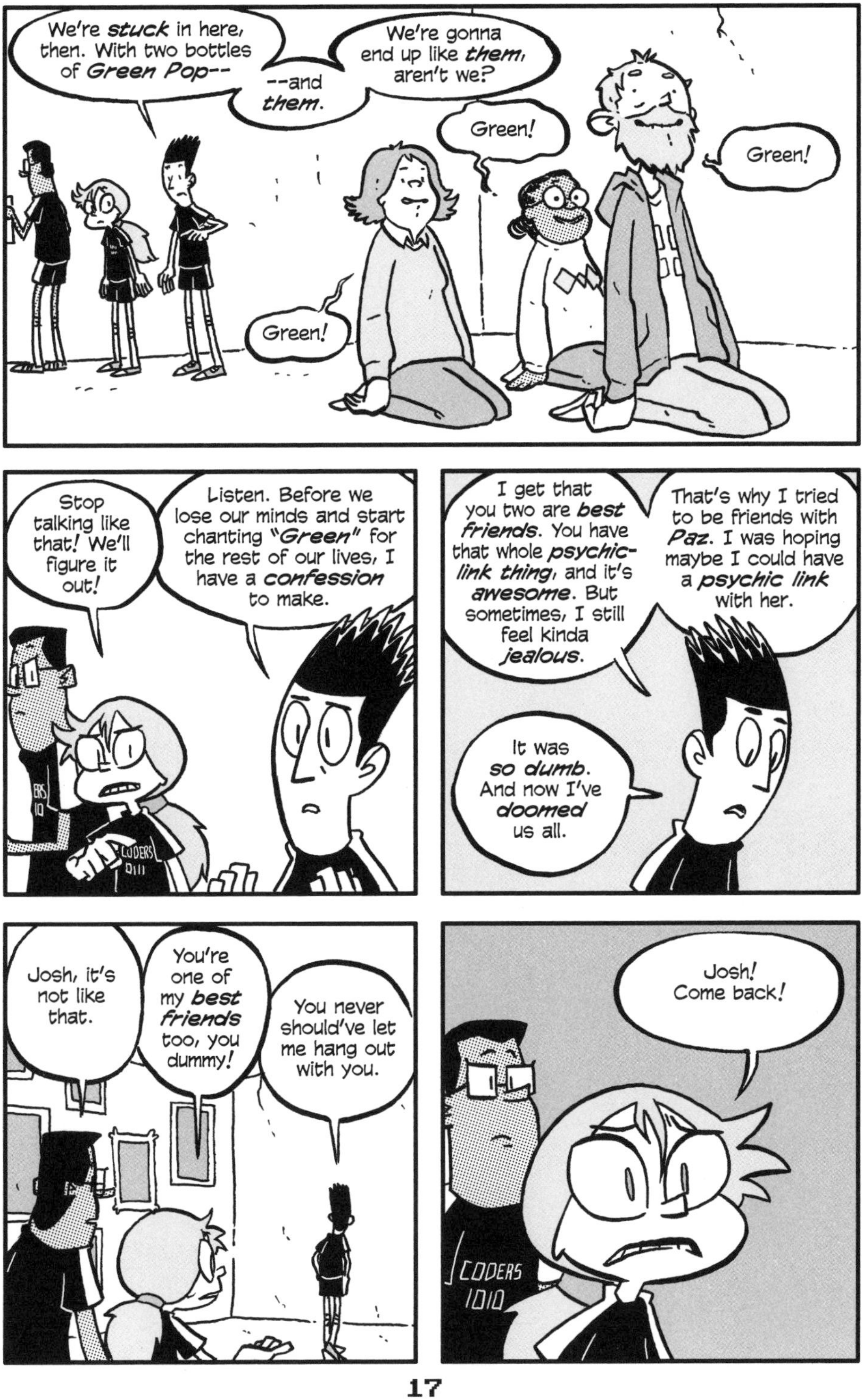
We're stuck in here, then. With two bottles of Green Pop--
--and them.
We're gonna end up like them, aren't we?
Green!
Green!
Green!
Stop talking like that! We'll figure it out!
Listen. Before we lose our minds and start chanting "Green" for the rest of our lives, I have a confession to make.
CODERS 1011
I get that you two are best friends. You have that whole psychic-link thing, and it's awesome. But sometimes, I still feel kinda jealous.
That's why I tried to be friends with Paz. I was hoping maybe I could have a psychic link with her.
It was so dumb. And now I've doomed us all.
Josh, it's not like that.
You're one of my best friends too, you dummy!
You never should've let me hang out with you.
Josh! Come back!
CODERS 1010

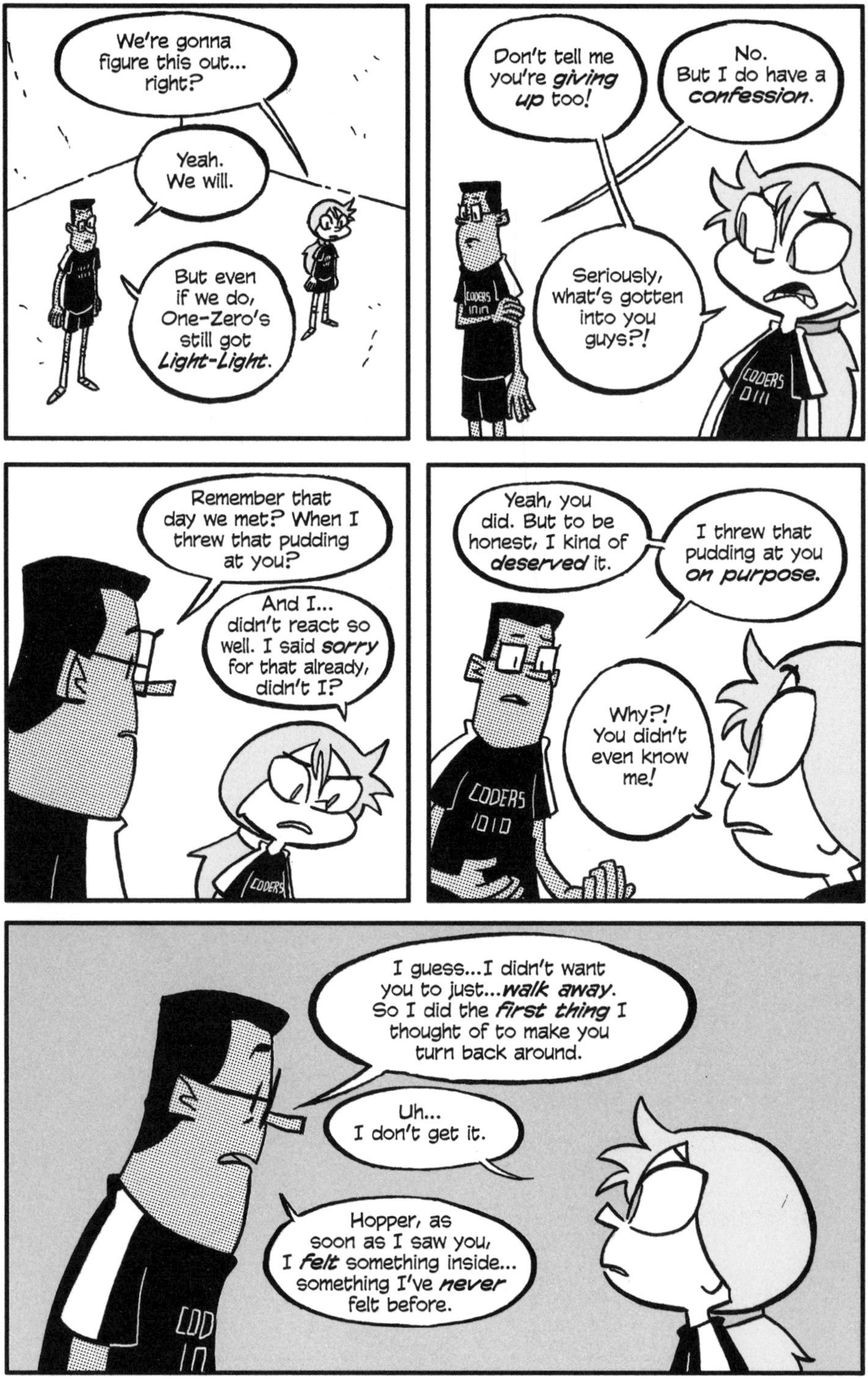
We're gonna figure this out... right?
Yeah. We will.
But even if we do, One-Zero's still got Light-Light.
Don't tell me you're giving up too!
No. But I do have a confession.
Seriously, what's gotten into you guys?!
CODERS 1010
CODERS 0111
Remember that day we met? When I threw that pudding at you?
And I... didn't react so well. I said sorry for that already, didn't I?
CODERS
Yeah, you did. But to be honest, I kind of deserved it.
I threw that pudding at you on purpose.
Why?! You didn't even know me!
CODERS 1010
I guess...I didn't want you to just...walk away. So I did the first thing I thought of to make you turn back around.
Uh... I don't get it.
Hopper, as soon as I saw you, I felt something inside... something I've never felt before.

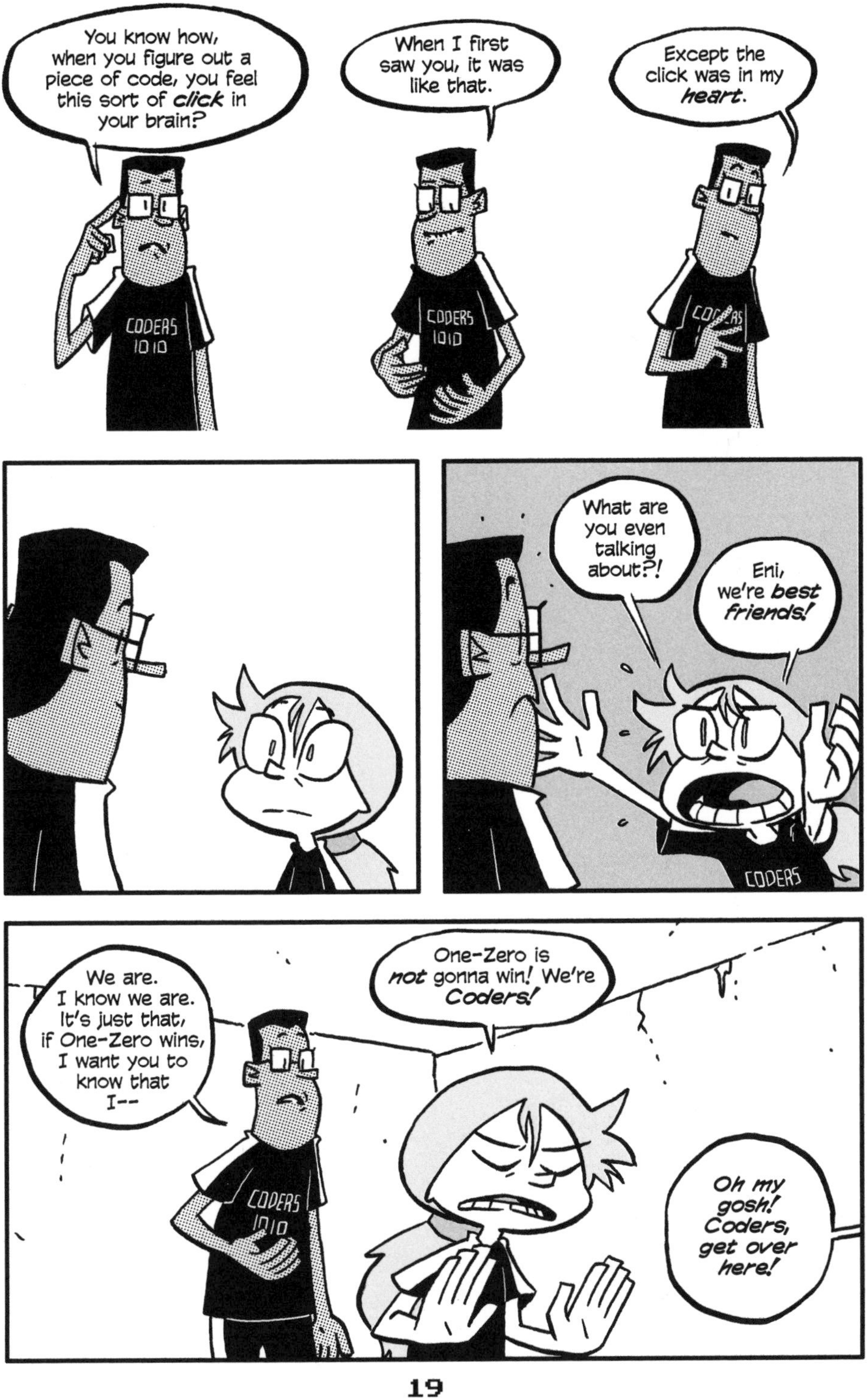
You know how, when you figure out a piece of code, you feel this sort of *click* in your brain?
CODERS 1010
When I first saw you, it was like that.
CODERS 1010
Except the click was in my *heart*.
What are you even talking about?!
Eni, we're *best friends!*
CODERS
We are. I know we are. It's just that, if One-Zero wins, I want you to know that I--
One-Zero is *not* gonna win! We're *Coders!*
CODERS 1010
Oh my gosh! Coders, get over here!

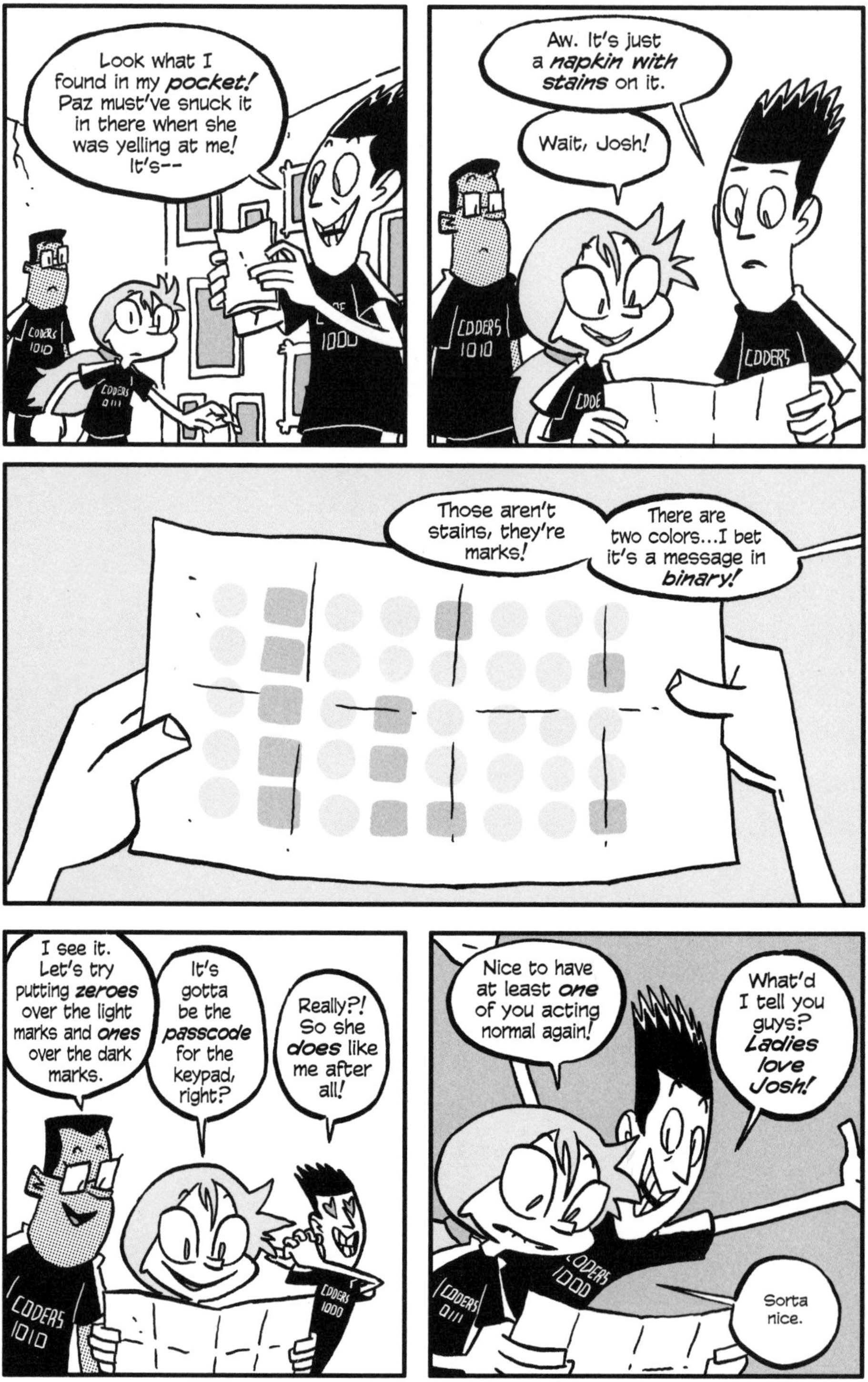
Look what I found in my pocket! Paz must've snuck it in there when she was yelling at me! It's--
CODERS 1010
CODERS 0111
CODERS 1000
Aw. It's just a napkin with stains on it.
Wait, Josh!
CODERS 1010
CODERS
CODERS
Those aren't stains, they're marks!
There are two colors...I bet it's a message in binary!
I see it. Let's try putting zeroes over the light marks and ones over the dark marks.
It's gotta be the passcode for the keypad, right?
Really?! So she does like me after all!
CODERS 1010
CODERS 1000
Nice to have at least one of you acting normal again!
What'd I tell you guys? Ladies love Josh!
CODERS 1000
CODERS 0111
Sorta nice.

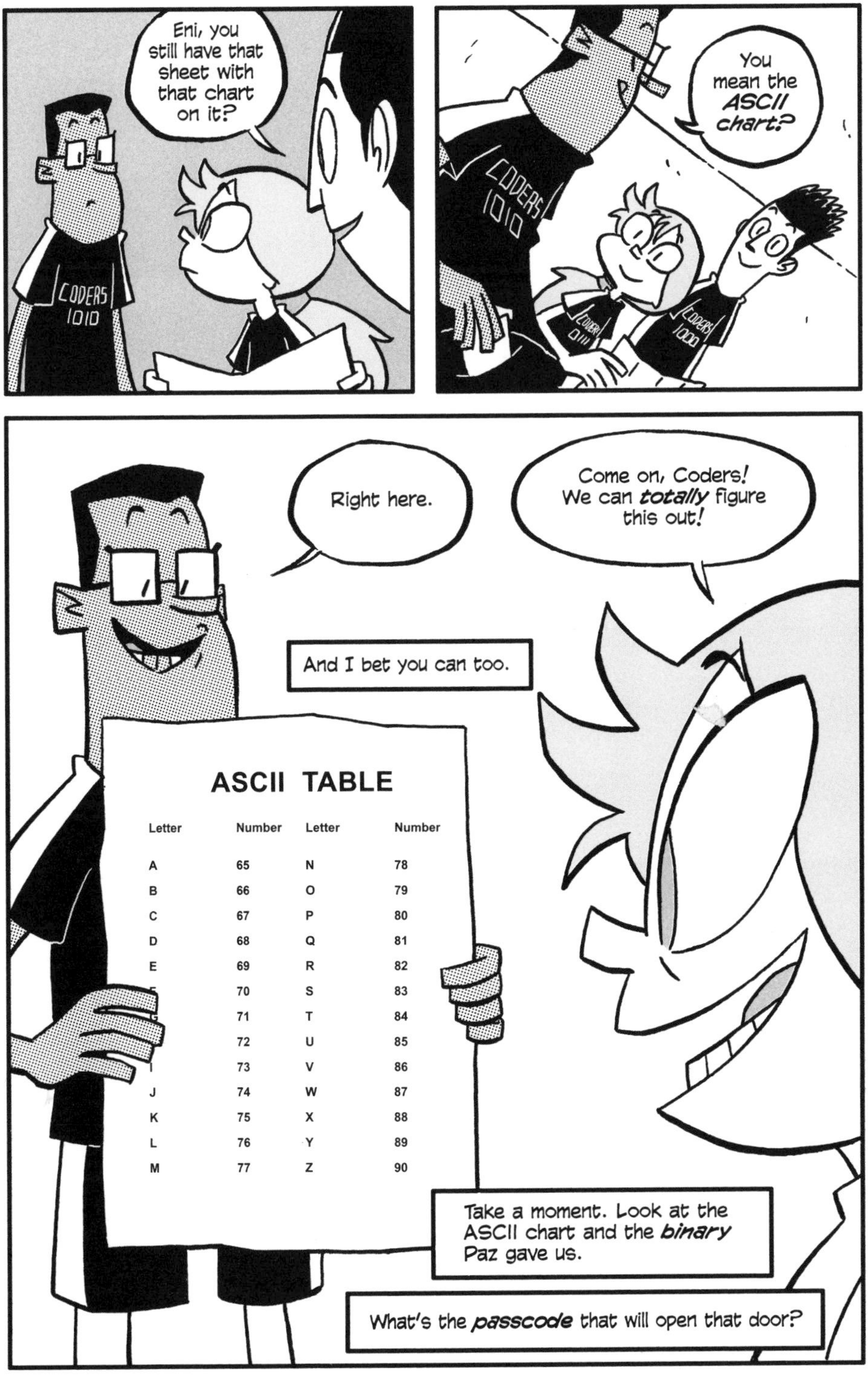
Eni, you still have that sheet with that chart on it?
You mean the ASCII chart?
CODERS 1010
Right here.
Come on, Coders! We can totally figure this out!
And I bet you can too.
ASCII TABLE
Letter Number Letter Number
A 65 N 78
B 66 O 79
C 67 P 80
D 68 Q 81
E 69 R 82
70 S 83
71 T 84
72 U 85
73 V 86
J 74 W 87
K 75 X 88
L 76 Y 89
M 77 Z 90
Take a moment. Look at the ASCII chart and the binary Paz gave us.
What's the passcode that will open that door?

Chapter

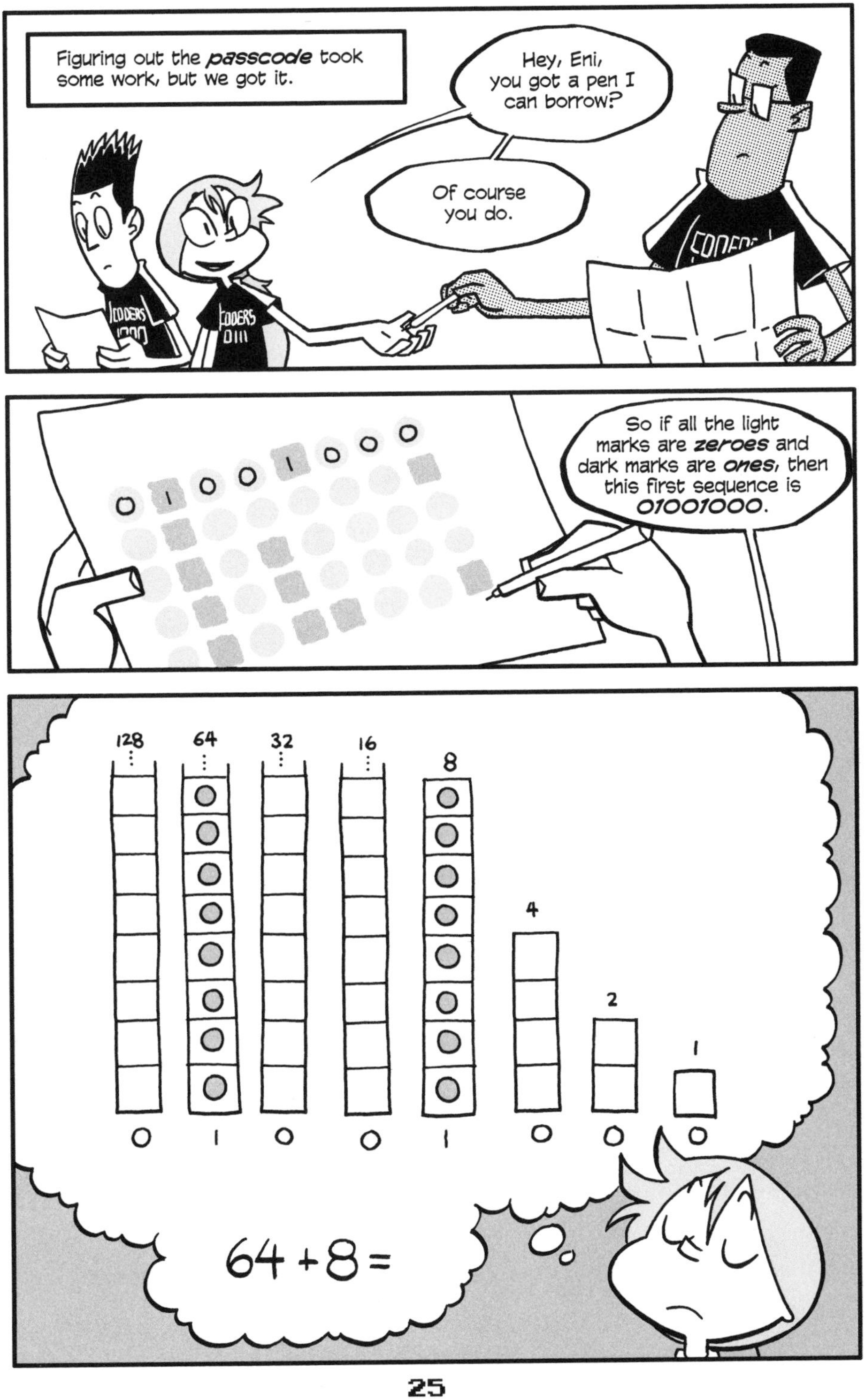

Figuring out the ***passcode*** took some work, but we got it.
Hey, Eni, you got a pen I can borrow?
Of course you do.
0 1 0 0 1 0 0 0
So if all the light marks are ***zeroes*** and dark marks are ***ones***, then this first sequence is ***01001000***.
128
64
32
16
8
4
2
1
0 1 0 0 1 0 0 0
64 + 8 =

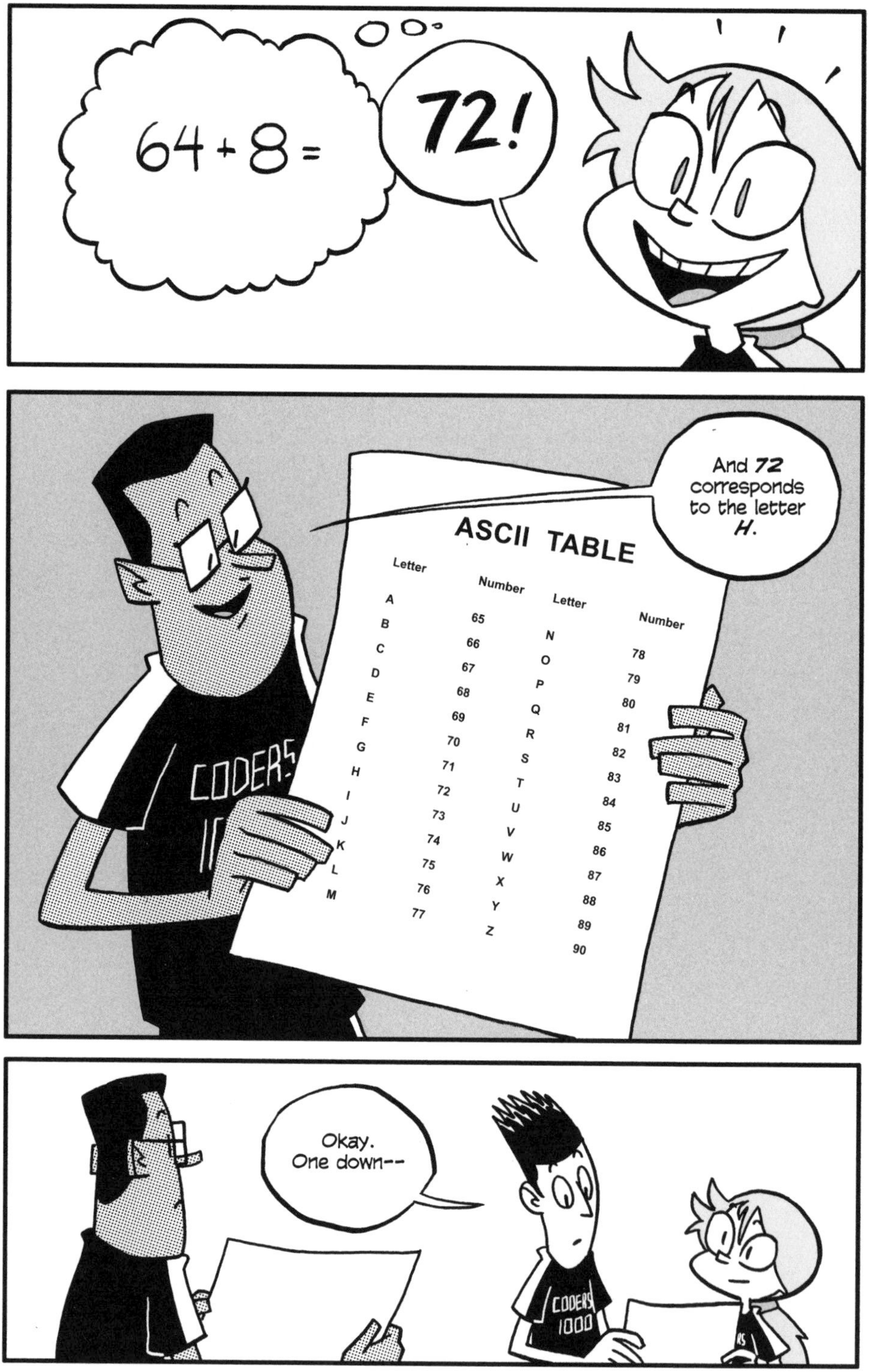
64 + 8 =
72!
And 72 corresponds to the letter H.
ASCII TABLE
Letter Number Letter Number
A 65 N 78
B 66 O 79
C 67 P 80
D 68 Q 81
E 69 R 82
F 70 S 83
G 71 T 84
H 72 U 85
I 73 V 86
J 74 W 87
K 75 X 88
L 76 Y 89
M 77 Z 90
CODERS
Okay.
One down--
CODERS
1000

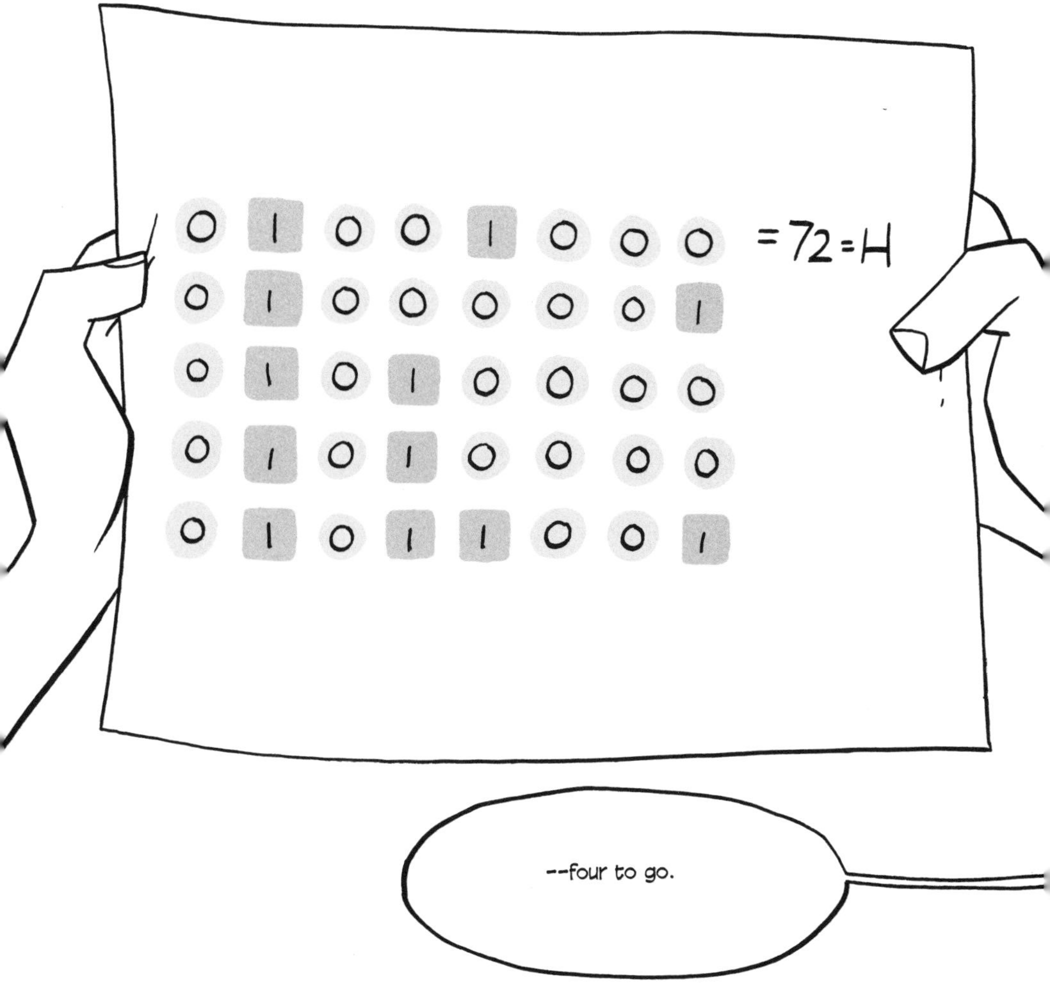
0 1 0 0 1 0 0 0 =72=H
0 1 0 0 0 0 0 1
0 1 0 1 0 0 0 0
0 1 0 1 0 0 0 0
0 1 0 1 1 0 0 1
--four to go.

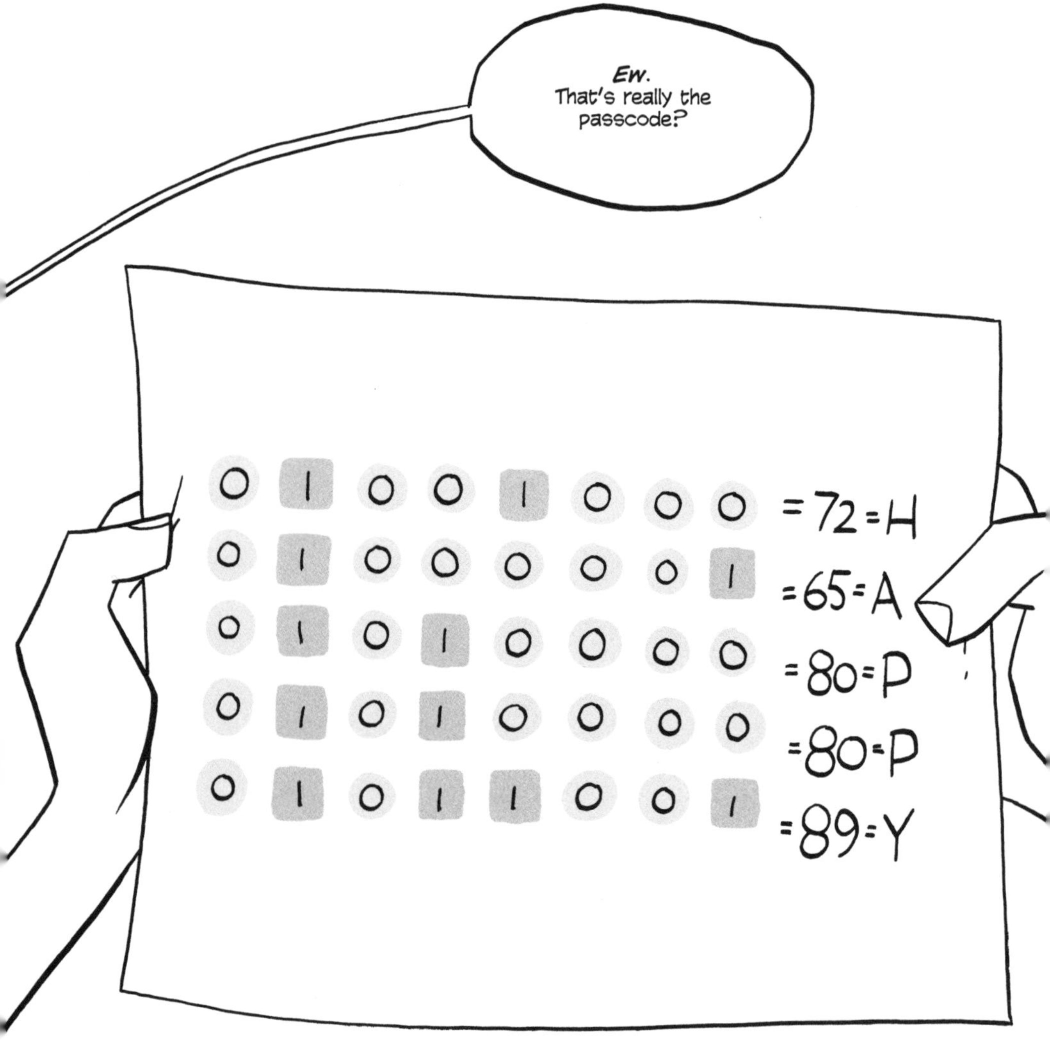
Ew.
That's really the passcode?
0 1 0 0 1 0 0 0 =72=H
0 1 0 0 0 0 0 1 =65=A
0 1 0 1 0 0 0 0 =80=P
0 1 0 1 0 0 0 0 =80=P
0 1 0 1 1 0 0 1 =89=Y

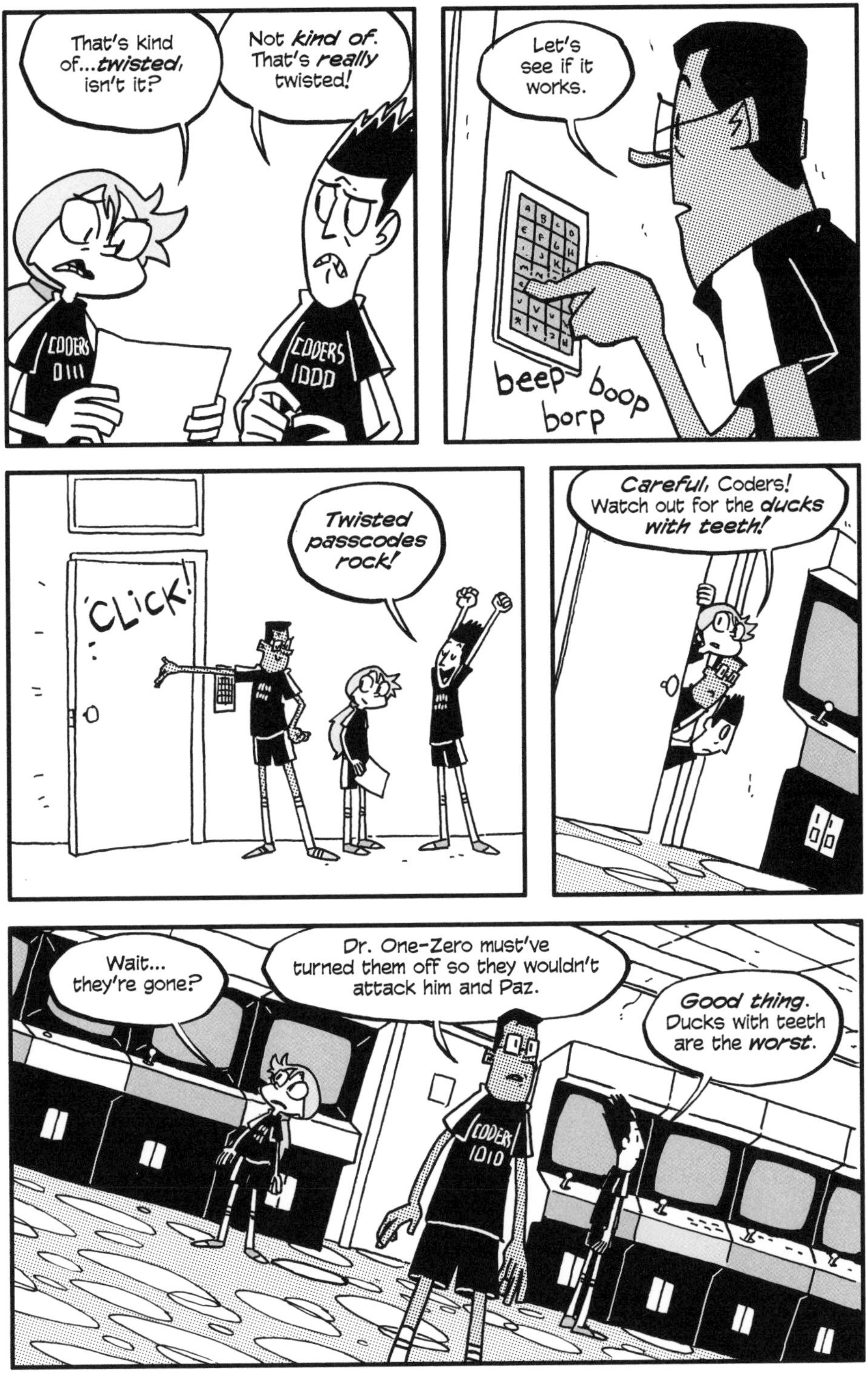
That's kind of...twisted, isn't it?
Not kind of. That's really twisted!
CODERS 0111
CODERS 1000
Let's see if it works.
beep boop borp
'CLICK!
Twisted passcodes rock!
Careful, Coders! Watch out for the ducks with teeth!
Wait... they're gone?
Dr. One-Zero must've turned them off so they wouldn't attack him and Paz.
Good thing. Ducks with teeth are the worst.
CODERS 1010

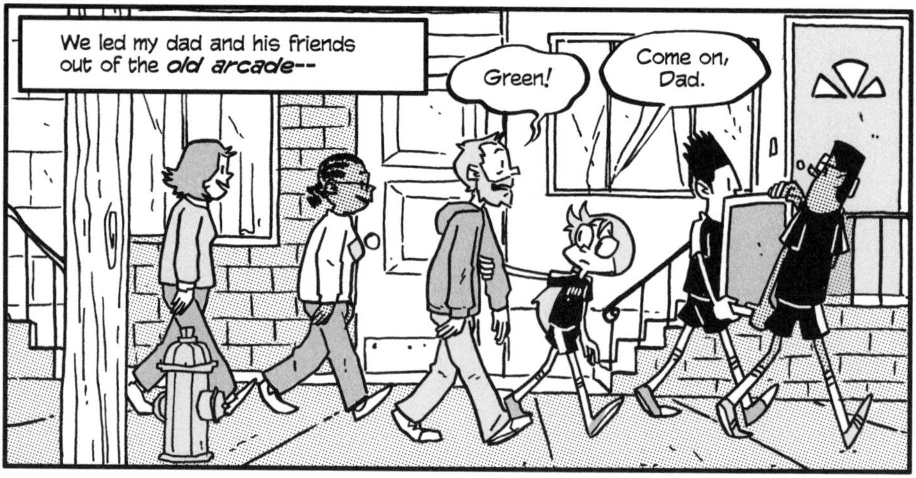
We led my dad and his friends out of the *old arcade*--
Green!
Come on, Dad.

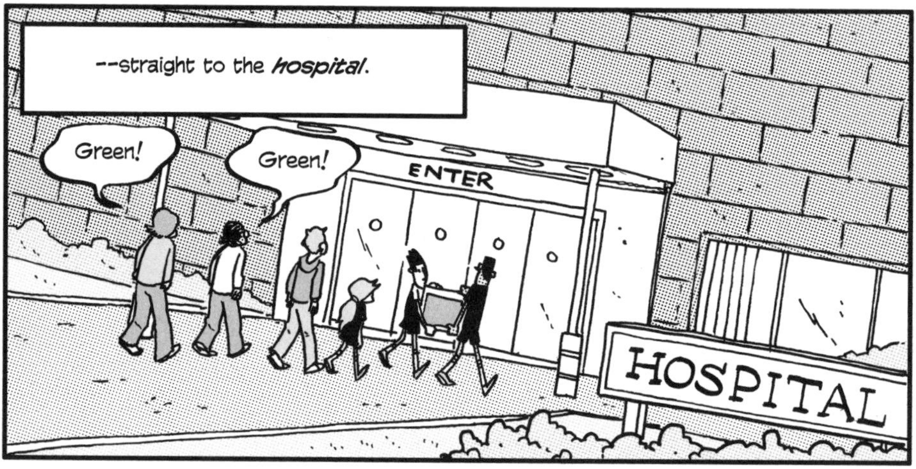
--straight to the *hospital*.
Green!
Green!
ENTER
HOSPITAL

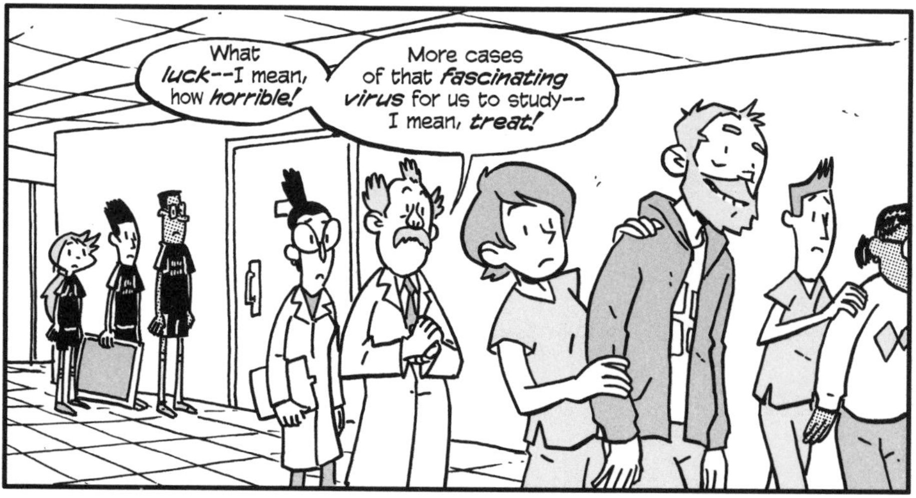
What *luck*--I mean, how *horrible!*
More cases of that *fascinating virus* for us to study--I mean, *treat!*

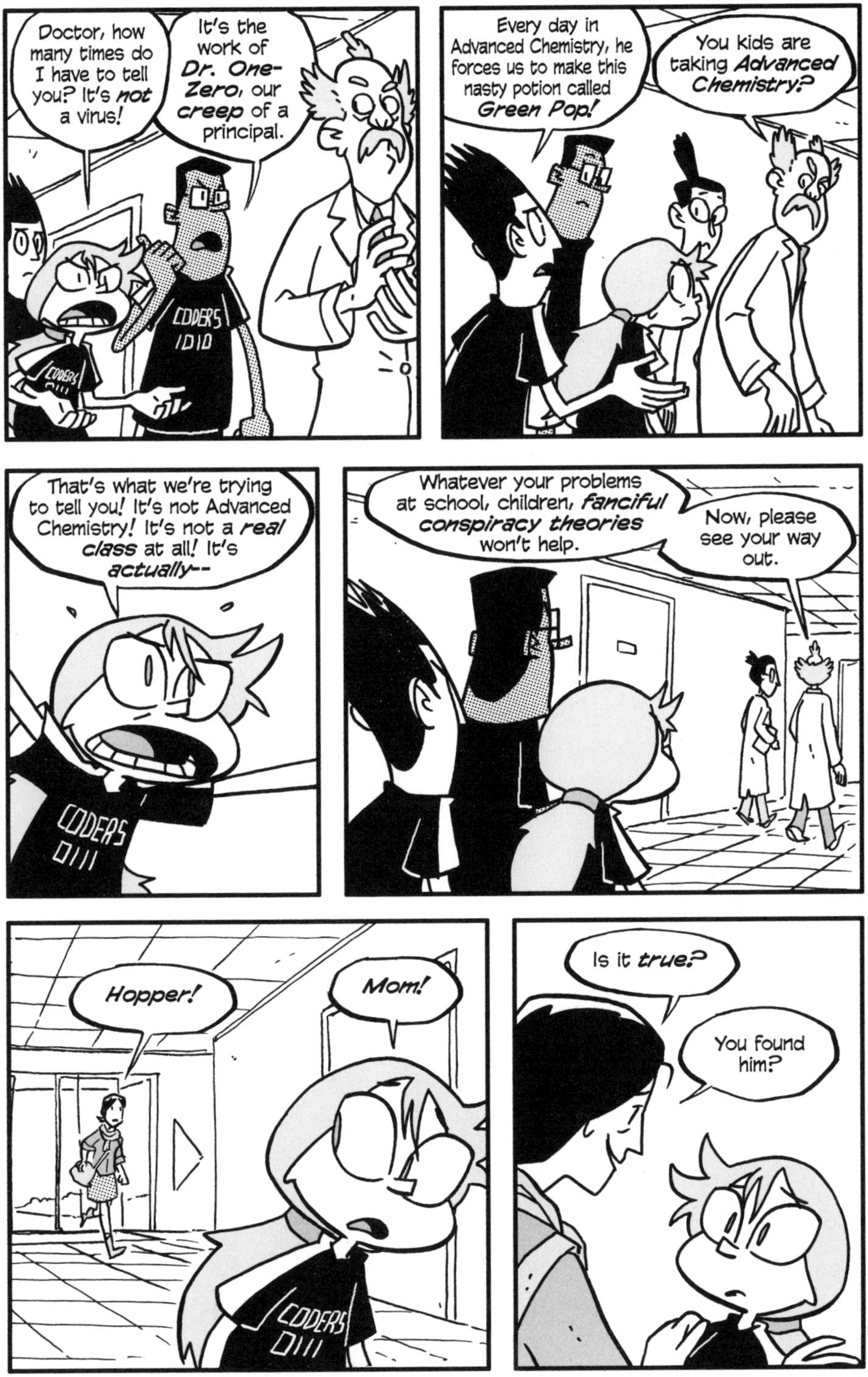
Doctor, how many times do I have to tell you? It's *not* a virus!
It's the work of *Dr. One-Zero*, our *creep* of a principal.
CODERS 1010
CODERS 0111
Every day in Advanced Chemistry, he forces us to make this nasty potion called *Green Pop!*
You kids are taking *Advanced Chemistry?*
That's what we're trying to tell you! It's not Advanced Chemistry! It's not a *real class* at all! It's *actually--*
CODERS 0111
Whatever your problems at school, children, *fanciful conspiracy theories* won't help.
Now, please see your way out.
Hopper!
Mom!
CODERS 0111
Is it *true?*
You found him?

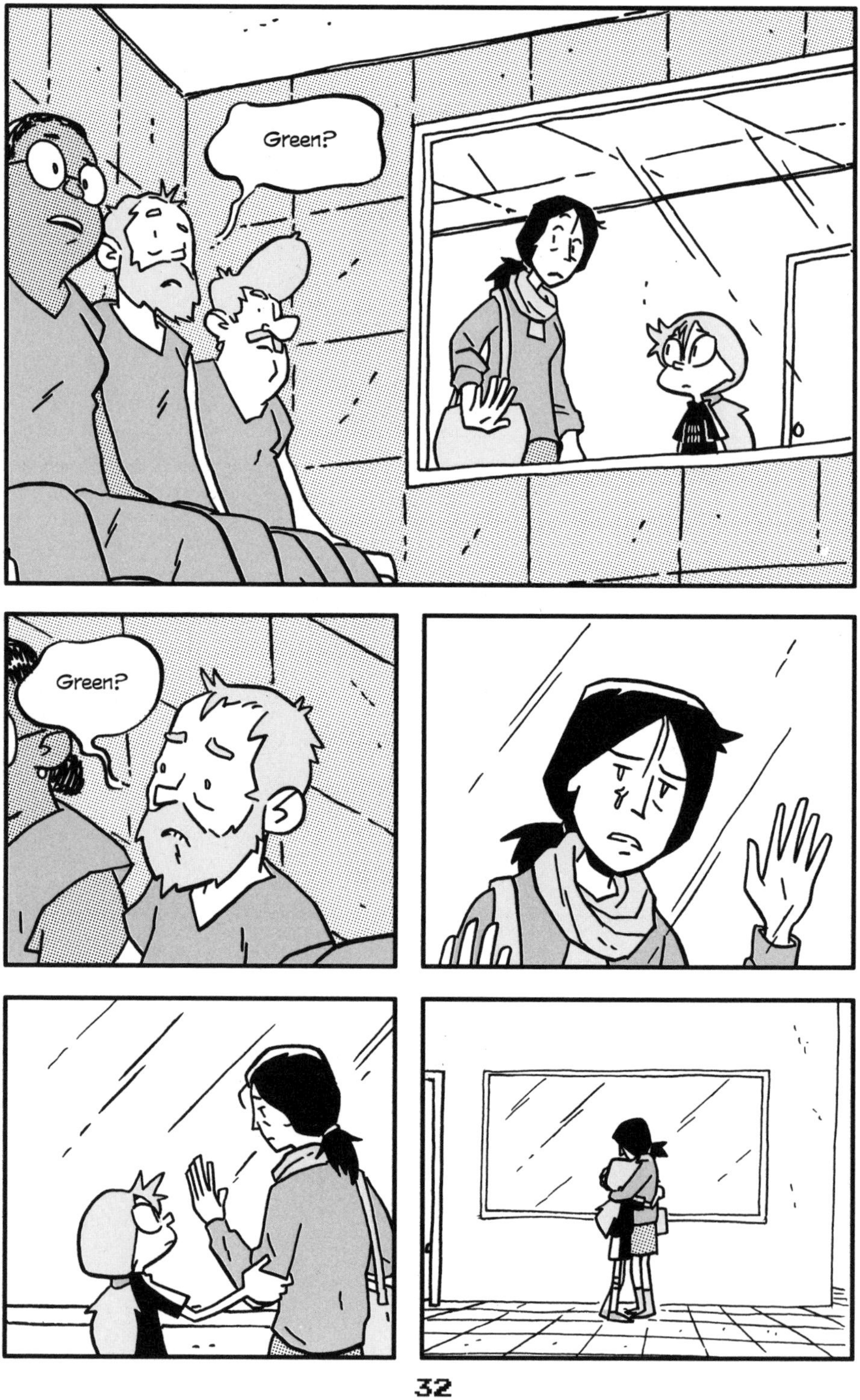
Green?
Green?

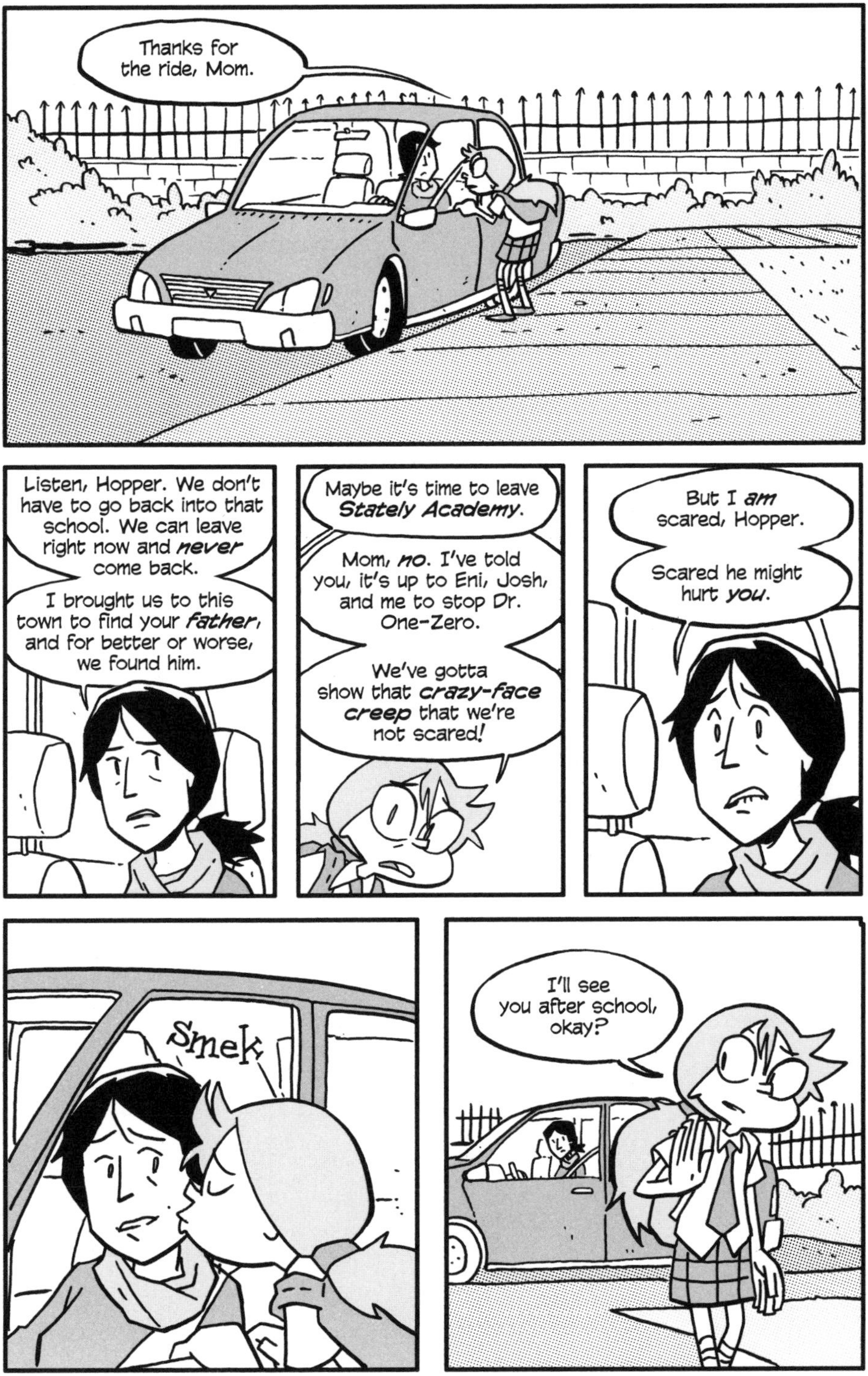

Thanks for the ride, Mom.
Listen, Hopper. We don't have to go back into that school. We can leave right now and *never* come back.
I brought us to this town to find your *father*, and for better or worse, we found him.
Maybe it's time to leave *Stately Academy*.
Mom, *no*. I've told you, it's up to Eni, Josh, and me to stop Dr. One-Zero.
We've gotta show that *crazy-face creep* that we're not scared!
But I *am* scared, Hopper.
Scared he might hurt *you*.
Smek
I'll see you after school, okay?

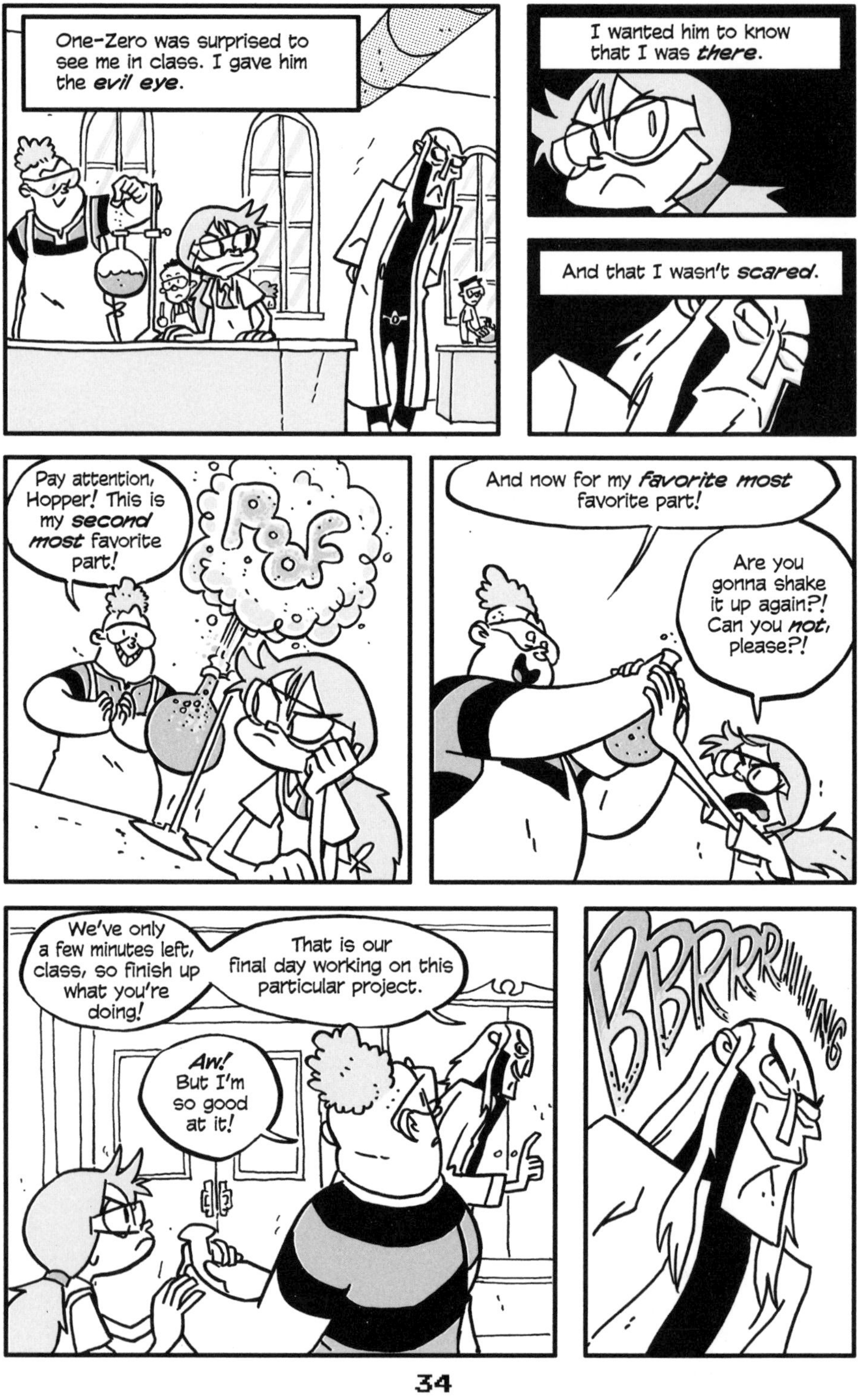

One-Zero was surprised to see me in class. I gave him the *evil eye*.
I wanted him to know that I was *there*.
And that I wasn't *scared*.
Pay attention, Hopper! This is my *second most* favorite part!
POOF
And now for my *favorite most* favorite part!
Are you gonna shake it up again?! Can you *not*, please?!
We've only a few minutes left, class, so finish up what you're doing!
That is our final day working on this particular project.
Aw! But I'm so good at it!
BBRRRIIIIIING

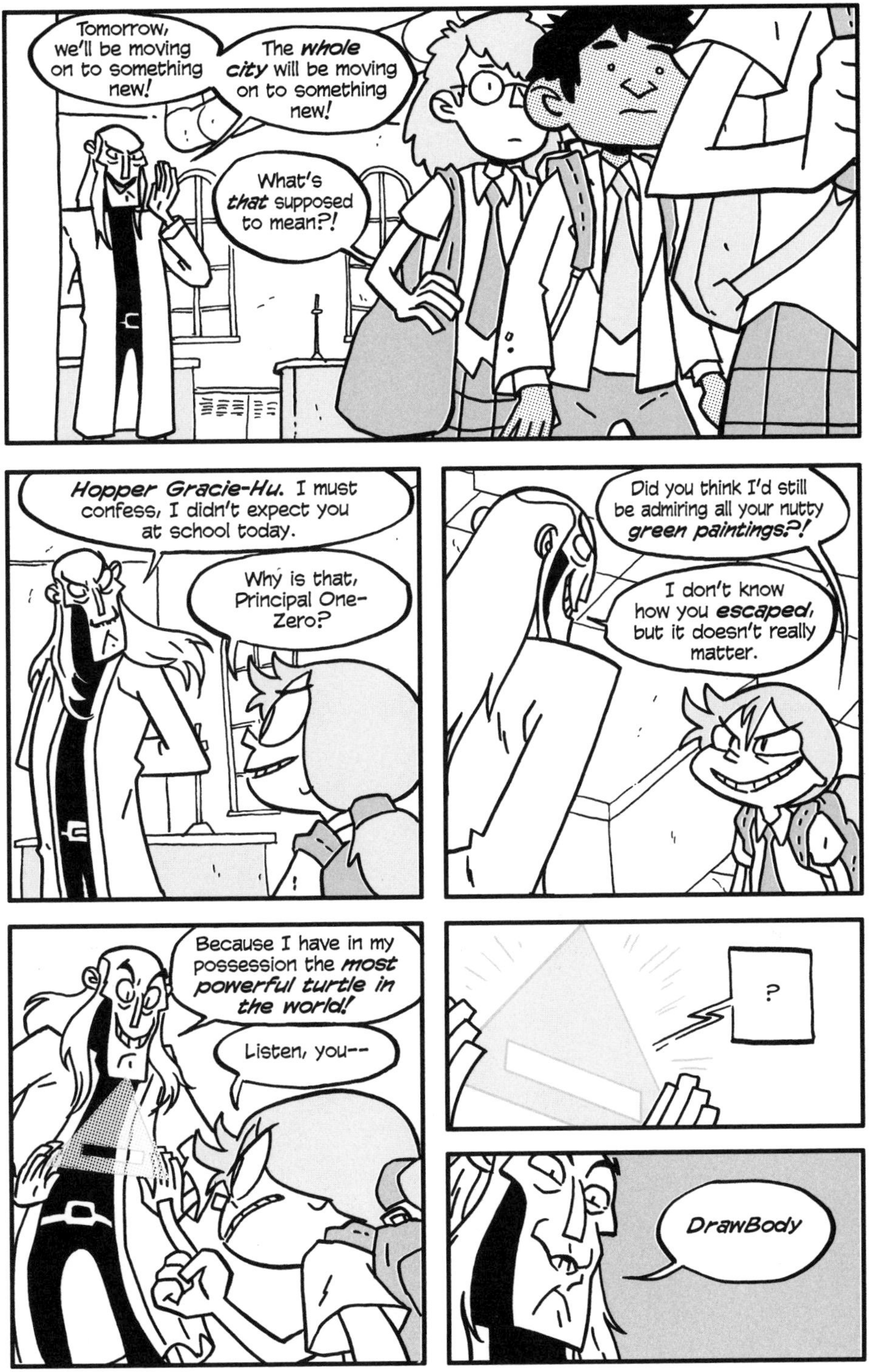
Tomorrow, we'll be moving on to something new!
The *whole city* will be moving on to something new!
What's *that* supposed to mean?!
Hopper Gracie-Hu. I must confess, I didn't expect you at school today.
Why is that, Principal One-Zero?
Did you think I'd still be admiring all your nutty *green paintings?!*
I don't know how you *escaped*, but it doesn't really matter.
Because I have in my possession the *most powerful turtle in the world!*
Listen, you--
?
DrawBody

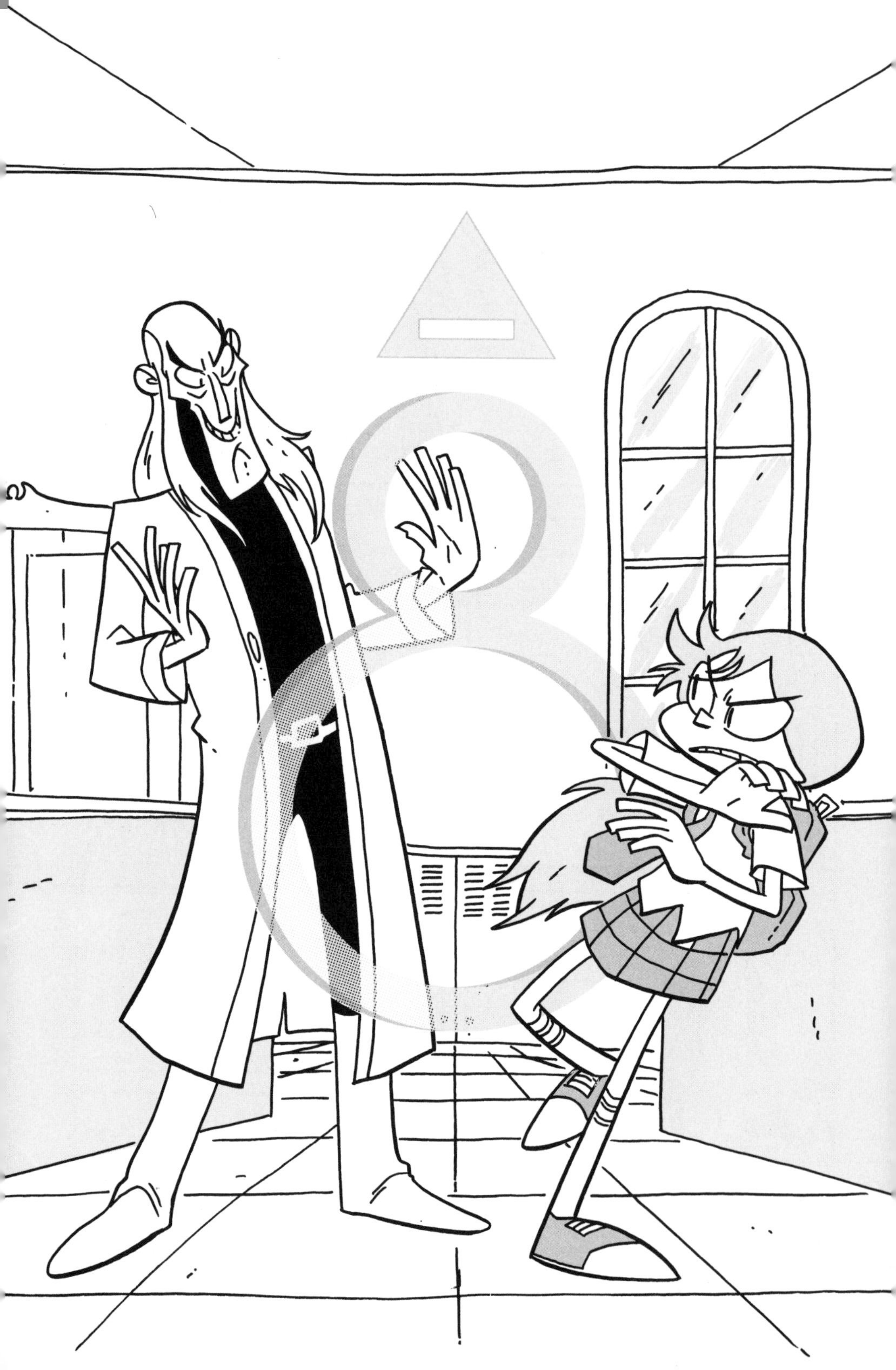

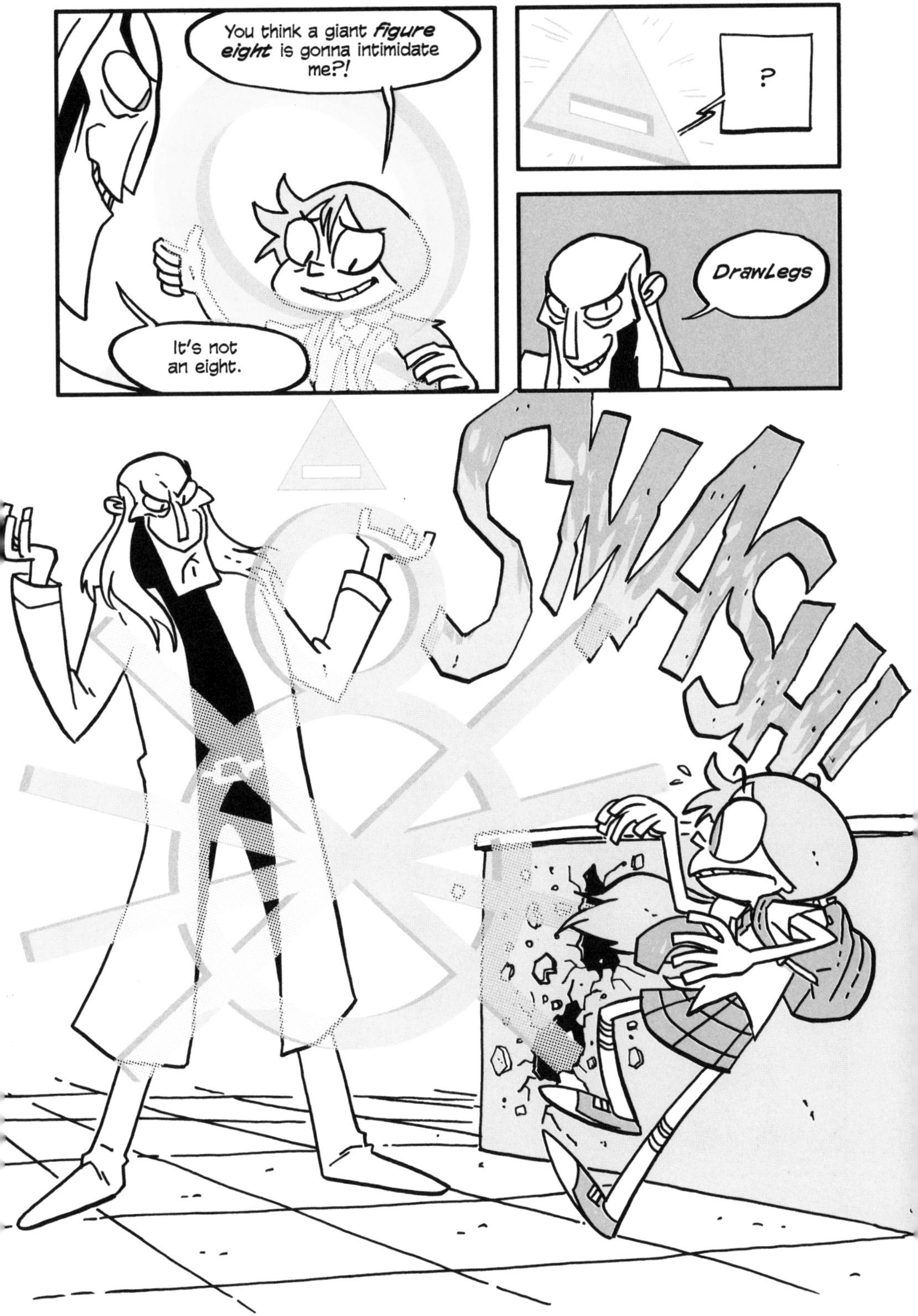

You think a giant *figure eight* is gonna intimidate me?!
It's not an eight.
?
DrawLegs
SMASH!!

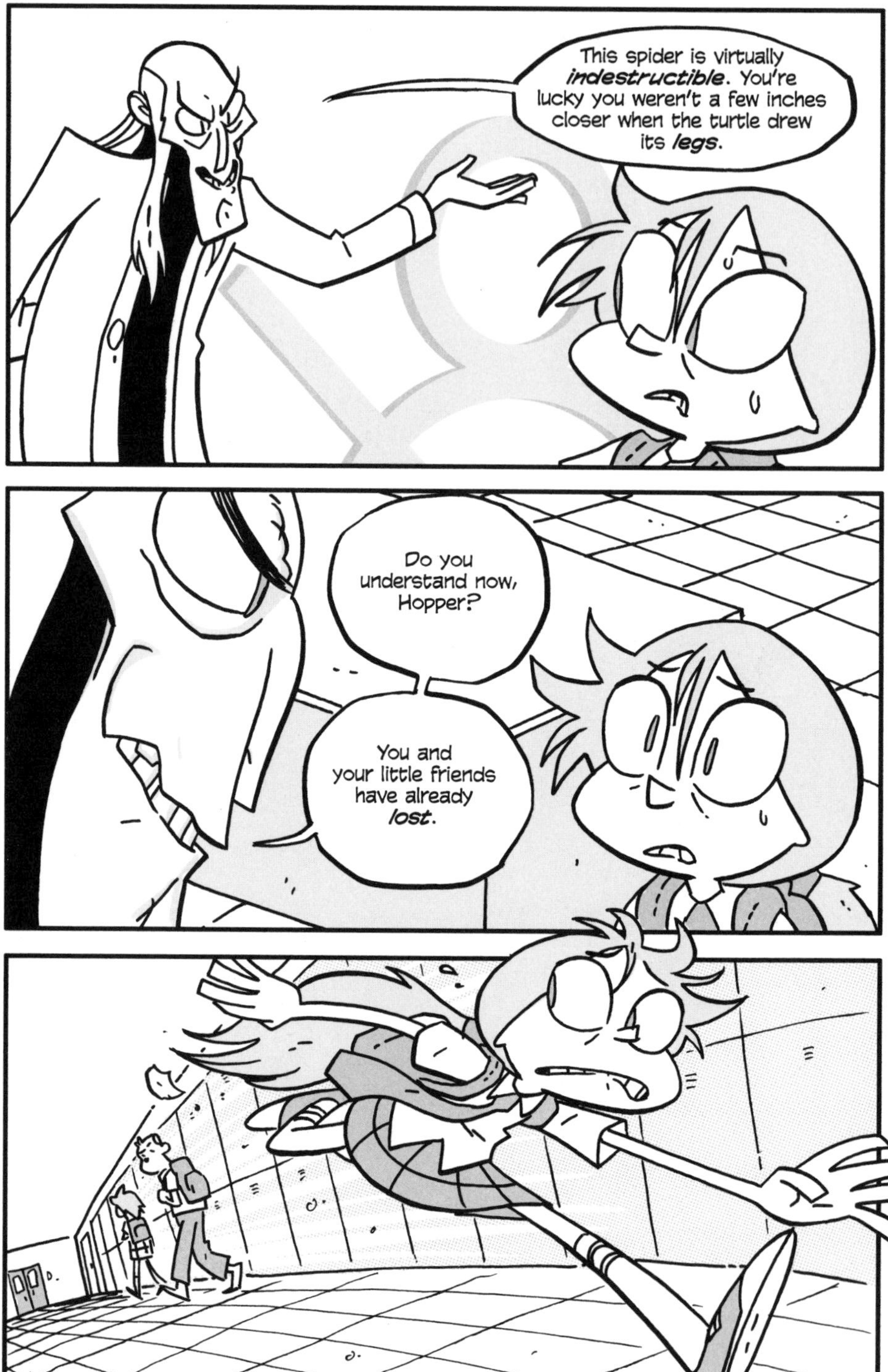
This spider is virtually *indestructible*. You're lucky you weren't a few inches closer when the turtle drew its *legs*.
Do you understand now, Hopper?
You and your little friends have already *lost*.

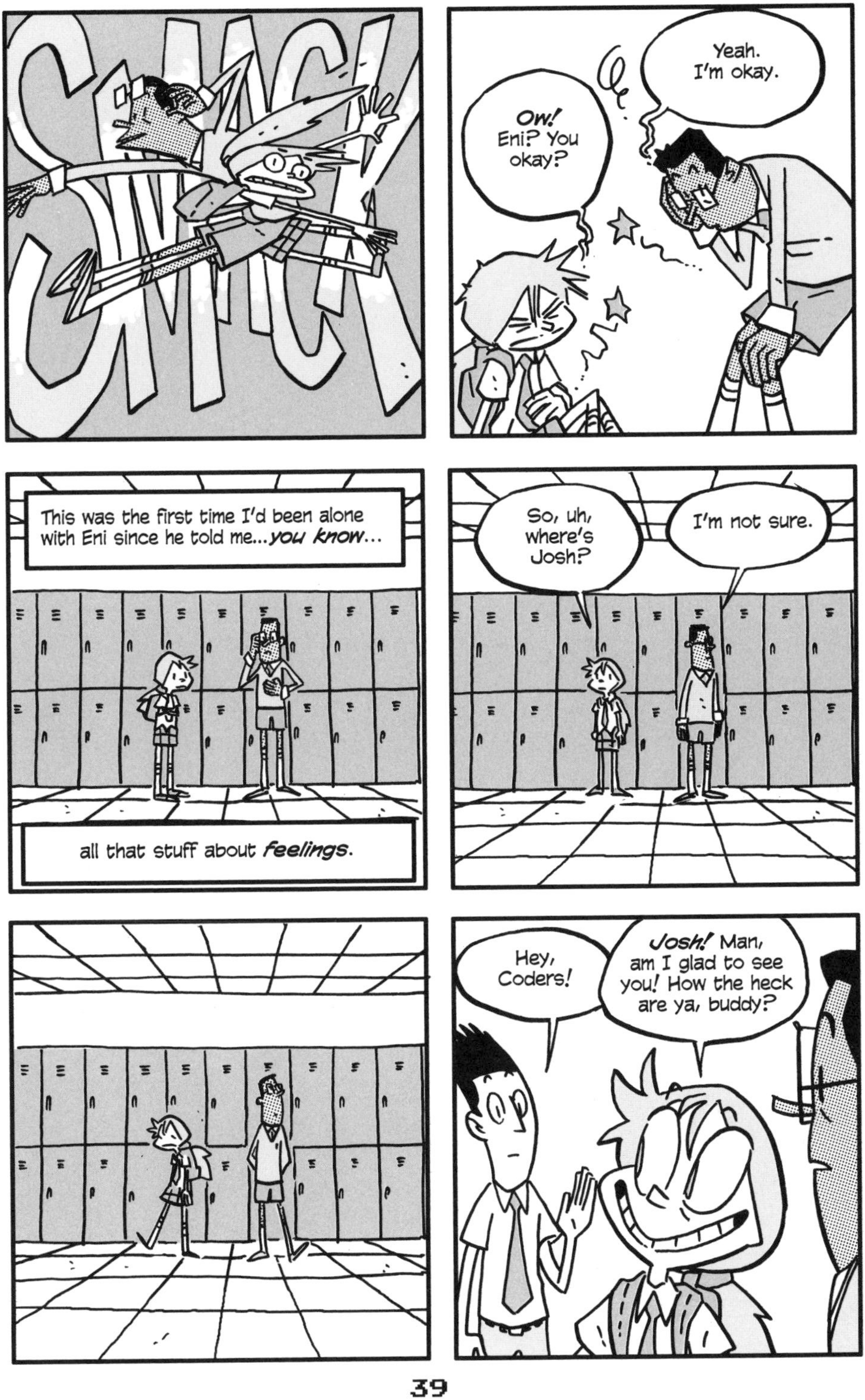
SMACK
Ow! Eni? You okay?
Yeah. I'm okay.
This was the first time I'd been alone with Eni since he told me...*you know*...
all that stuff about *feelings*.
So, uh, where's Josh?
I'm not sure.
Hey, Coders!
Josh! Man, am I glad to see you! How the heck are ya, buddy?

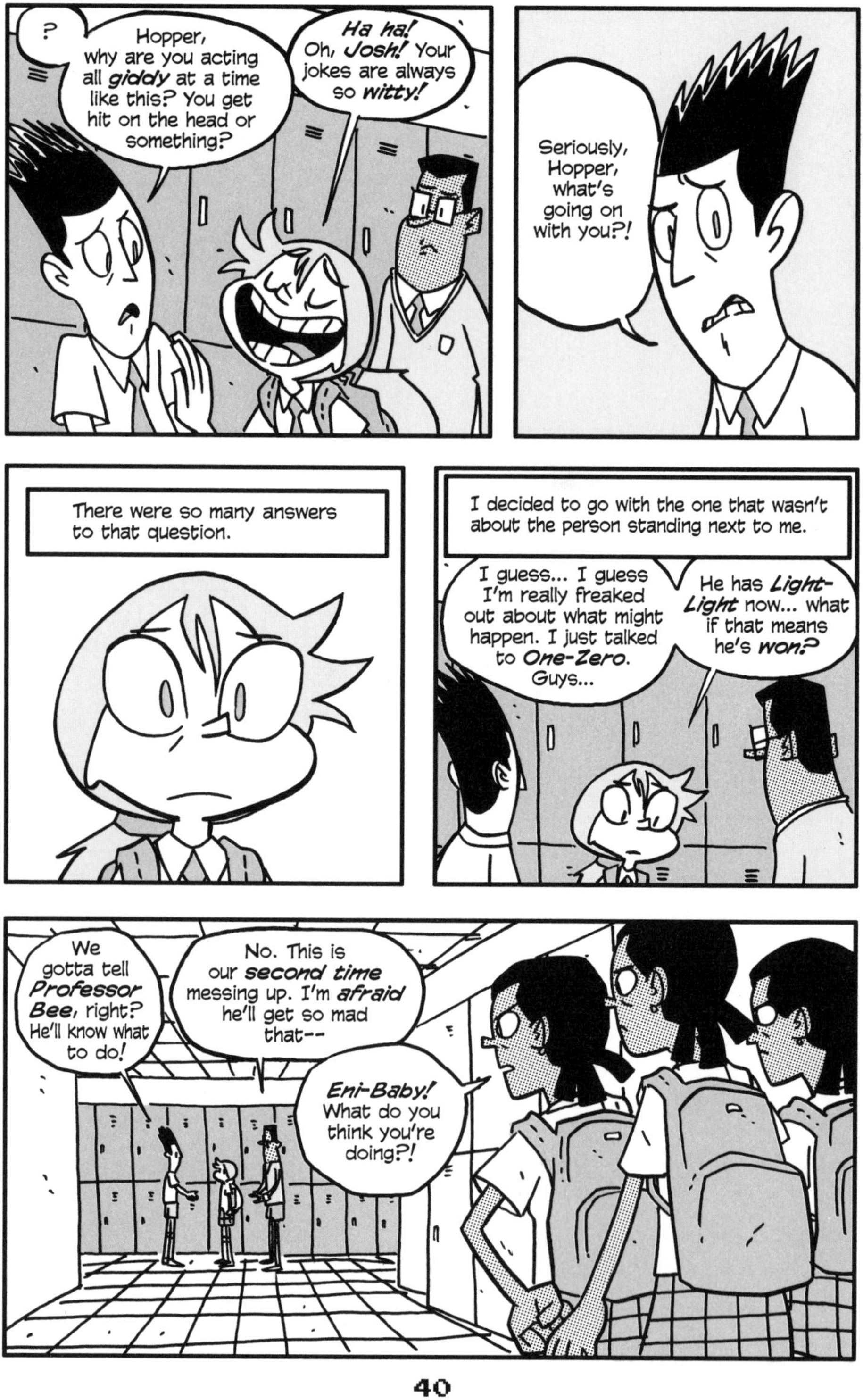
?
Hopper, why are you acting all *giddy* at a time like this? You get hit on the head or something?
Ha ha! Oh, *Josh!* Your jokes are always so *witty!*
Seriously, Hopper, what's going on with you?!
There were so many answers to that question.
I decided to go with the one that wasn't about the person standing next to me.
I guess... I guess I'm really freaked out about what might happen. I just talked to *One-Zero*. Guys...
He has *Light-Light* now... what if that means he's *won?*
We gotta tell *Professor Bee*, right? He'll know what to do!
No. This is our *second time* messing up. I'm *afraid* he'll get so mad that--
Eni-Baby! What do you think you're doing?!

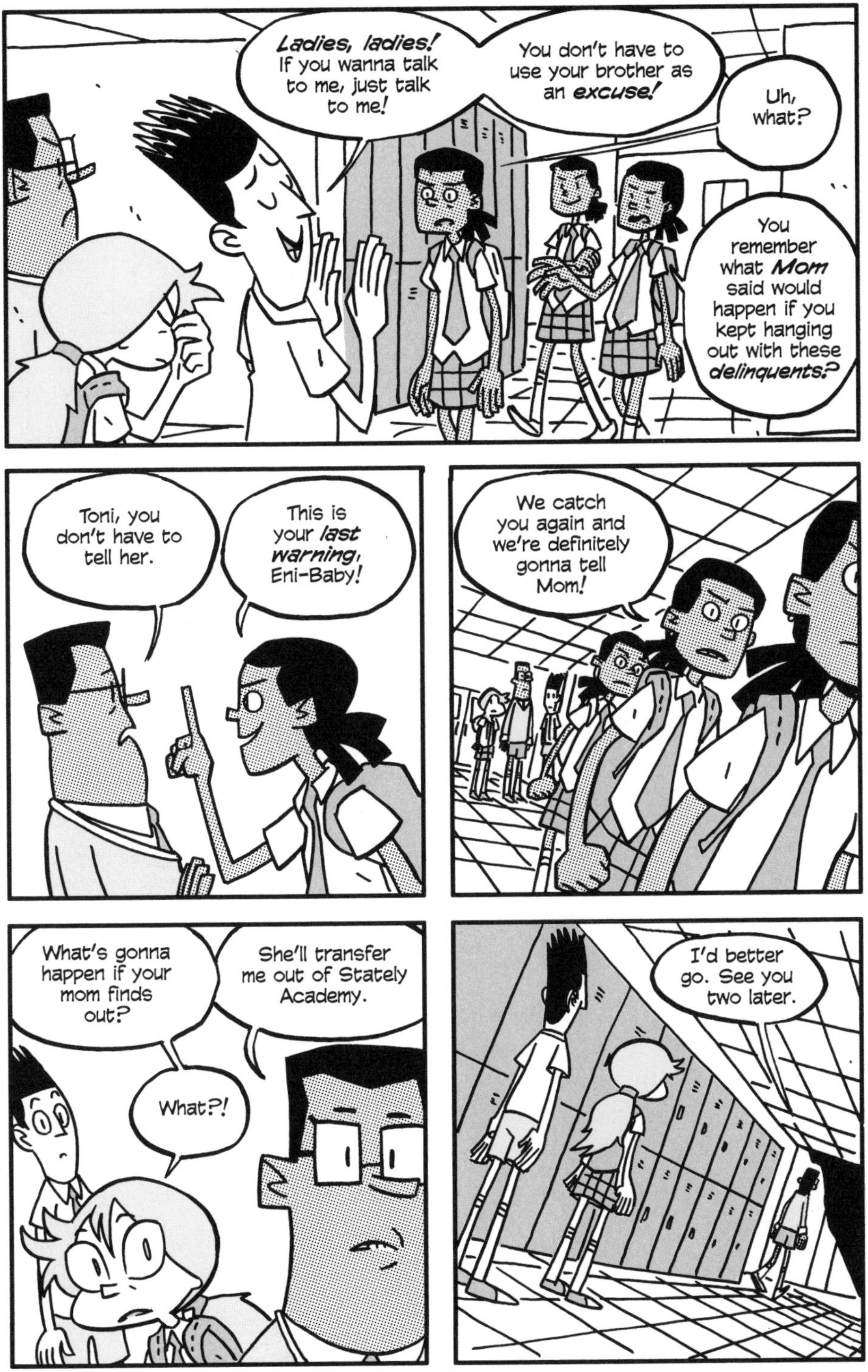
Ladies, ladies! If you wanna talk to me, just talk to me!
You don't have to use your brother as an excuse!
Uh, what?
You remember what Mom said would happen if you kept hanging out with these delinquents?
Toni, you don't have to tell her.
This is your last warning, Eni-Baby!
We catch you again and we're definitely gonna tell Mom!
What's gonna happen if your mom finds out?
She'll transfer me out of Stately Academy.
What?!
I'd better go. See you two later.

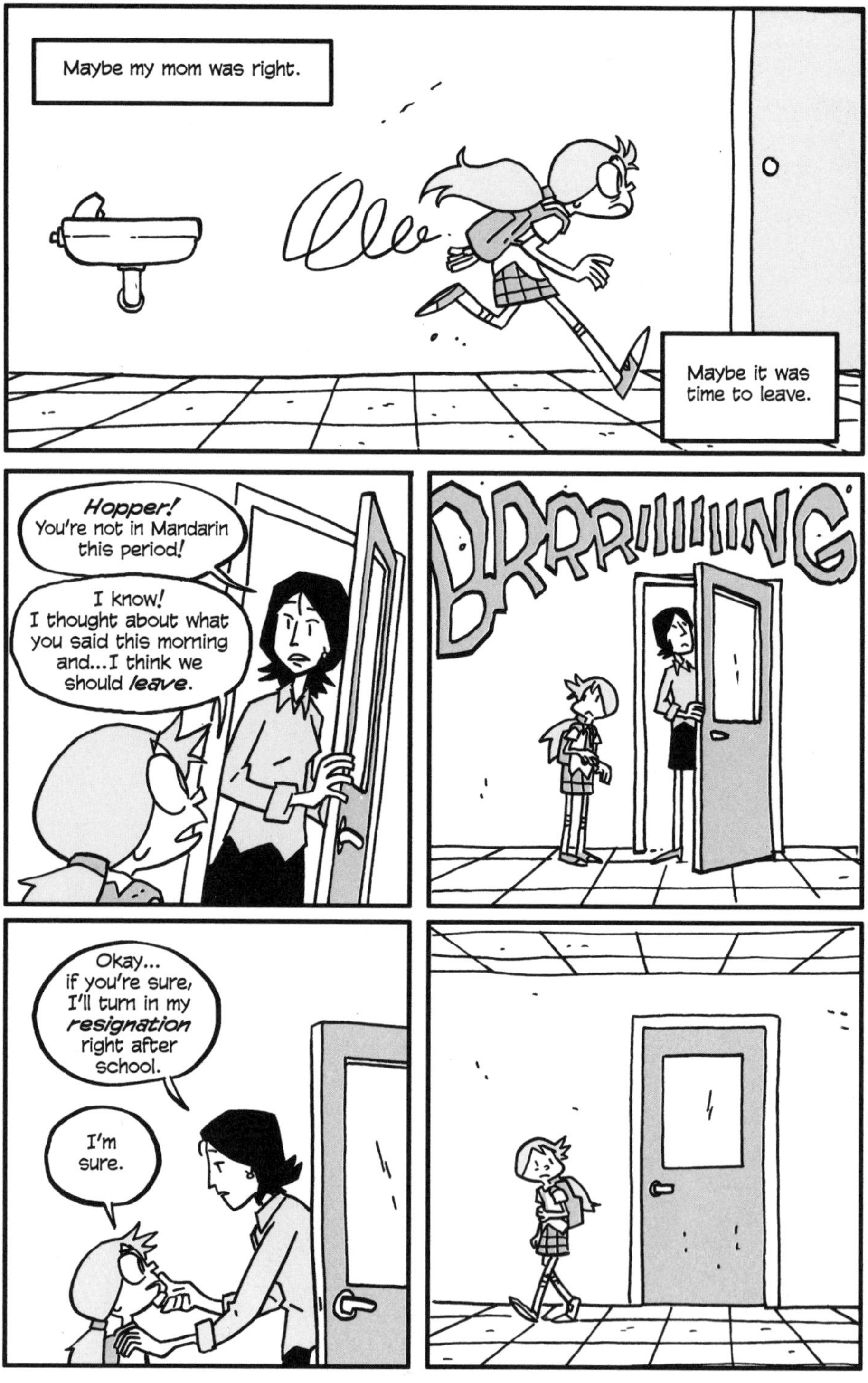
Maybe my mom was right.
Maybe it was time to leave.
Hopper! You're not in Mandarin this period!
I know! I thought about what you said this morning and...I think we should *leave*.
BRRRIIIIING
Okay... if you're sure, I'll turn in my *resignation* right after school.
I'm sure.

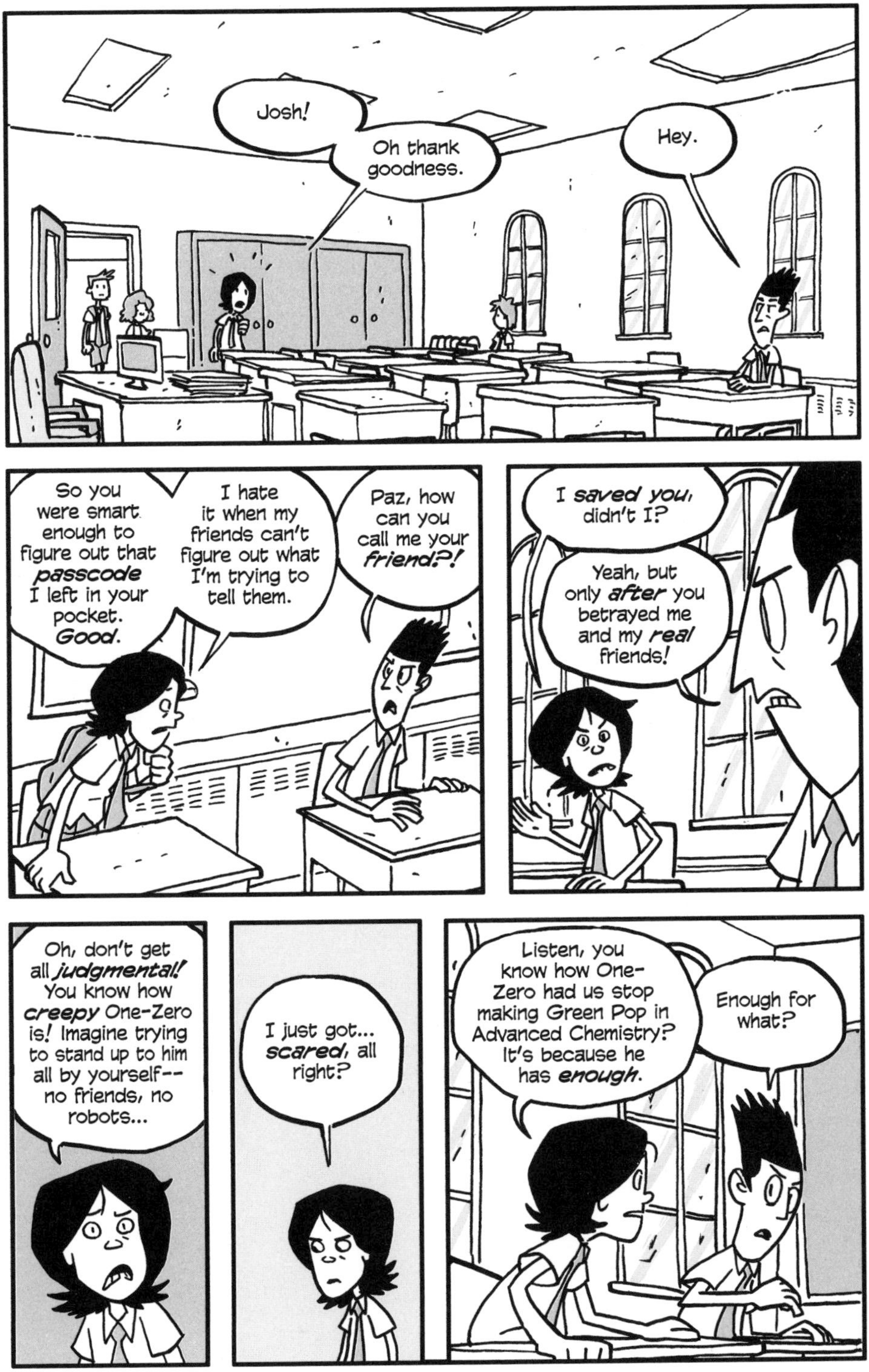
Josh!
Oh thank goodness.
Hey.
So you were smart enough to figure out that *passcode* I left in your pocket. *Good*.
I hate it when my friends can't figure out what I'm trying to tell them.
Paz, how can you call me your *friend?!*
I *saved you*, didn't I?
Yeah, but only *after* you betrayed me and my *real* friends!
Oh, don't get all *judgmental!* You know how *creepy* One-Zero is! Imagine trying to stand up to him all by yourself-- no friends, no robots...
I just got... *scared*, all right?
Listen, you know how One-Zero had us stop making Green Pop in Advanced Chemistry? It's because he has *enough*.
Enough for what?

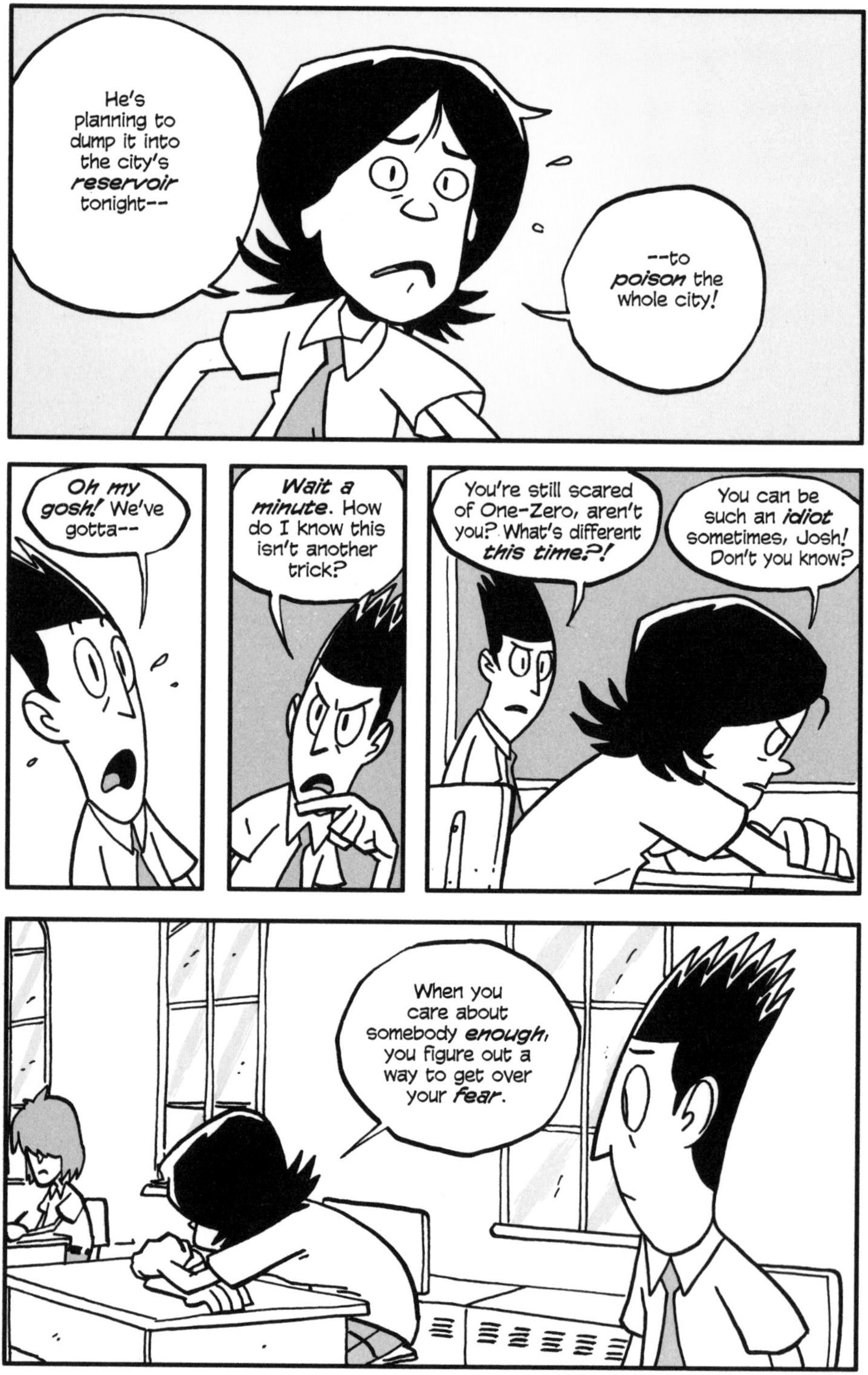
He's planning to dump it into the city's *reservoir* tonight--
--to *poison* the whole city!
Oh my gosh! We've gotta--
Wait a minute. How do I know this isn't another trick?
You're still scared of One-Zero, aren't you? What's different *this time?!*
You can be such an *idiot* sometimes, Josh! Don't you know?
When you care about somebody *enough*, you figure out a way to get over your *fear*.

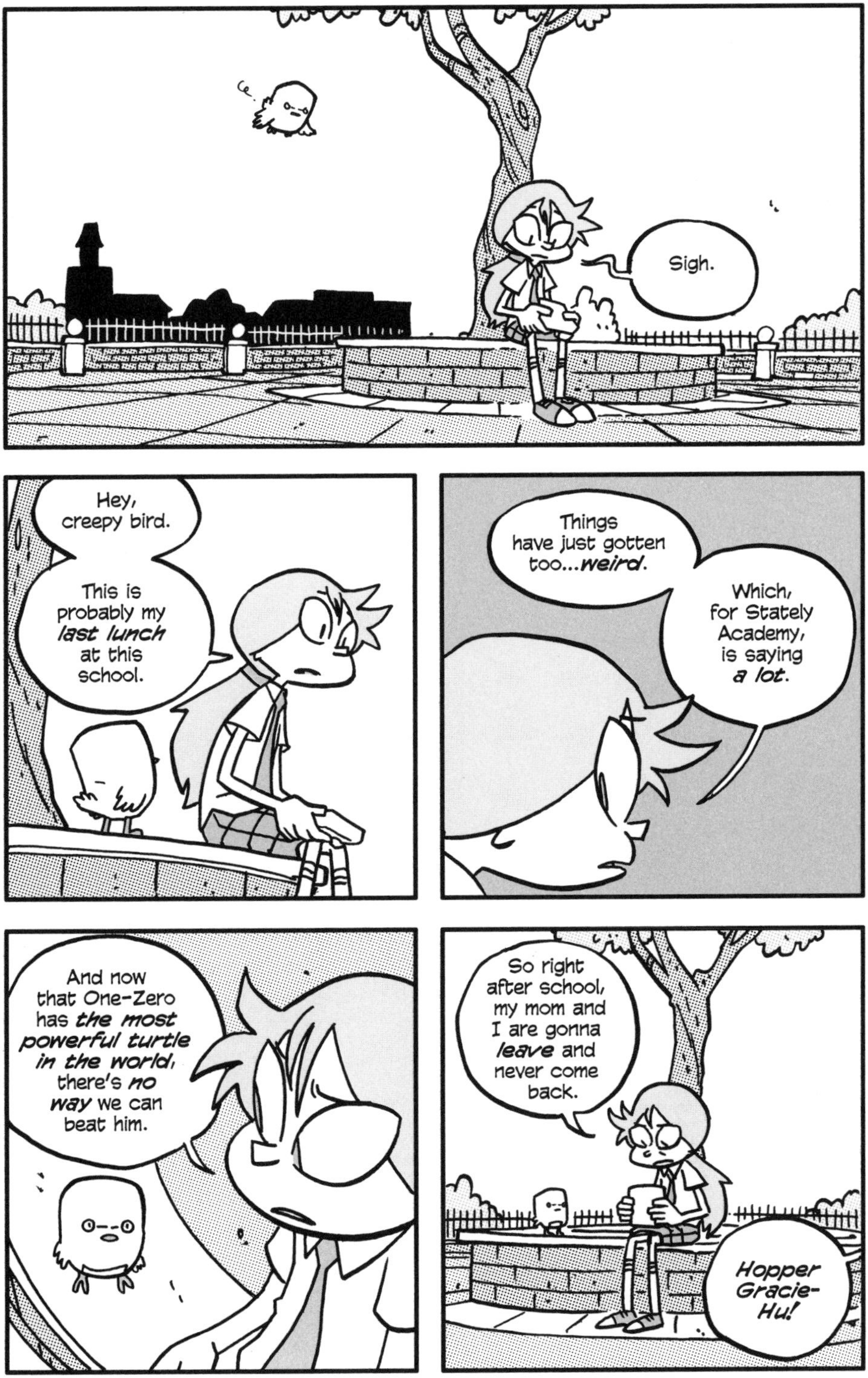
Sigh.
Hey, creepy bird.
This is probably my *last lunch* at this school.
Things have just gotten too...*weird*.
Which, for Stately Academy, is saying *a lot*.
And now that One-Zero has *the most powerful turtle in the world*, there's *no way* we can beat him.
So right after school, my mom and I are gonna *leave* and never come back.
Hopper Gracie-Hu!

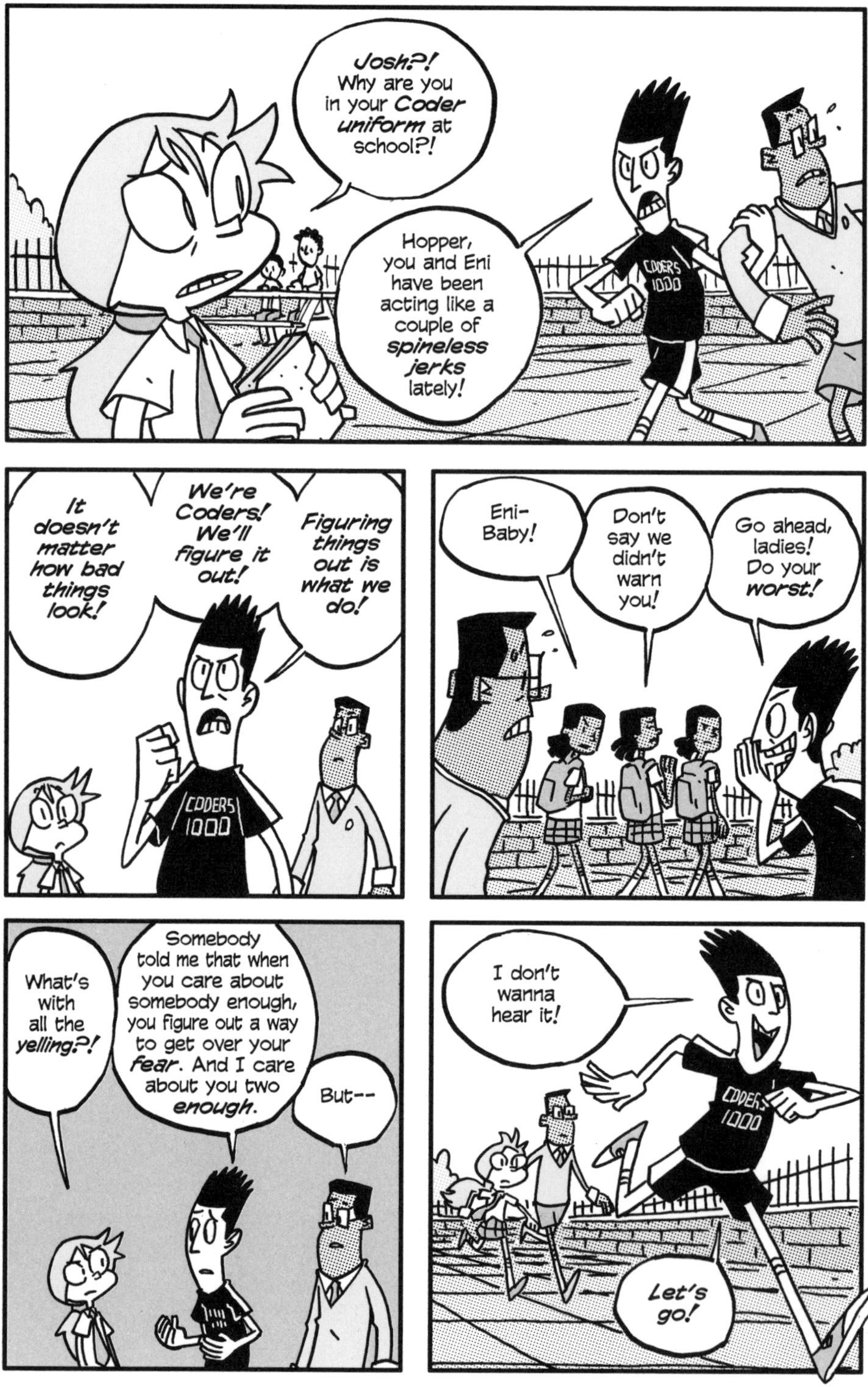
Josh?! Why are you in your Coder uniform at school?!
Hopper, you and Eni have been acting like a couple of spineless jerks lately!
It doesn't matter how bad things look!
We're Coders! We'll figure it out!
Figuring things out is what we do!
Eni-Baby!
Don't say we didn't warn you!
Go ahead, ladies! Do your worst!
What's with all the yelling?!
Somebody told me that when you care about somebody enough, you figure out a way to get over your fear. And I care about you two enough.
But--
I don't wanna hear it!
Let's go!

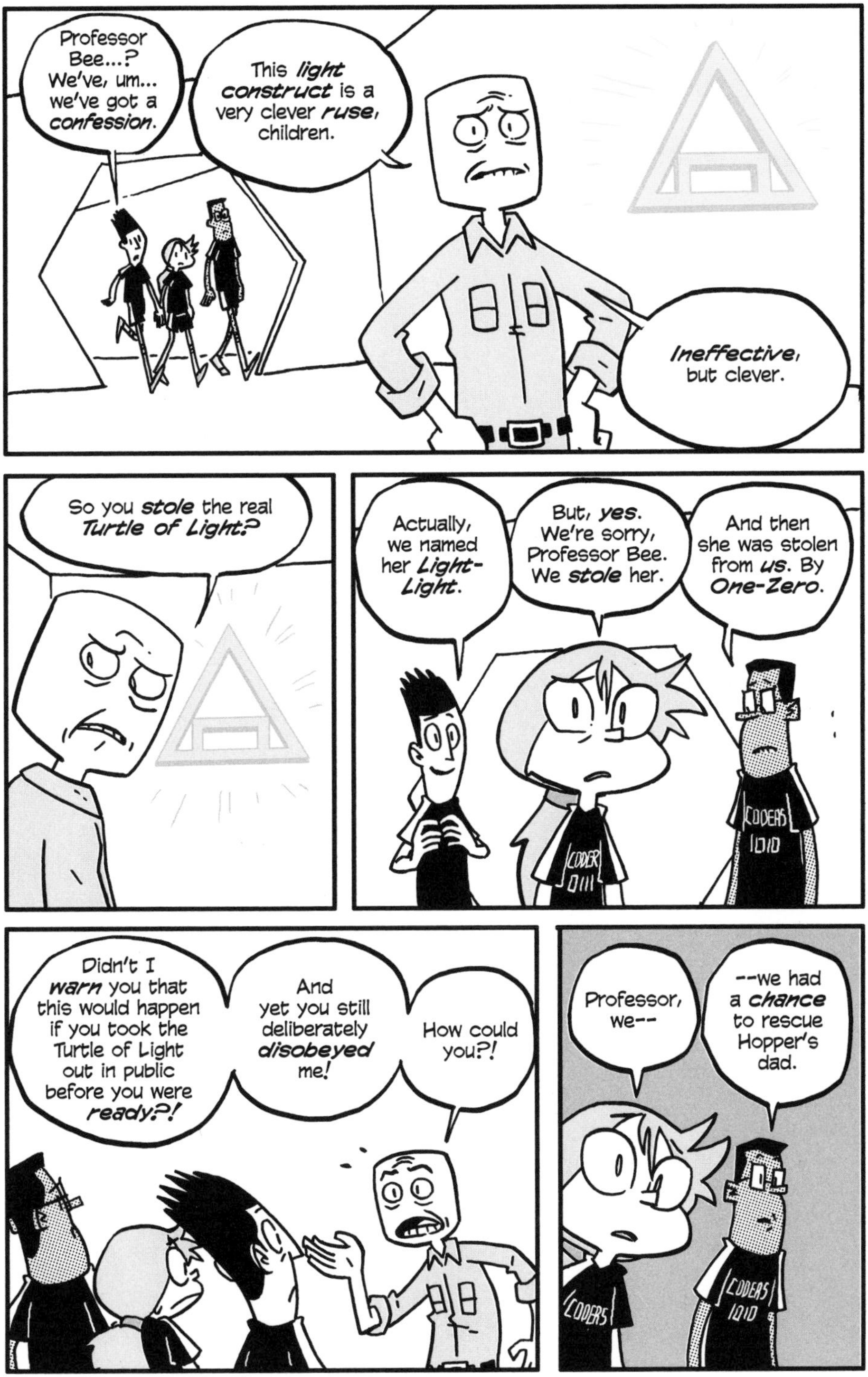
Professor Bee...? We've, um... we've got a confession.
This light construct is a very clever ruse, children.
Ineffective, but clever.
So you stole the real Turtle of Light?
Actually, we named her Light-Light.
But, yes. We're sorry, Professor Bee. We stole her.
And then she was stolen from us. By One-Zero.
CODER 0111
CODERS 1010
Didn't I warn you that this would happen if you took the Turtle of Light out in public before you were ready?!
And yet you still deliberately disobeyed me!
How could you?!
Professor, we--
--we had a chance to rescue Hopper's dad.
CODERS
CODERS 1010

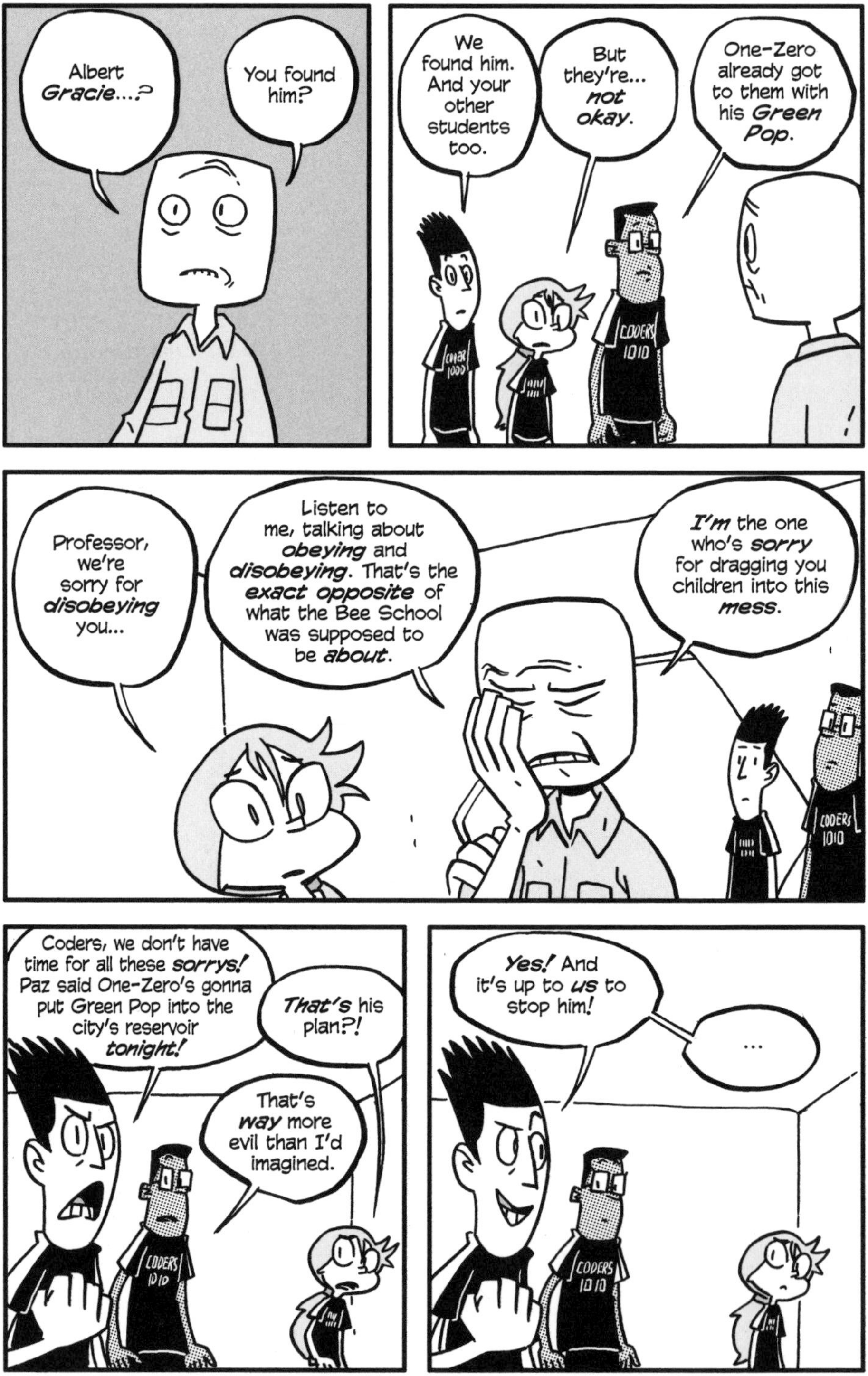
Albert *Gracie*...?
You found him?
We found him. And your other students too.
But they're... *not okay*.
One-Zero already got to them with his *Green Pop*.
Professor, we're sorry for *disobeying* you...
Listen to me, talking about *obeying* and *disobeying*. That's the *exact opposite* of what the Bee School was supposed to be *about*.
I'm the one who's *sorry* for dragging you children into this *mess*.
Coders, we don't have time for all these *sorrys!* Paz said One-Zero's gonna put Green Pop into the city's reservoir *tonight!*
That's his plan?!
That's *way* more evil than I'd imagined.
Yes! And it's up to *us* to stop him!
...

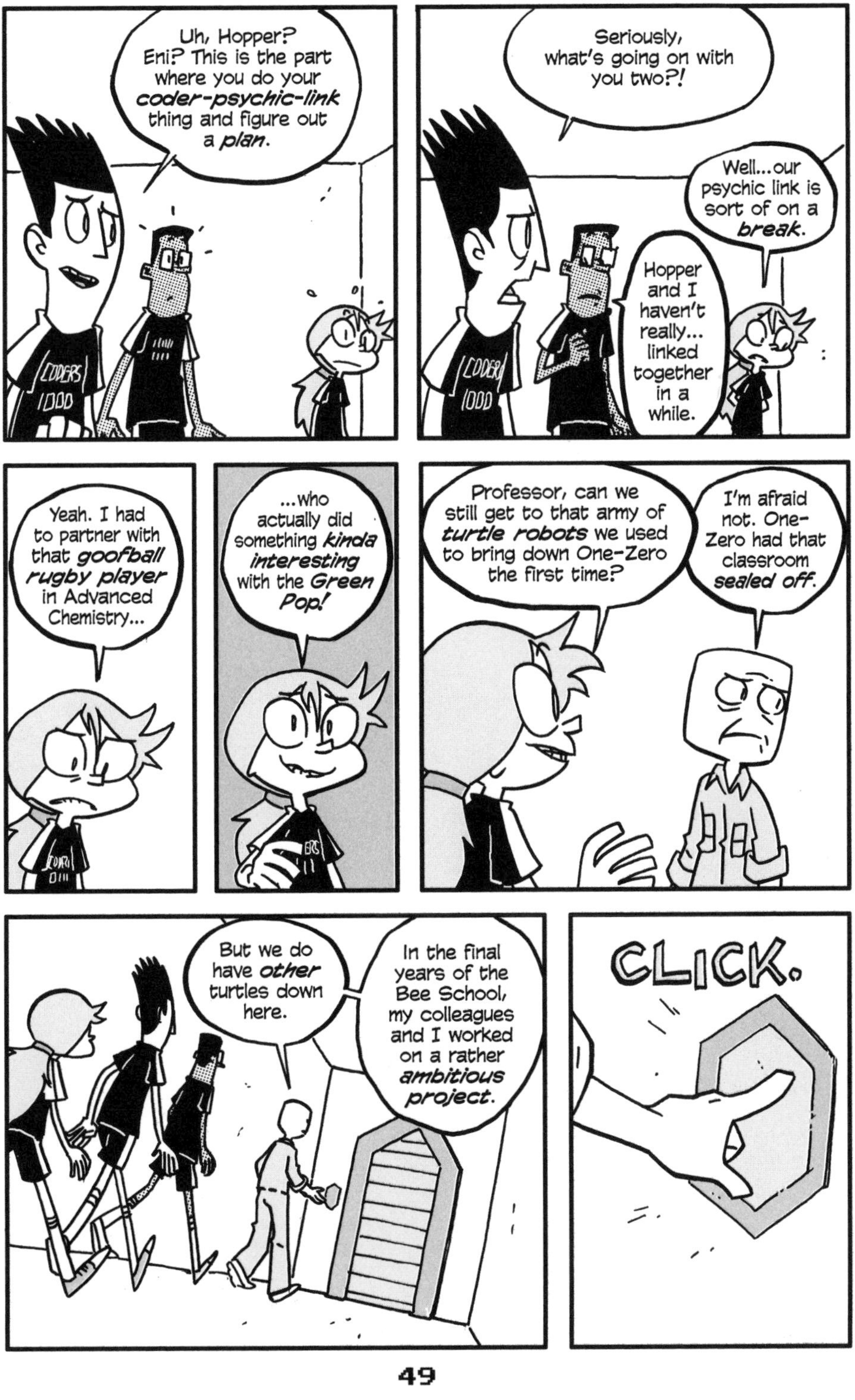
Uh, Hopper? Eni? This is the part where you do your coder-psychic-link thing and figure out a plan.
CODERS 1000
Seriously, what's going on with you two?!
Well...our psychic link is sort of on a break.
Hopper and I haven't really... linked together in a while.
Yeah. I had to partner with that goofball rugby player in Advanced Chemistry...
...who actually did something kinda interesting with the Green Pop!
Professor, can we still get to that army of turtle robots we used to bring down One-Zero the first time?
I'm afraid not. One-Zero had that classroom sealed off.
But we do have other turtles down here.
In the final years of the Bee School, my colleagues and I worked on a rather ambitious project.
CLICK.

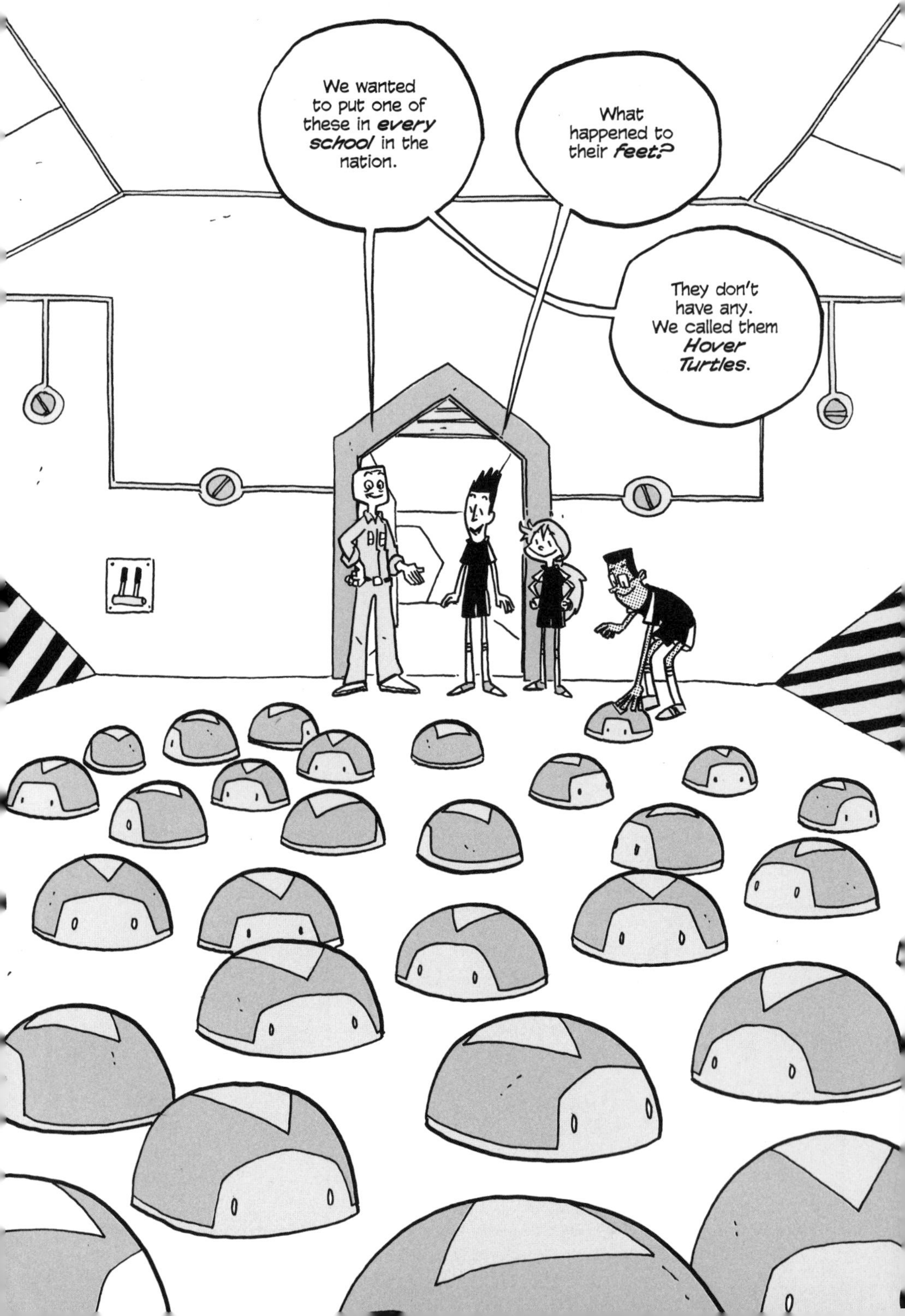
We wanted to put one of these in *every school* in the nation.
What happened to their *feet?*
They don't have any. We called them *Hover Turtles*.

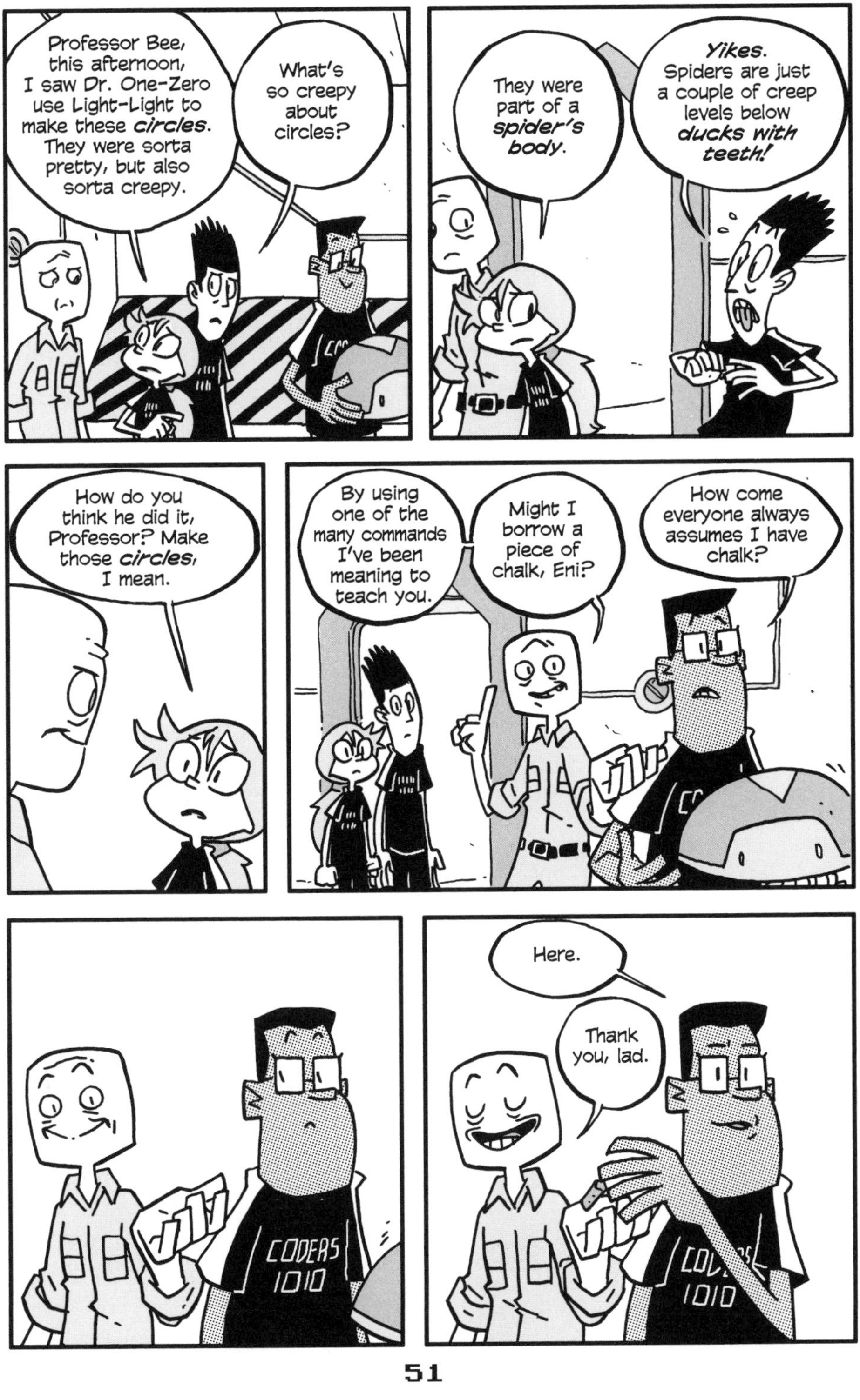
Professor Bee, this afternoon, I saw Dr. One-Zero use Light-Light to make these *circles*. They were sorta pretty, but also sorta creepy.
What's so creepy about circles?
They were part of a *spider's body*.
Yikes. Spiders are just a couple of creep levels below *ducks with teeth!*
How do you think he did it, Professor? Make those *circles*, I mean.
By using one of the many commands I've been meaning to teach you.
Might I borrow a piece of chalk, Eni?
How come everyone always assumes I have chalk?
CODERS 1010
Here.
Thank you, lad.

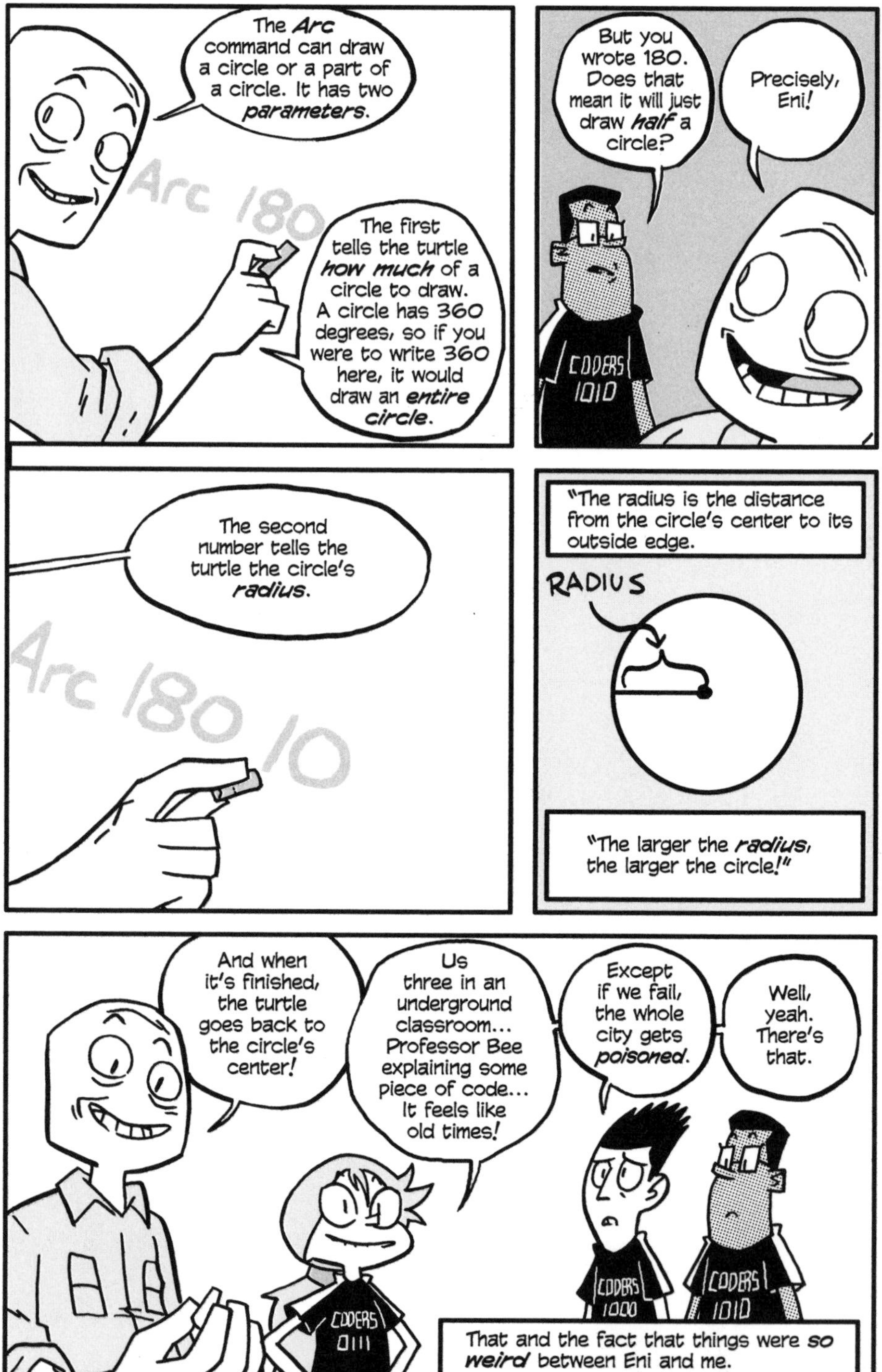
The Arc command can draw a circle or a part of a circle. It has two parameters.
Arc 180
The first tells the turtle how much of a circle to draw. A circle has 360 degrees, so if you were to write 360 here, it would draw an entire circle.
But you wrote 180. Does that mean it will just draw half a circle?
Precisely, Eni!
CODERS 1010
The second number tells the turtle the circle's radius.
Arc 180 10
"The radius is the distance from the circle's center to its outside edge.
RADIUS
"The larger the radius, the larger the circle!"
And when it's finished, the turtle goes back to the circle's center!
Us three in an underground classroom... Professor Bee explaining some piece of code... It feels like old times!
Except if we fail, the whole city gets poisoned.
Well, yeah. There's that.
CODERS 0111
CODERS 1000
CODERS 1010
That and the fact that things were so weird between Eni and me.

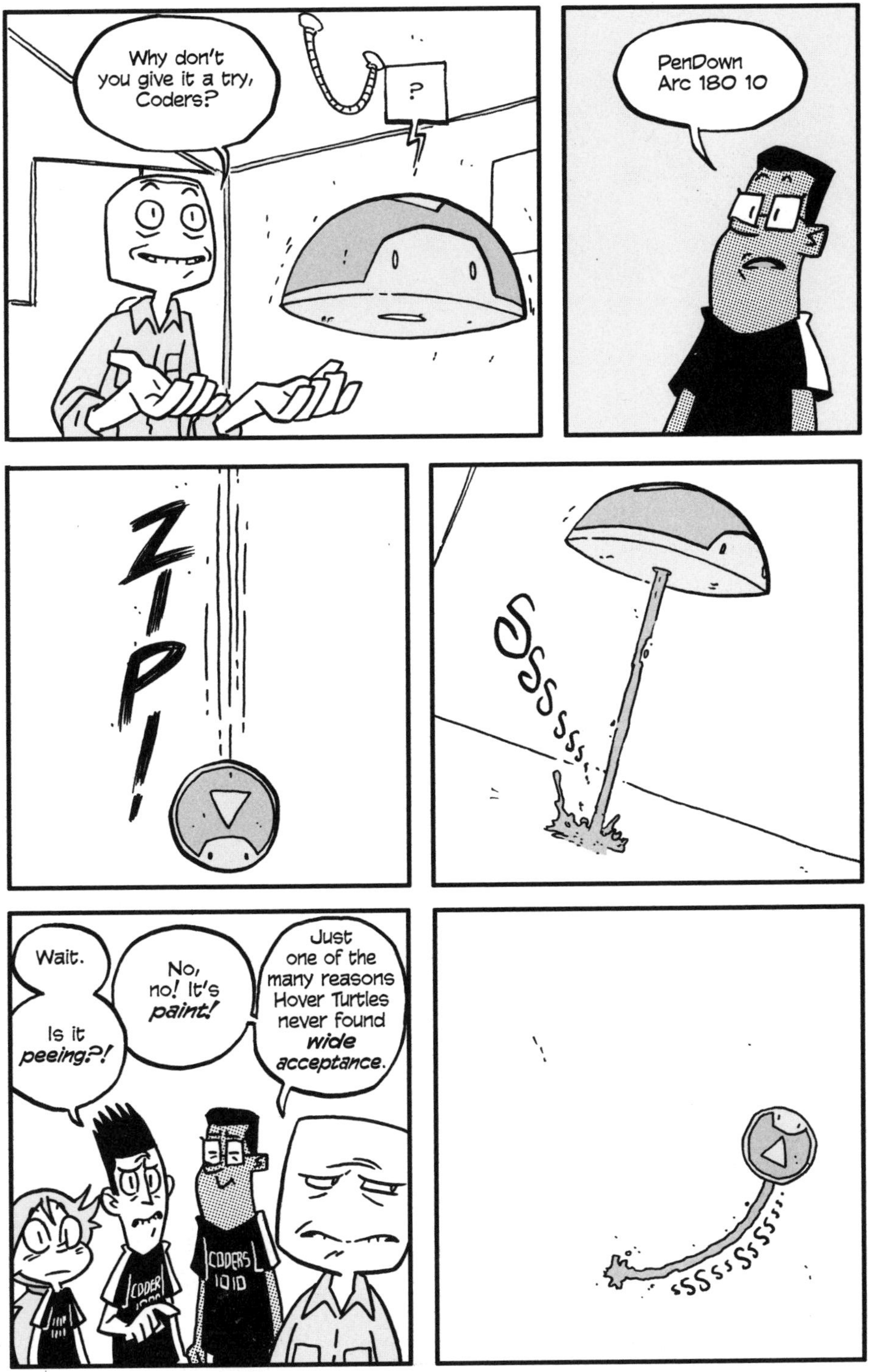

Why don't you give it a try, Coders?
?
PenDown Arc 180 10
ZIP!
SSSSSS
Wait.
Is it *peeing?!*
No, no! It's ***paint!***
Just one of the many reasons Hover Turtles never found ***wide acceptance***.
CODERS 1010
sSSSSSSSSSS

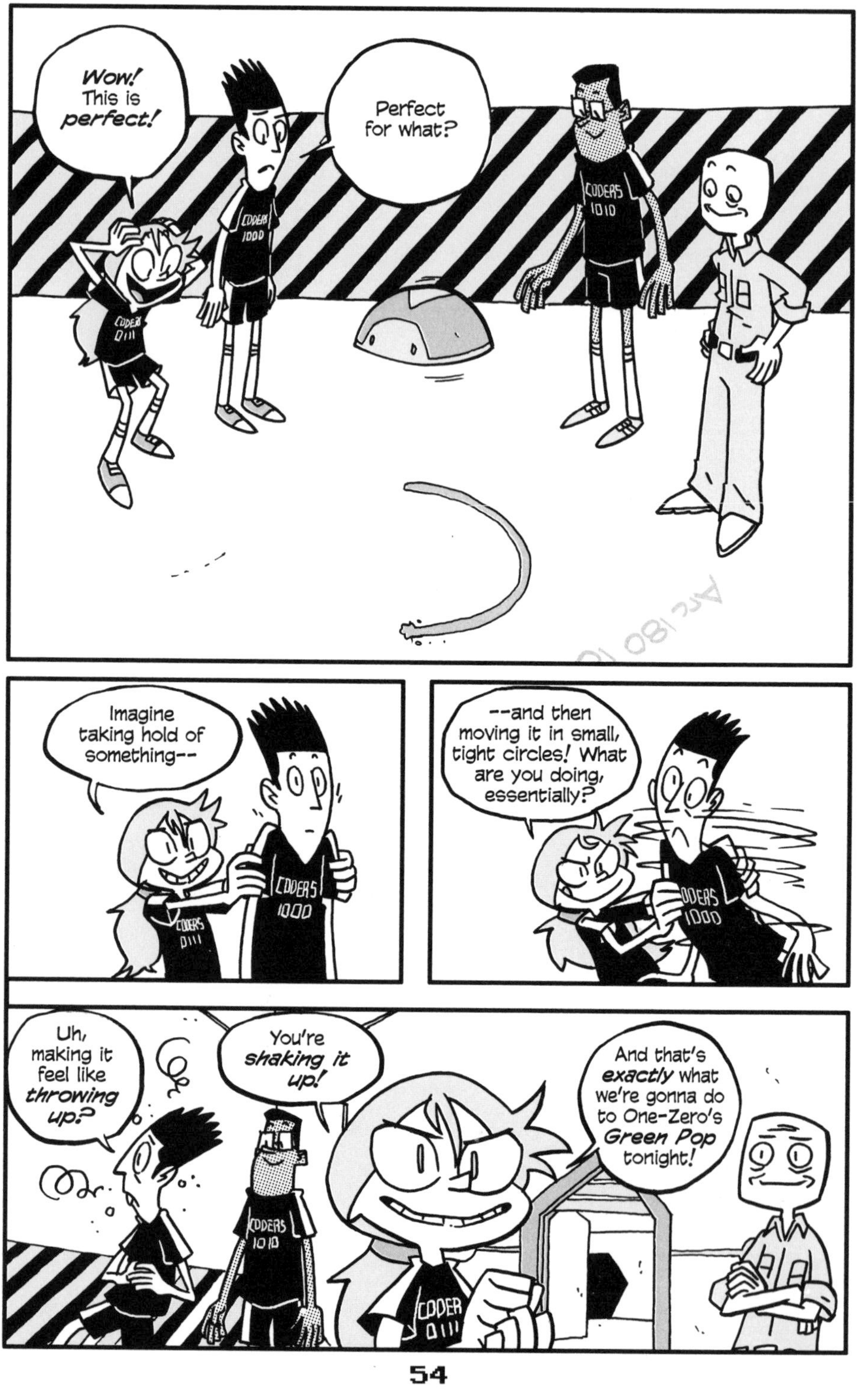
Wow! This is perfect!
Perfect for what?
Arc 180
Imagine taking hold of something--
--and then moving it in small, tight circles! What are you doing, essentially?
Uh, making it feel like throwing up?
You're shaking it up!
And that's exactly what we're gonna do to One-Zero's Green Pop tonight!

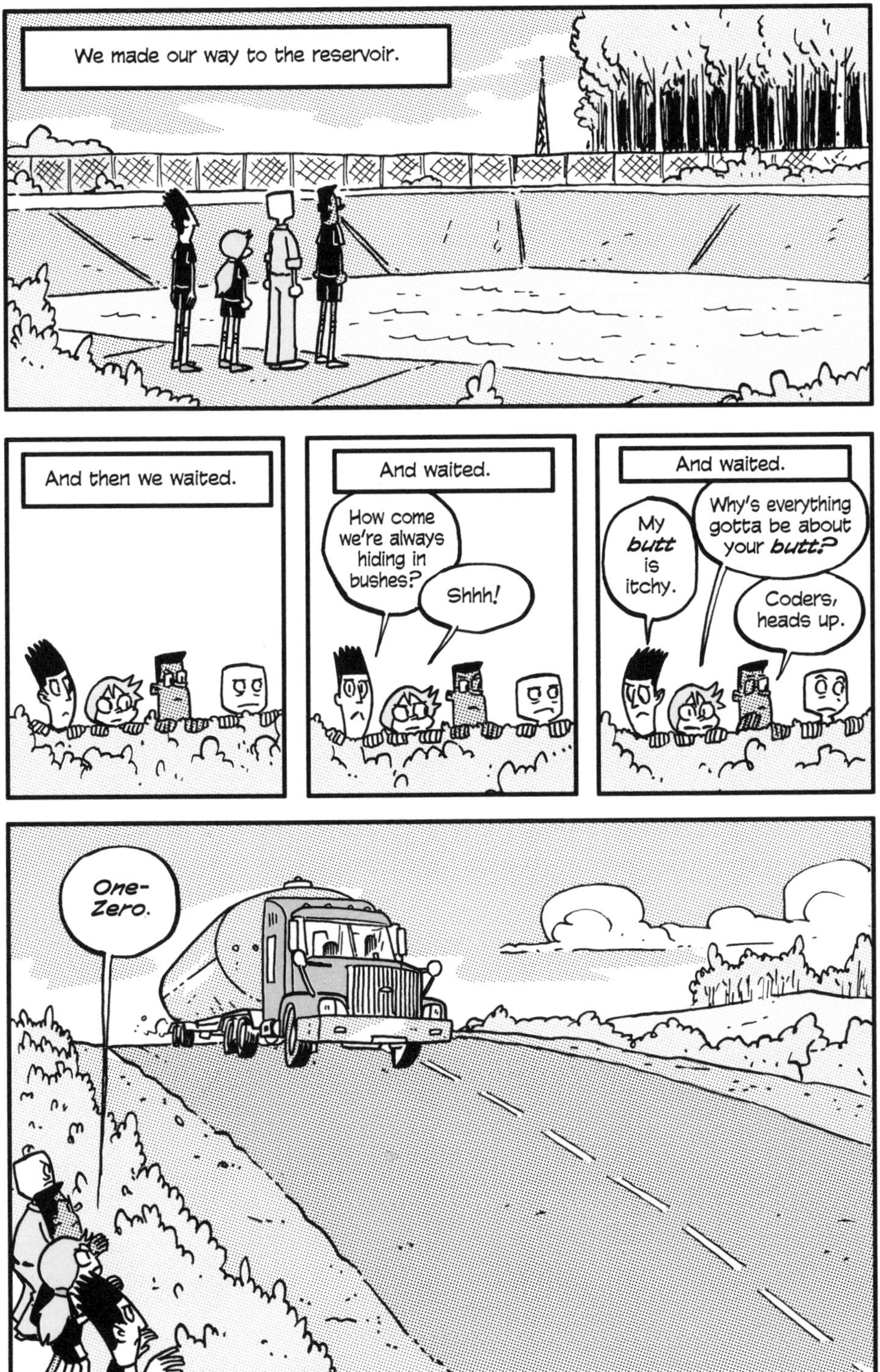
We made our way to the reservoir.
And then we waited.
And waited.
How come we're always hiding in bushes?
Shhh!
And waited.
My *butt* is itchy.
Why's everything gotta be about your *butt?*
Coders, heads up.
One-Zero.

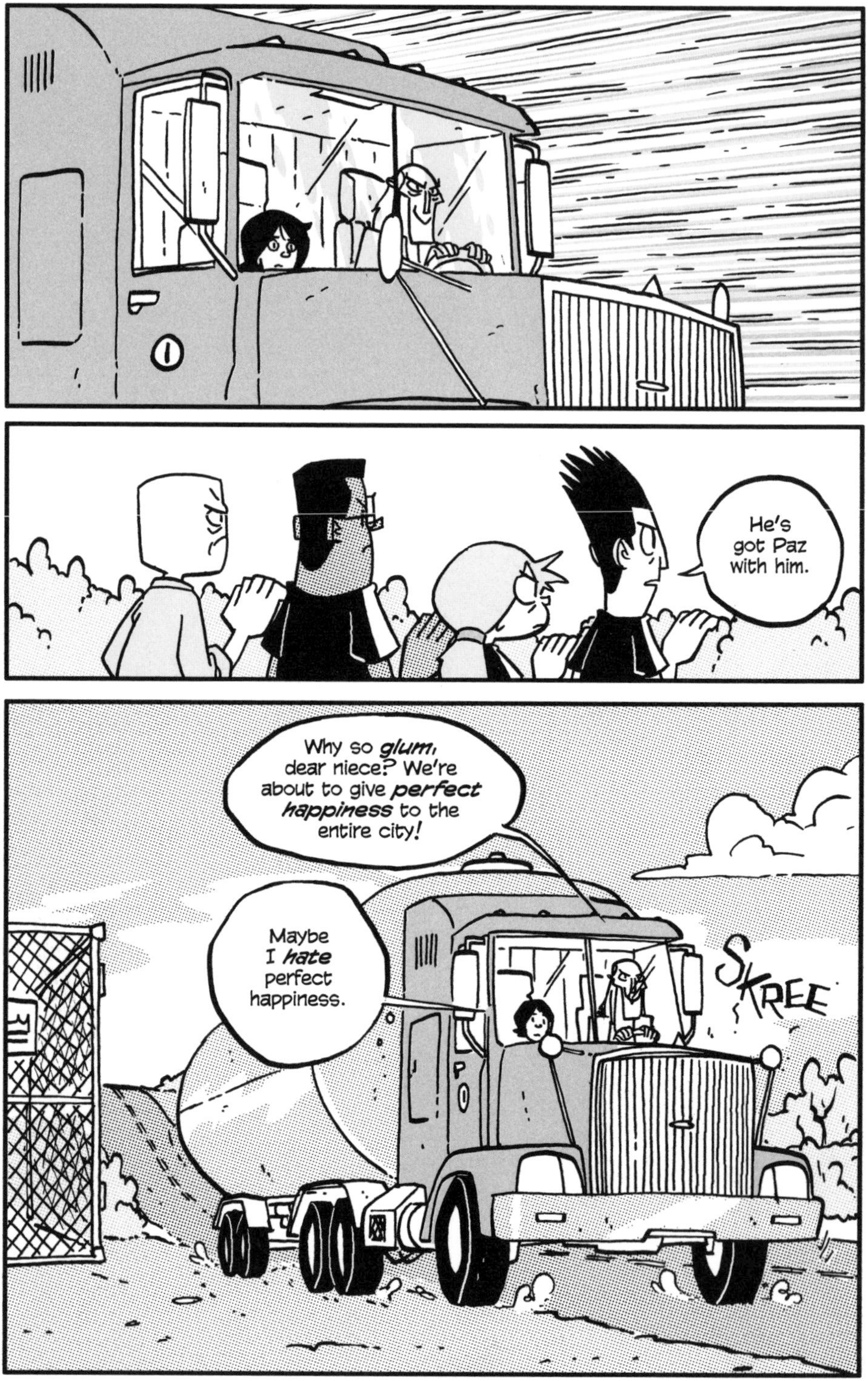
He's got Paz with him.
Why so *glum*, dear niece? We're about to give *perfect happiness* to the entire city!
Maybe I *hate* perfect happiness.
SKREE

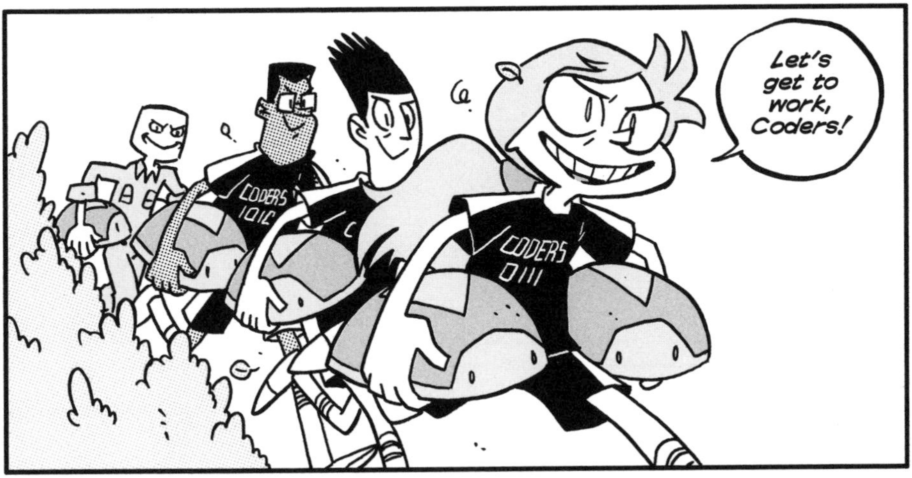
Let's get to work, Coders!
CODERS 1010
CODERS 0111

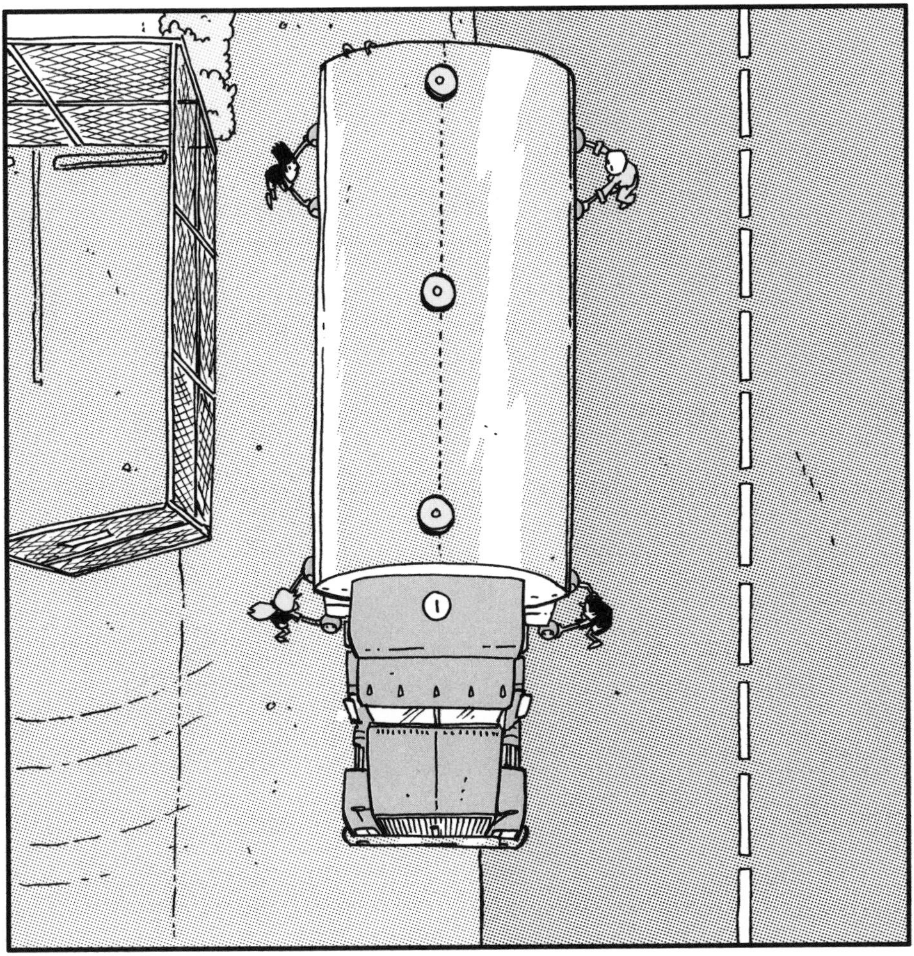

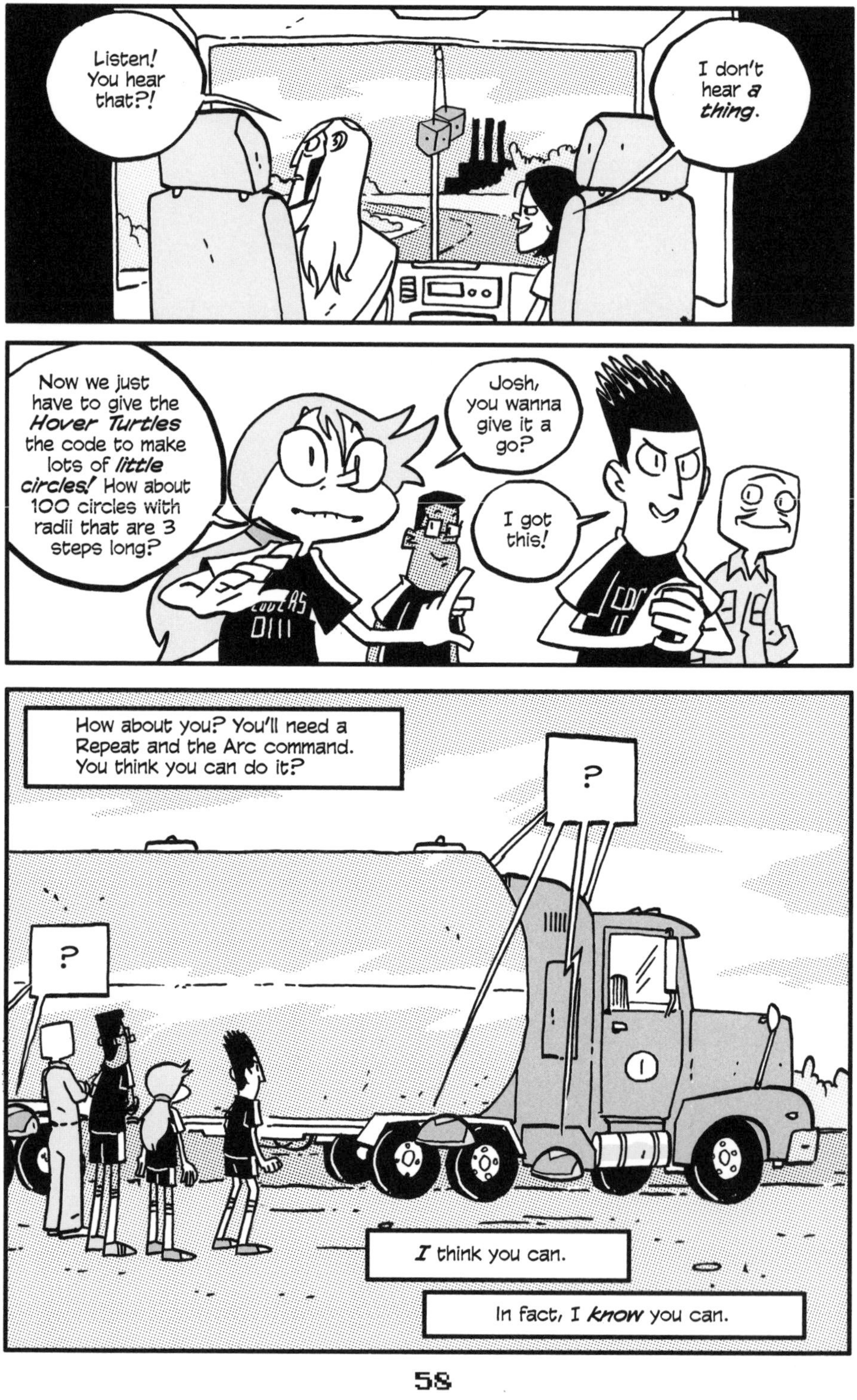

Listen! You hear that?!
I don't hear *a thing*.
Now we just have to give the *Hover Turtles* the code to make lots of *little circles!* How about 100 circles with radii that are 3 steps long?
Josh, you wanna give it a go?
I got this!
How about you? You'll need a Repeat and the Arc command. You think you can do it?
?
?
I think you can.
In fact, I *know* you can.

Chapter

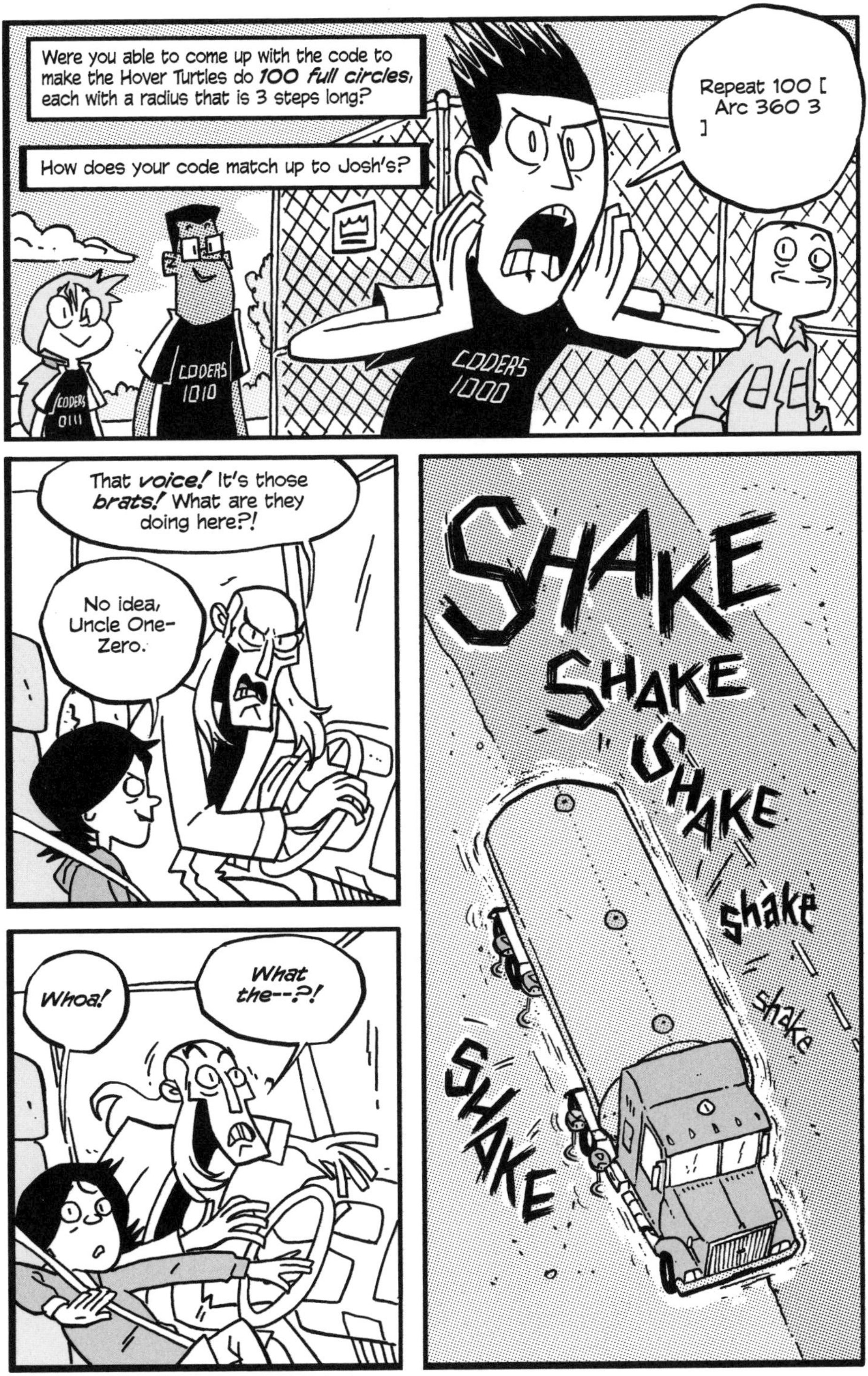

Were you able to come up with the code to make the Hover Turtles do 100 full circles, each with a radius that is 3 steps long?
How does your code match up to Josh's?
Repeat 100 [
Arc 360 3
]
CODERS 0111
CODERS 1010
CODERS 1000
That voice! It's those brats! What are they doing here?!
No idea, Uncle One-Zero.
Whoa!
What the--?!
SHAKE
SHAKE
SHAKE
shake
shake
SHAKE

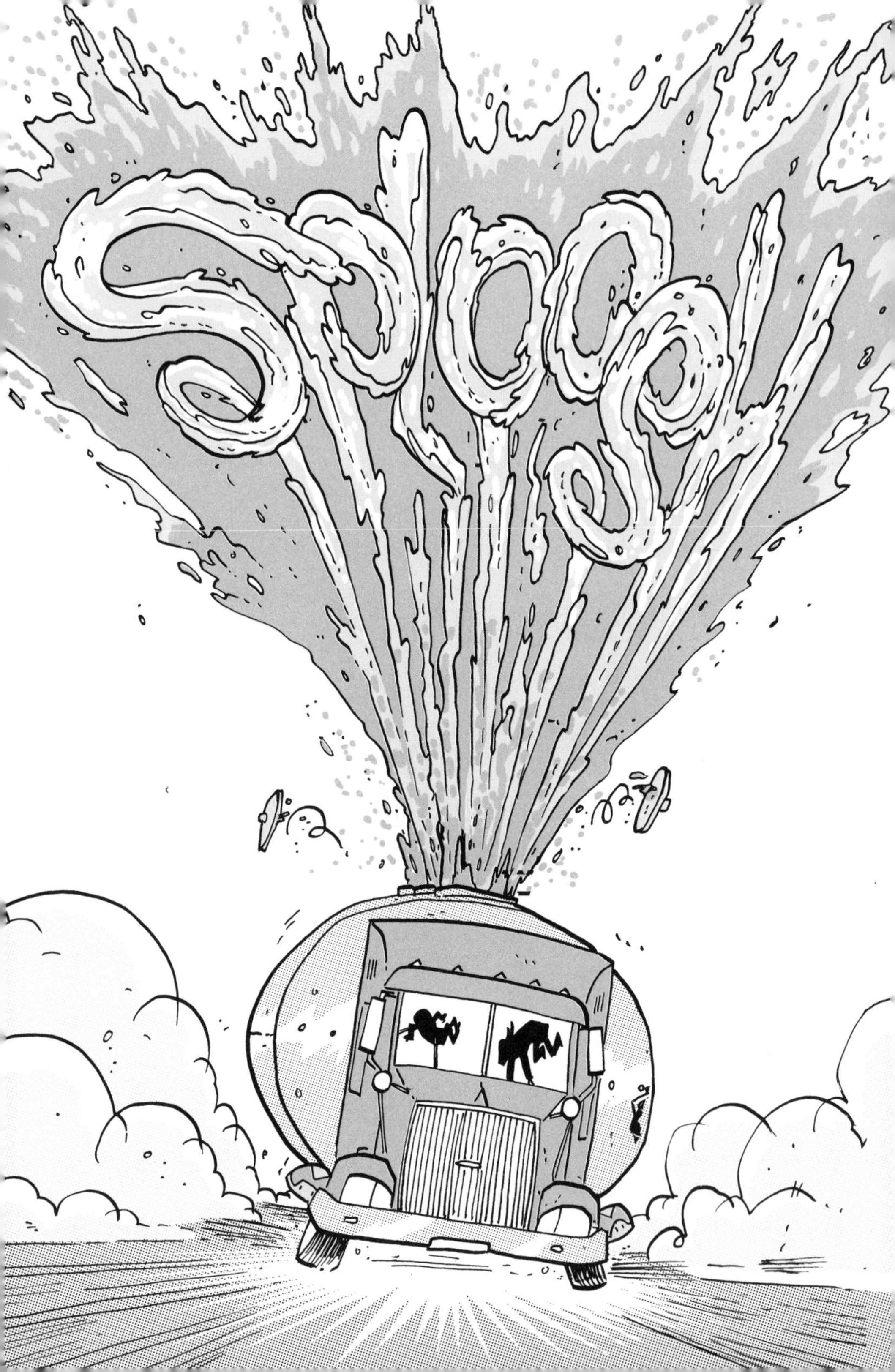
SPLOOSH

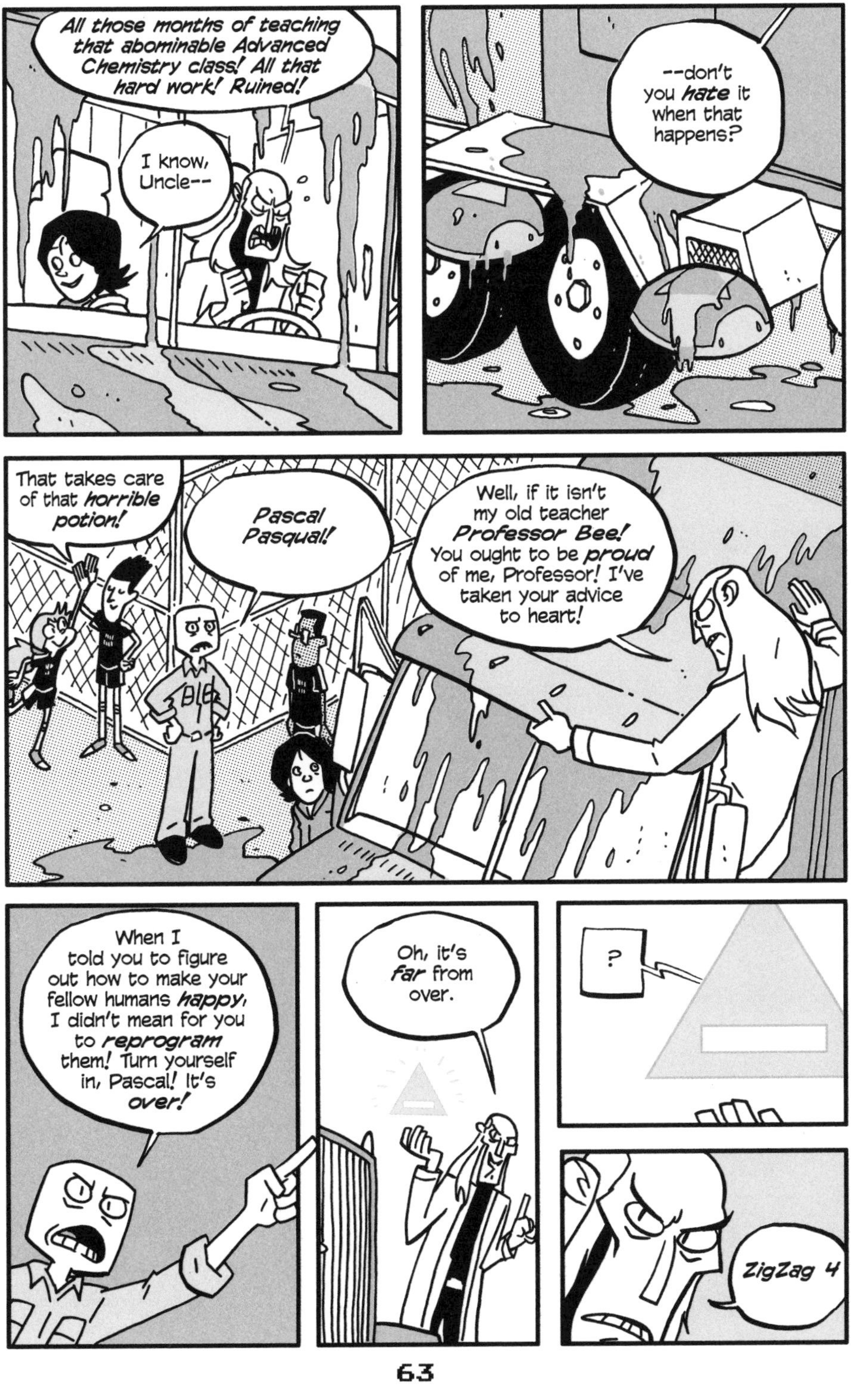
All those months of teaching that abominable Advanced Chemistry class! All that hard work! Ruined!
I know, Uncle--
--don't you hate it when that happens?
That takes care of that horrible potion!
Pascal Pasqual!
Well, if it isn't my old teacher Professor Bee! You ought to be proud of me, Professor! I've taken your advice to heart!
When I told you to figure out how to make your fellow humans happy, I didn't mean for you to reprogram them! Turn yourself in, Pascal! It's over!
Oh, it's far from over.
?
ZigZag 4

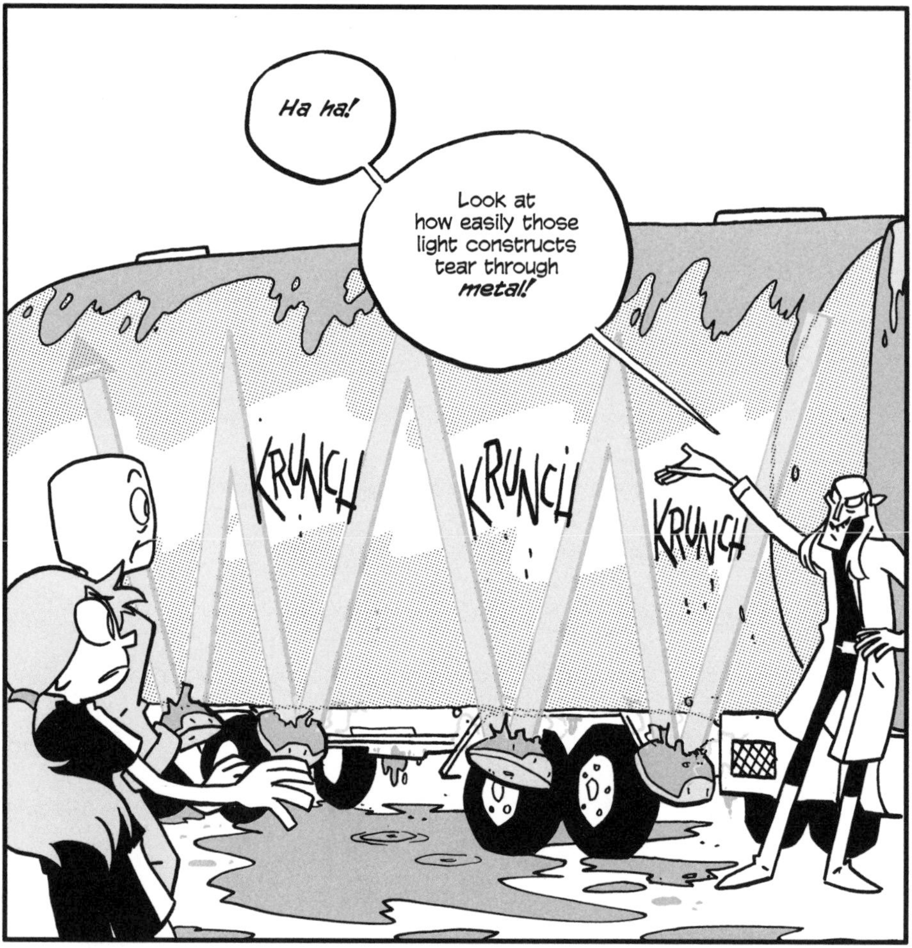
Ha ha!
Look at how easily those light constructs tear through *metal!*
KRUNCH
KRUNCH
KRUNCH

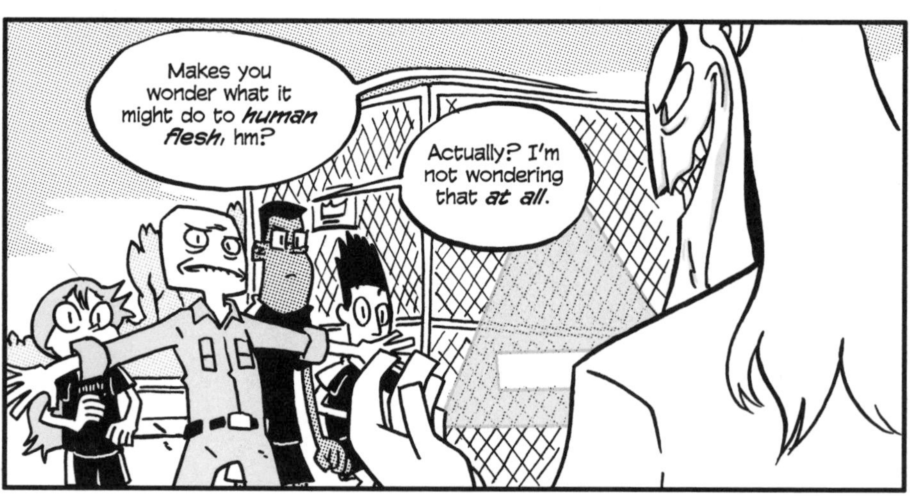
Makes you wonder what it might do to *human flesh*, hm?
Actually? I'm not wondering that *at all*.

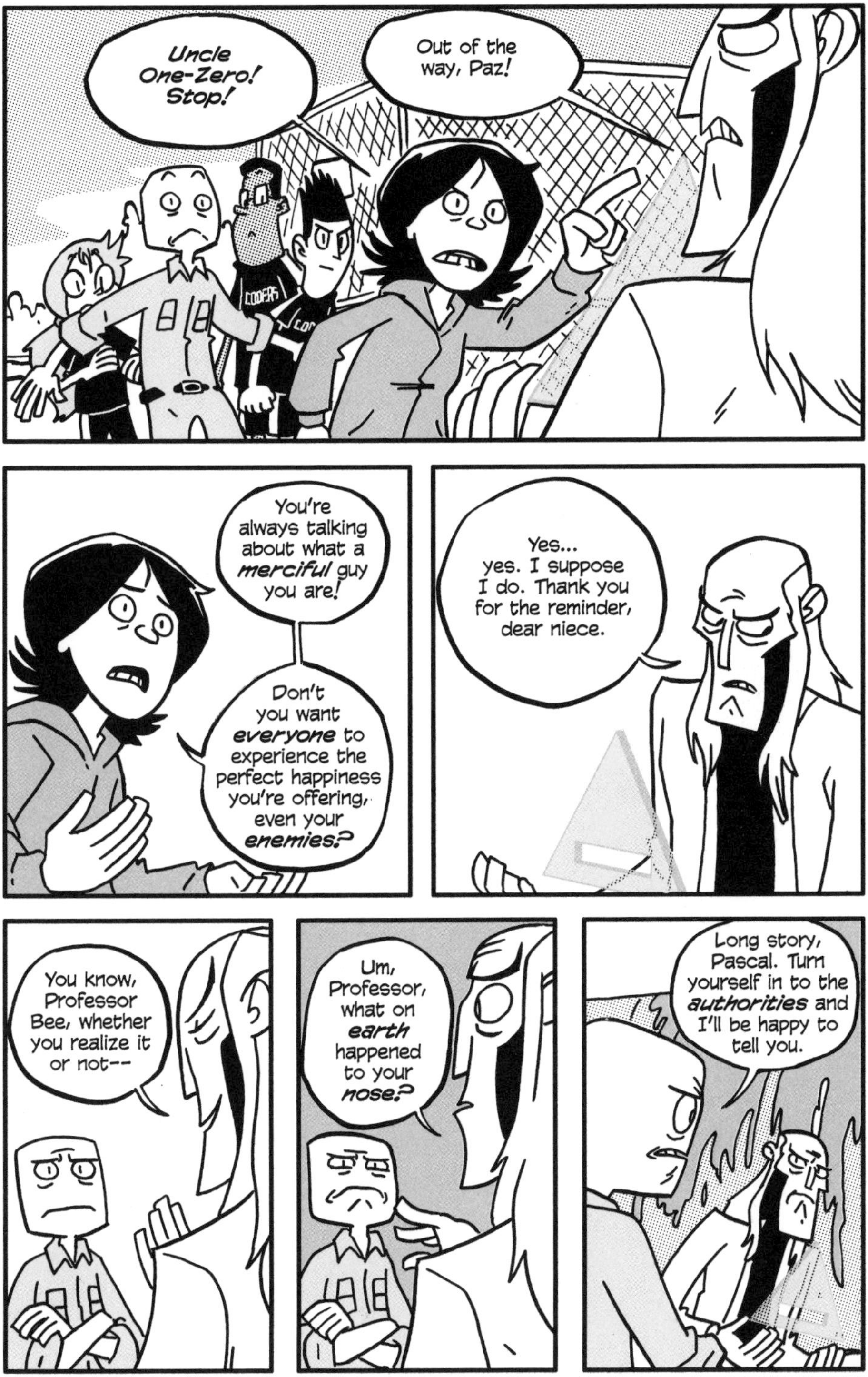
Uncle One-Zero! Stop!
Out of the way, Paz!
COOPERS
You're always talking about what a merciful guy you are!
Don't you want everyone to experience the perfect happiness you're offering, even your enemies?
Yes... yes. I suppose I do. Thank you for the reminder, dear niece.
You know, Professor Bee, whether you realize it or not--
Um, Professor, what on earth happened to your nose?
Long story, Pascal. Turn yourself in to the authorities and I'll be happy to tell you.

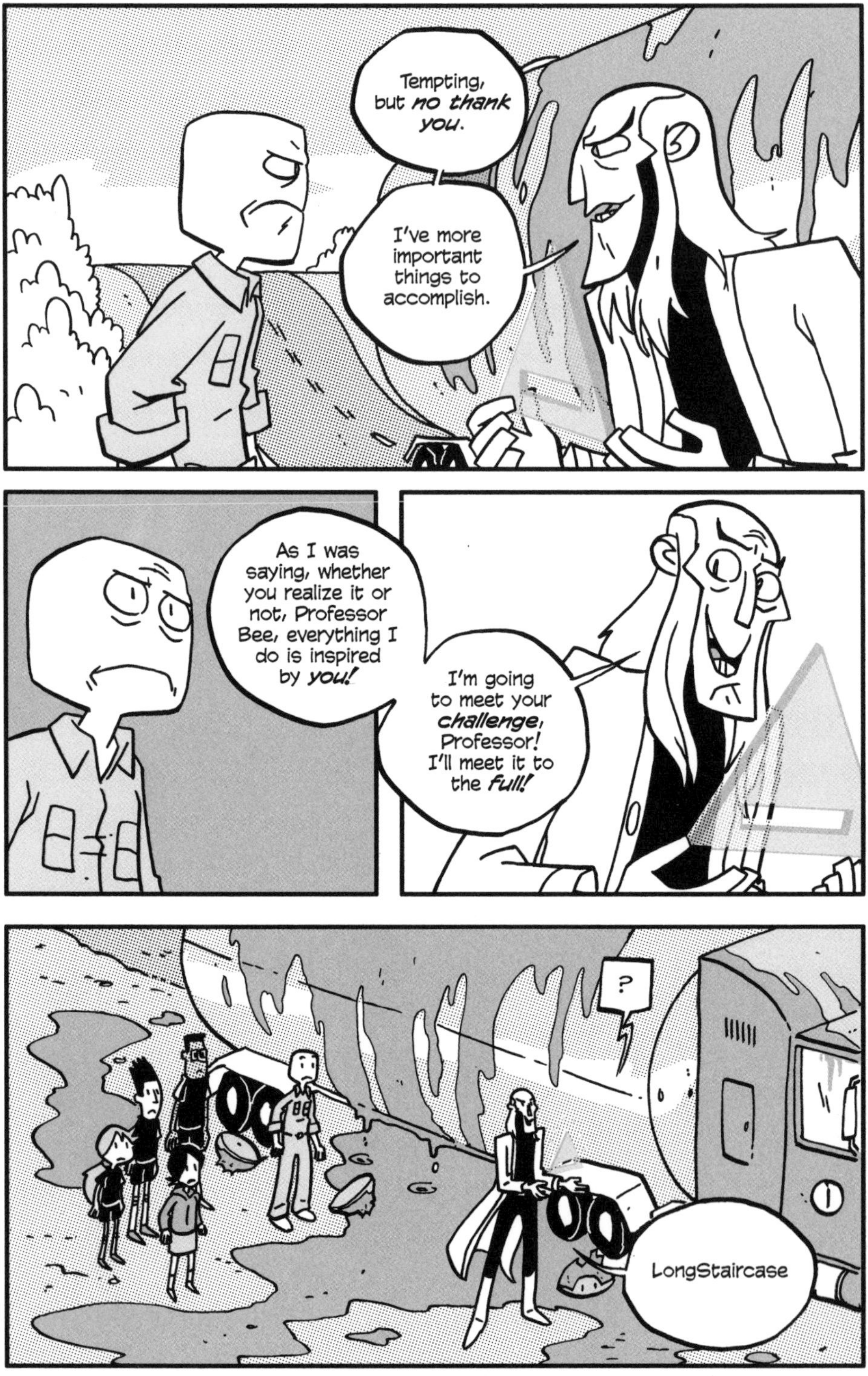
Tempting, but *no thank you*.
I've more important things to accomplish.
As I was saying, whether you realize it or not, Professor Bee, everything I do is inspired by *you!*
I'm going to meet your *challenge*, Professor! I'll meet it to the *full!*
?
LongStaircase

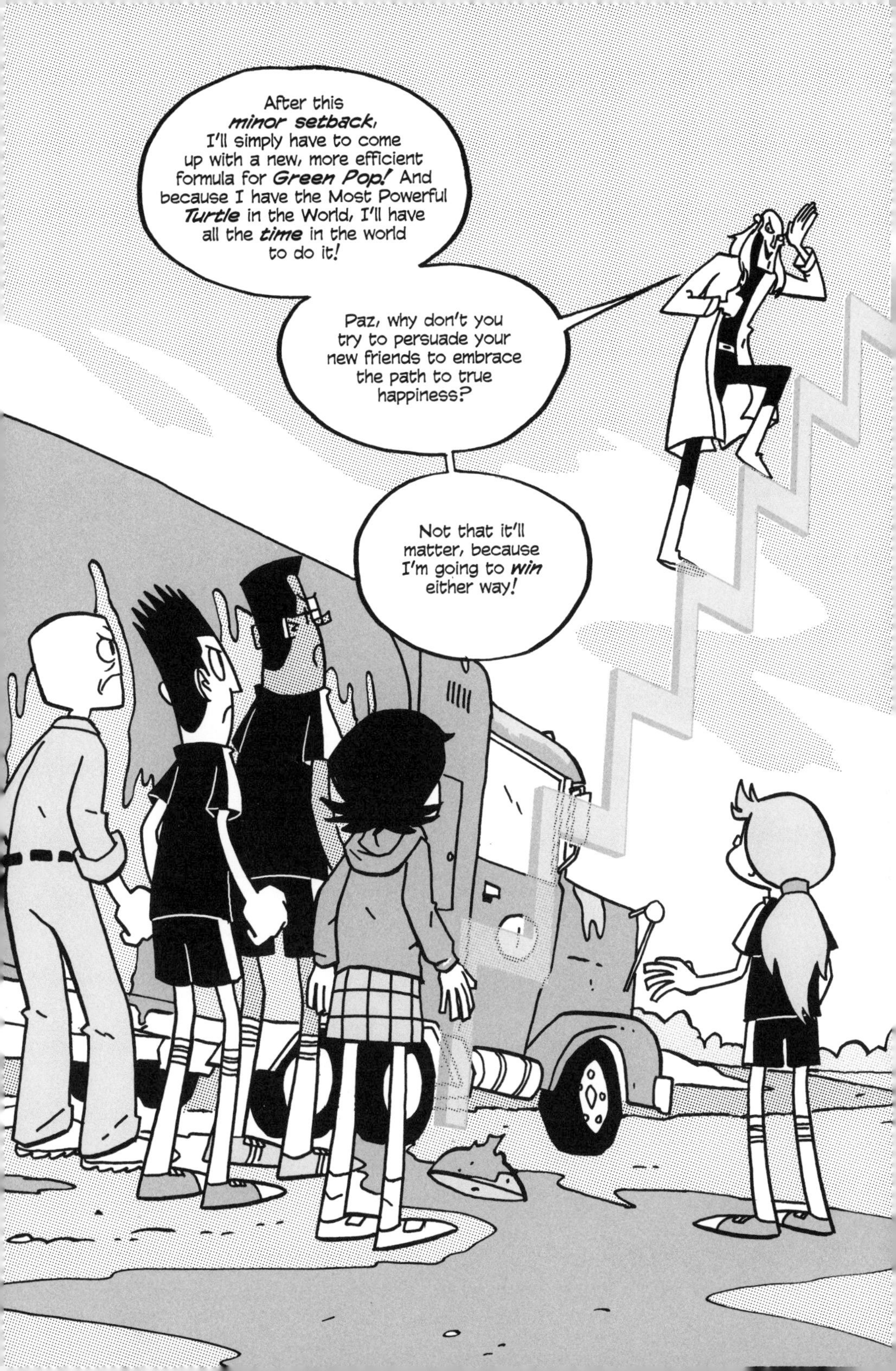
After this *minor setback*, I'll simply have to come up with a new, more efficient formula for *Green Pop!* And because I have the Most Powerful *Turtle* in the World, I'll have all the *time* in the world to do it!
Paz, why don't you try to persuade your new friends to embrace the path to true happiness?
Not that it'll matter, because I'm going to *win* either way!

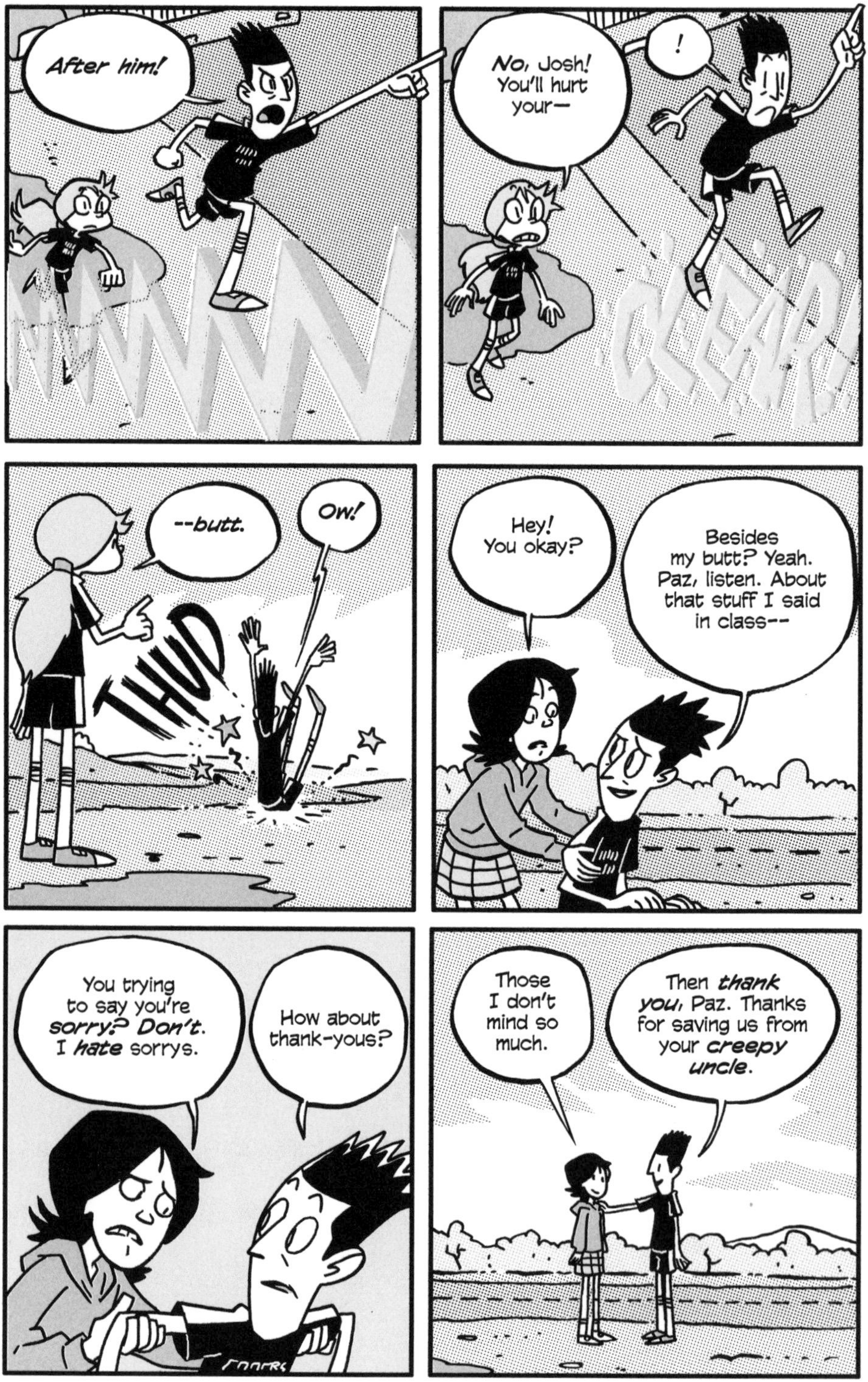
After him!
No, Josh! You'll hurt your—
!
CLEAR!
--butt.
Ow!
THUD
Hey! You okay?
Besides my butt? Yeah. Paz, listen. About that stuff I said in class--
You trying to say you're *sorry? Don't*. I *hate* sorrys.
How about thank-yous?
Those I don't mind so much.
Then *thank you*, Paz. Thanks for saving us from your *creepy uncle*.

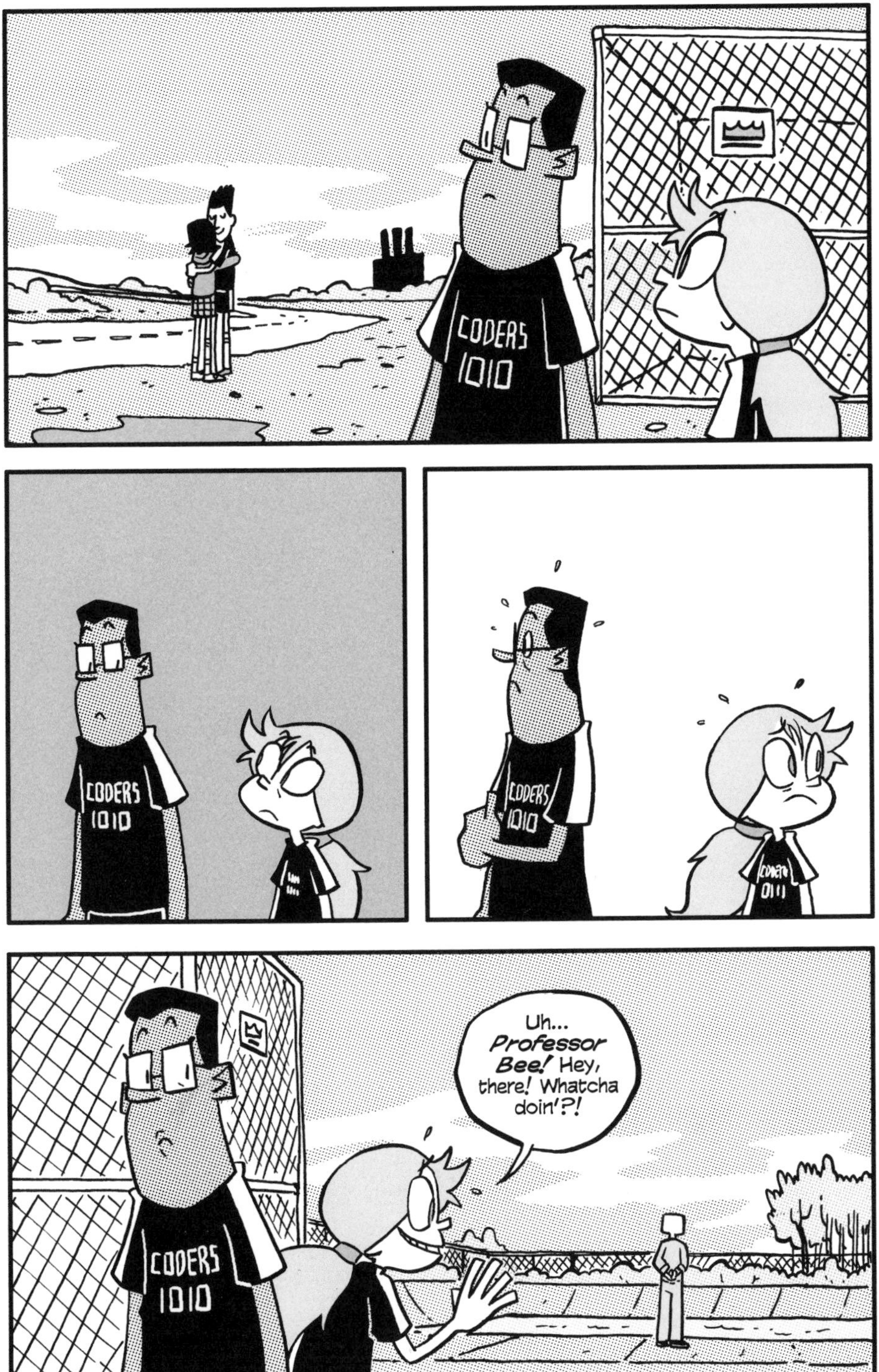
CODERS 1010
Uh... *Professor Bee!* Hey, there! Whatcha doin'?!

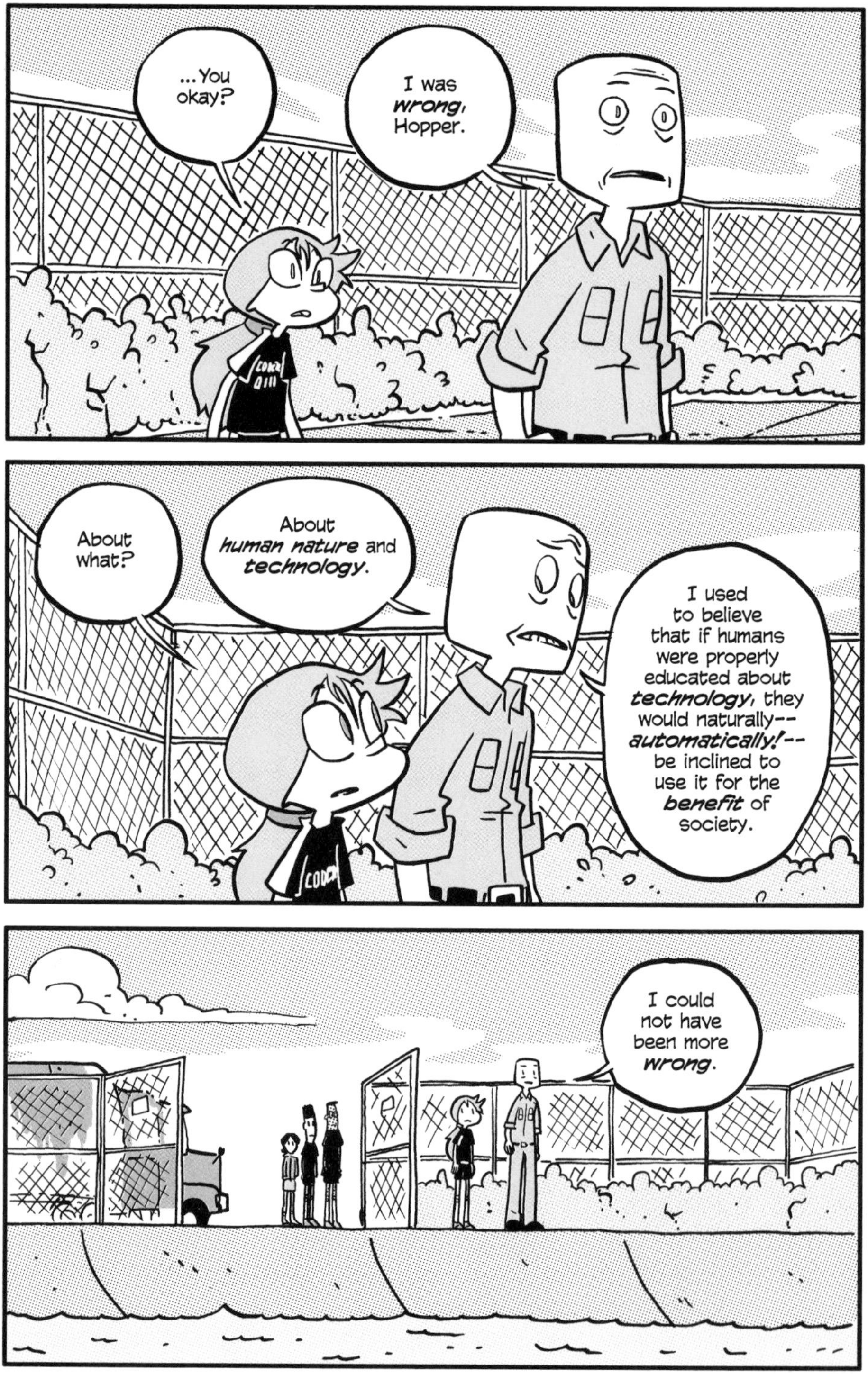
...You okay?
I was *wrong*, Hopper.
About what?
About *human nature* and *technology*.
I used to believe that if humans were properly educated about *technology*, they would naturally-- *automatically!*-- be inclined to use it for the *benefit* of society.
I could not have been more *wrong*.

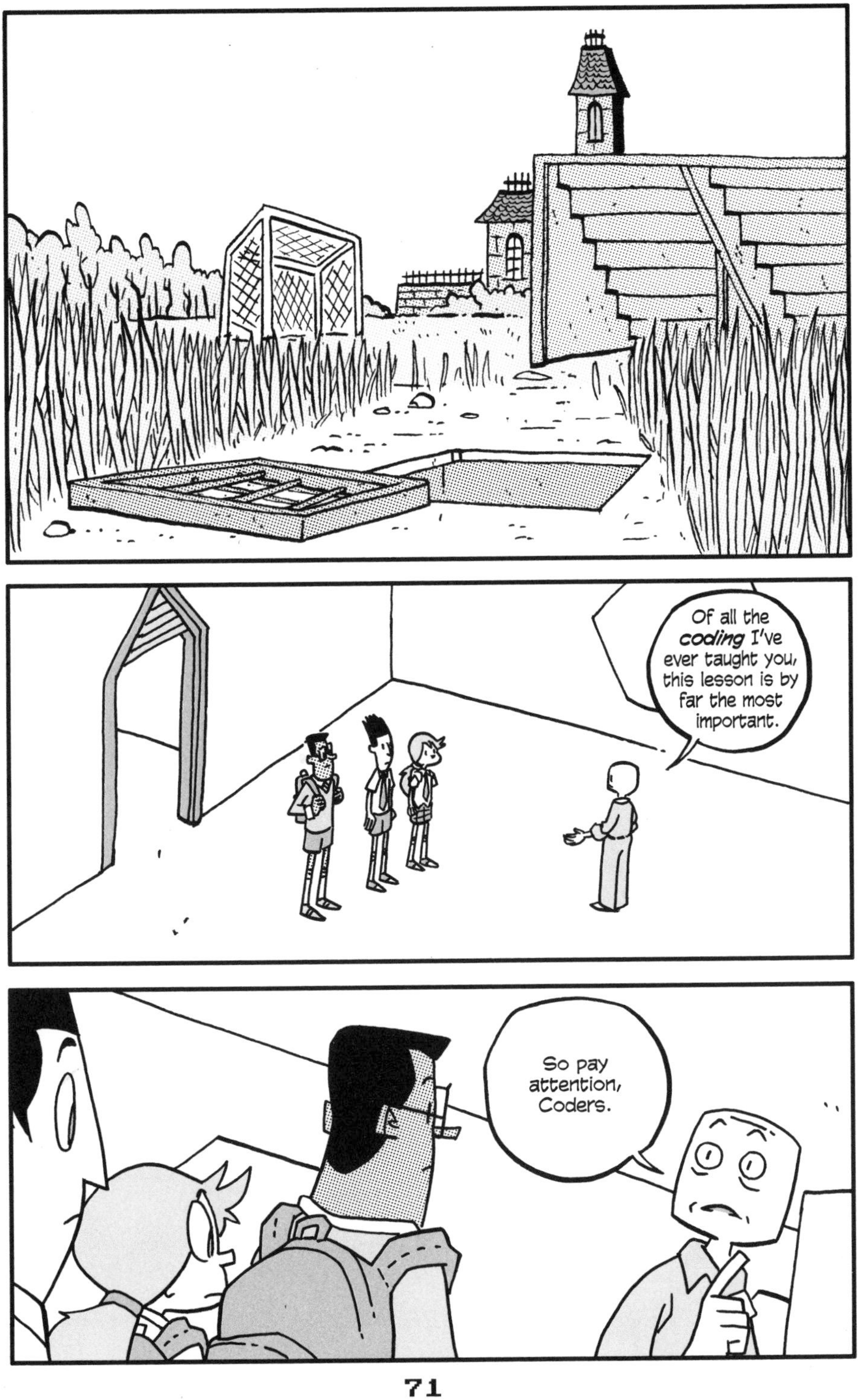
Of all the *coding* I've ever taught you, this lesson is by far the most important.
So pay attention, Coders.

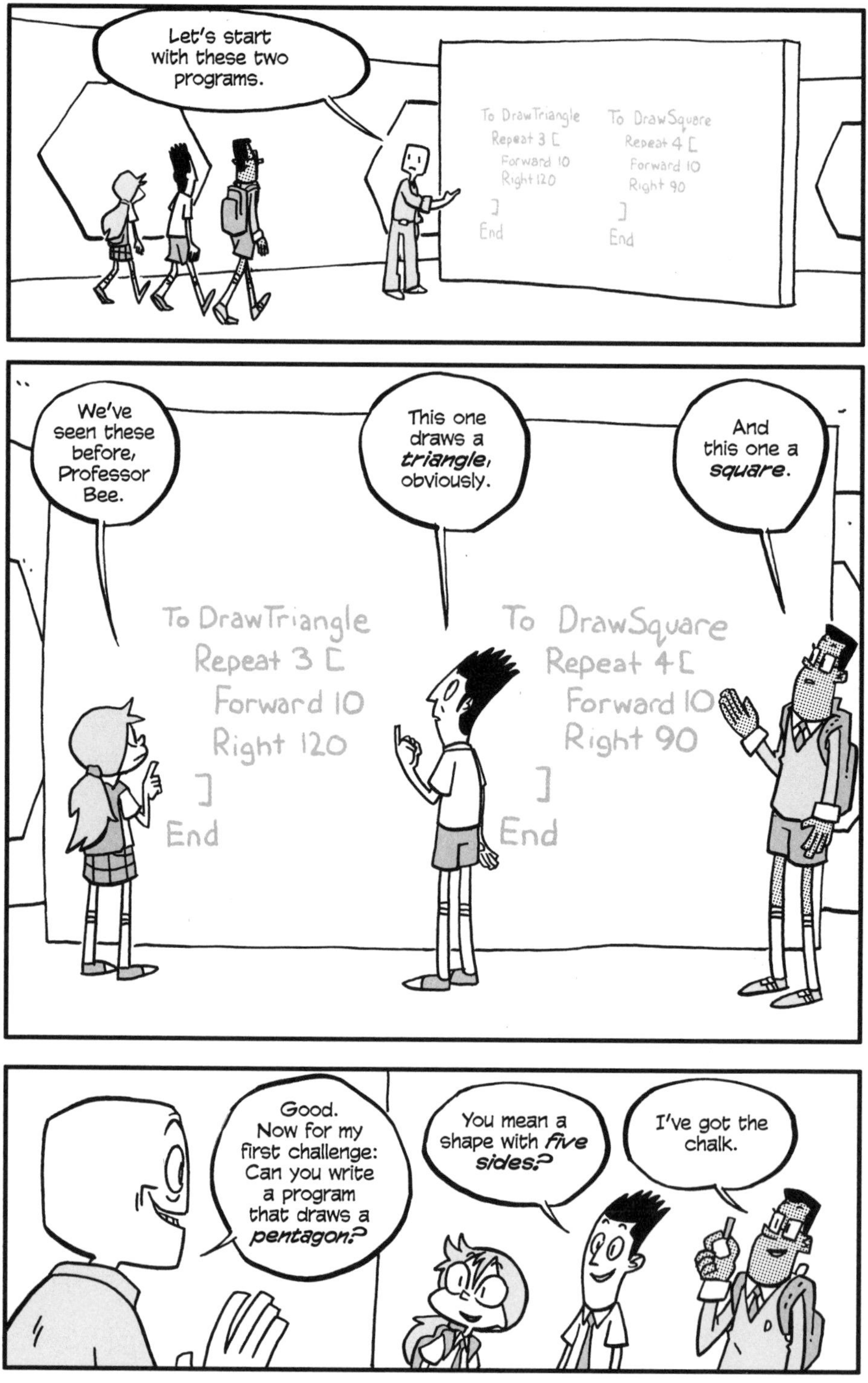
Let's start with these two programs.
To DrawTriangle
Repeat 3 [
Forward 10
Right 120
]
End
To DrawSquare
Repeat 4 [
Forward 10
Right 90
]
End
We've seen these before, Professor Bee.
This one draws a *triangle*, obviously.
And this one a *square*.
Good. Now for my first challenge: Can you write a program that draws a *pentagon?*
You mean a shape with *five sides?*
I've got the chalk.

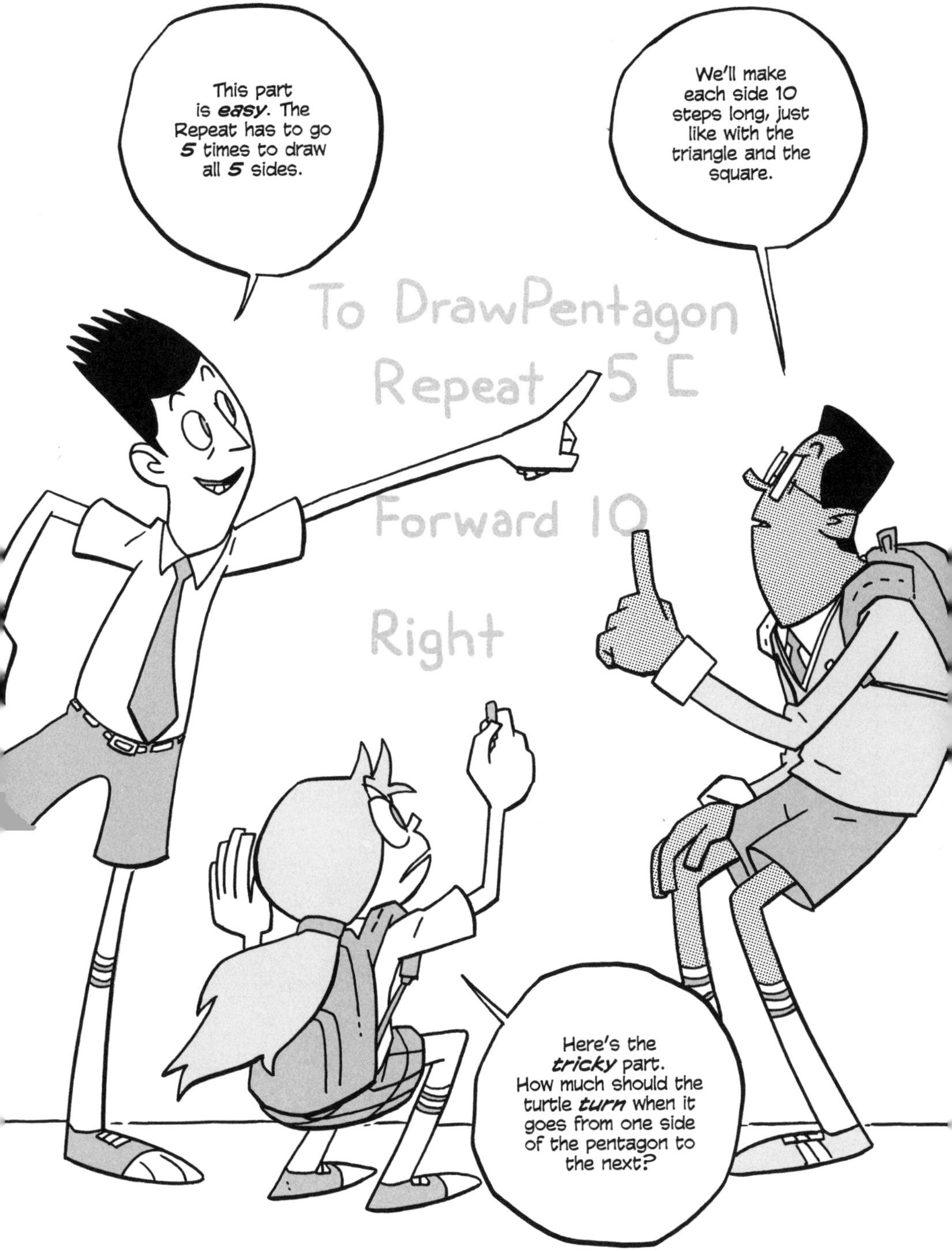
This part is *easy*. The Repeat has to go *5* times to draw all *5* sides.
We'll make each side 10 steps long, just like with the triangle and the square.
To DrawPentagon
Repeat 5 [
Forward 10
Right
Here's the *tricky* part. How much should the turtle *turn* when it goes from one side of the pentagon to the next?

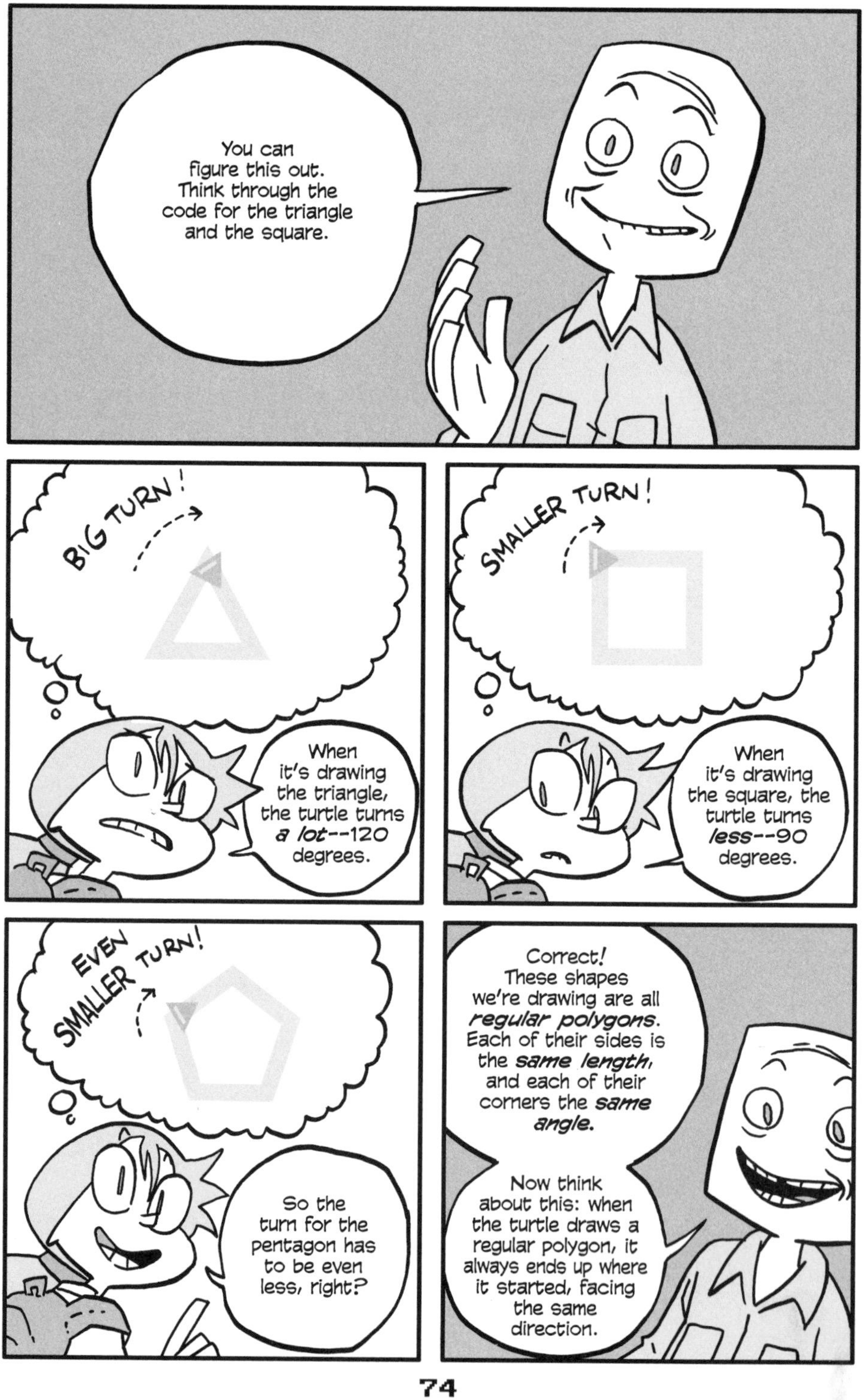
You can figure this out. Think through the code for the triangle and the square.
BIG TURN!
When it's drawing the triangle, the turtle turns *a lot*--120 degrees.
SMALLER TURN!
When it's drawing the square, the turtle turns *less*--90 degrees.
EVEN SMALLER TURN!
So the turn for the pentagon has to be even less, right?
Correct! These shapes we're drawing are all ***regular polygons***. Each of their sides is the ***same length***, and each of their corners the ***same angle***.
Now think about this: when the turtle draws a regular polygon, it always ends up where it started, facing the same direction.

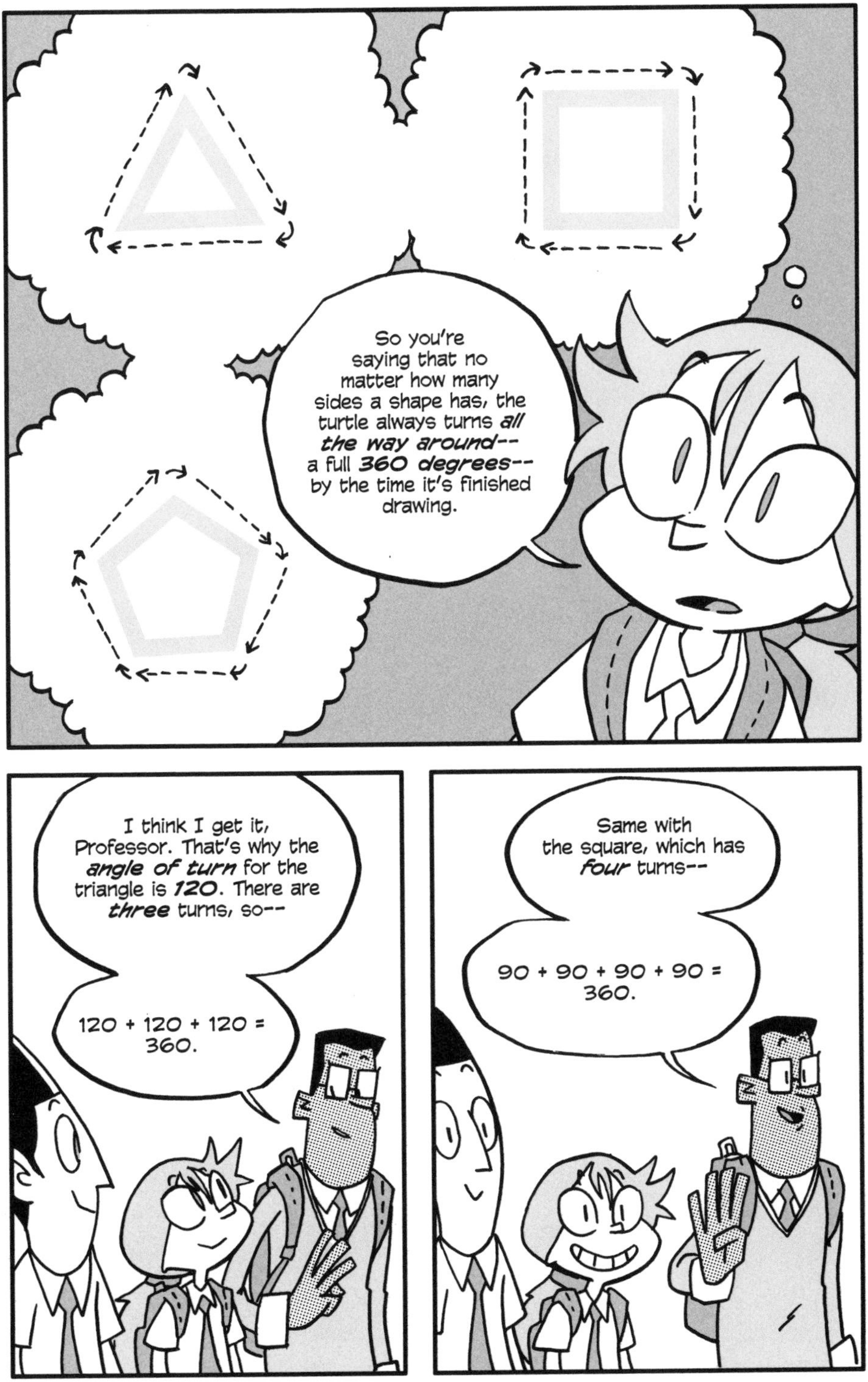
So you're saying that no matter how many sides a shape has, the turtle always turns *all the way around*-- a full **360 degrees**-- by the time it's finished drawing.
I think I get it, Professor. That's why the *angle of turn* for the triangle is *120*. There are *three* turns, so--
120 + 120 + 120 = 360.
Same with the square, which has *four* turns--
90 + 90 + 90 + 90 = 360.

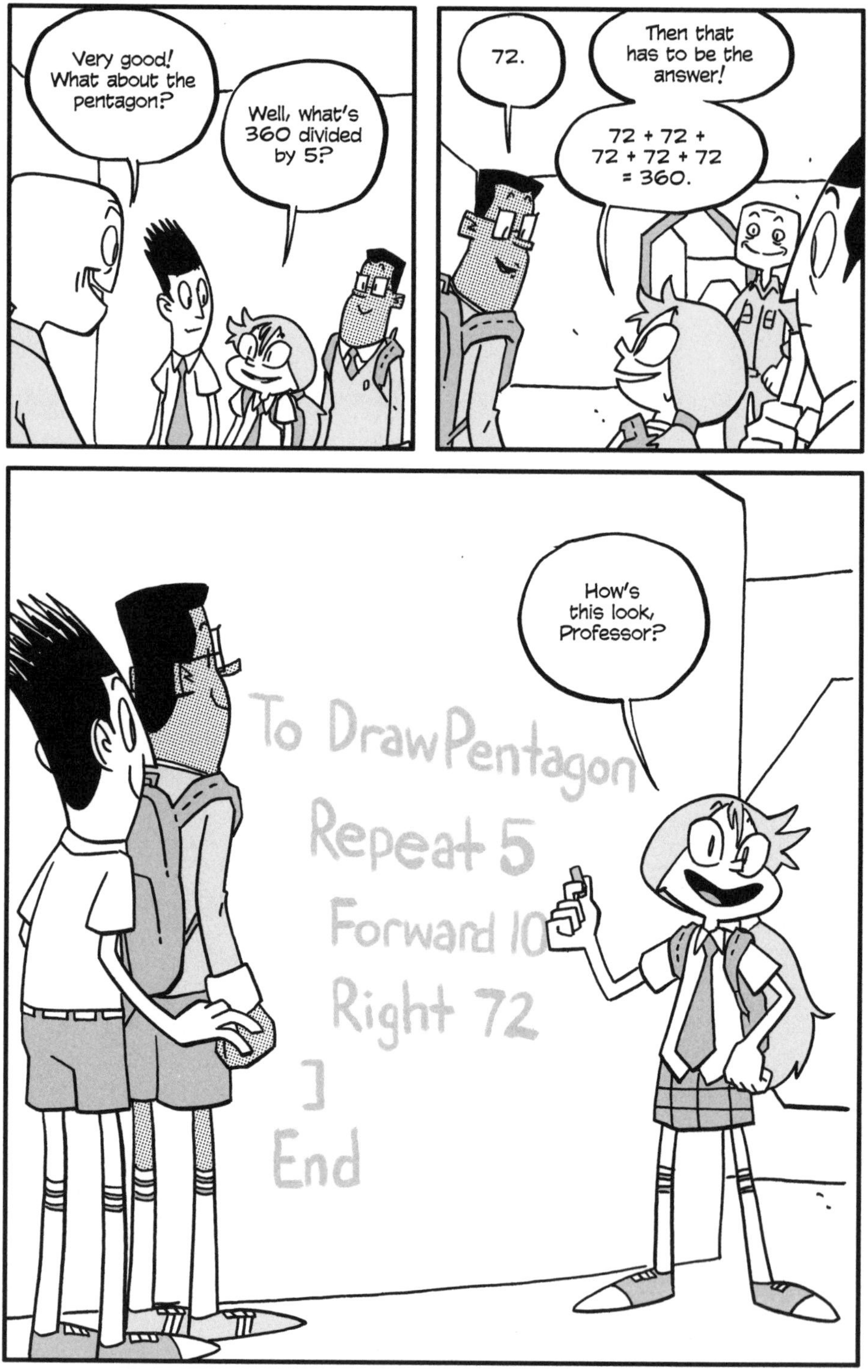
Very good! What about the pentagon?
Well, what's 360 divided by 5?
72.
Then that has to be the answer!
72 + 72 + 72 + 72 + 72 = 360.
How's this look, Professor?
To DrawPentagon
Repeat 5
Forward 10
Right 72
]
End

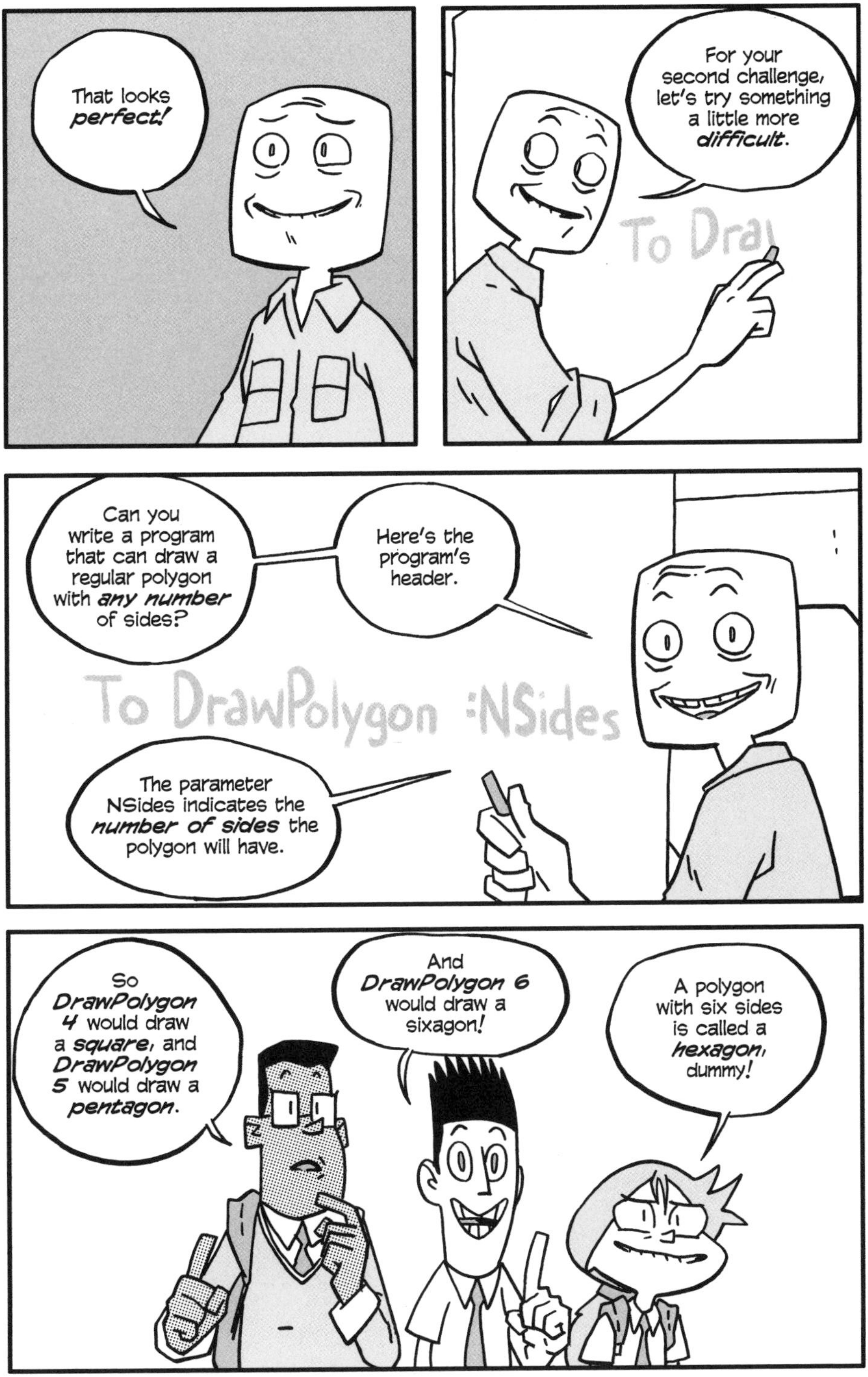
That looks perfect!
For your second challenge, let's try something a little more difficult.
To Draw
Can you write a program that can draw a regular polygon with any number of sides?
Here's the program's header.
To DrawPolygon :NSides
The parameter NSides indicates the number of sides the polygon will have.
So DrawPolygon 4 would draw a square, and DrawPolygon 5 would draw a pentagon.
And DrawPolygon 6 would draw a sixagon!
A polygon with six sides is called a hexagon, dummy!

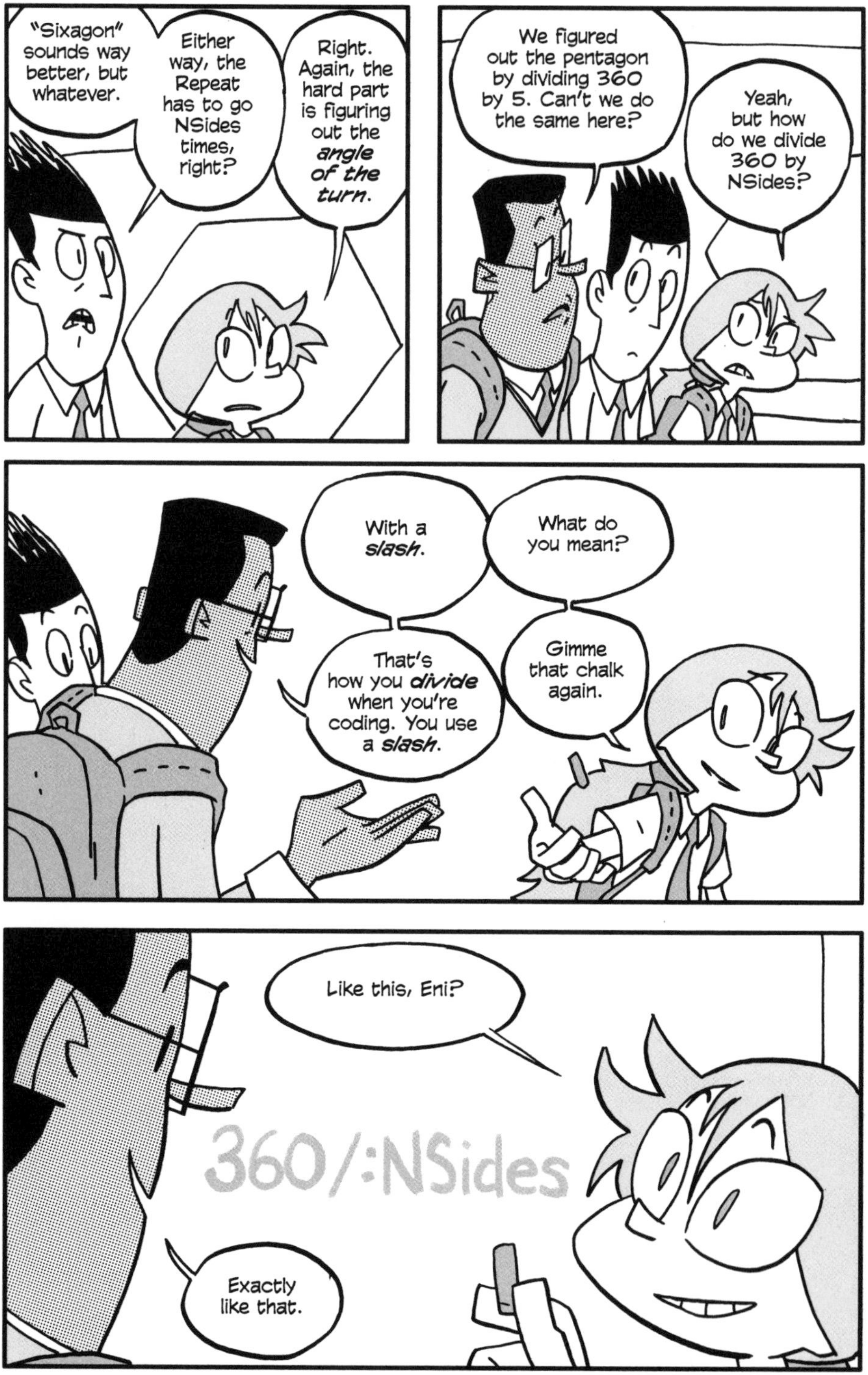
"Sixagon" sounds way better, but whatever.
Either way, the Repeat has to go NSides times, right?
Right. Again, the hard part is figuring out the *angle of the turn*.
We figured out the pentagon by dividing 360 by 5. Can't we do the same here?
Yeah, but how do we divide 360 by NSides?
With a *slash*.
What do you mean?
That's how you *divide* when you're coding. You use a *slash*.
Gimme that chalk again.
Like this, Eni?
360/:NSides
Exactly like that.

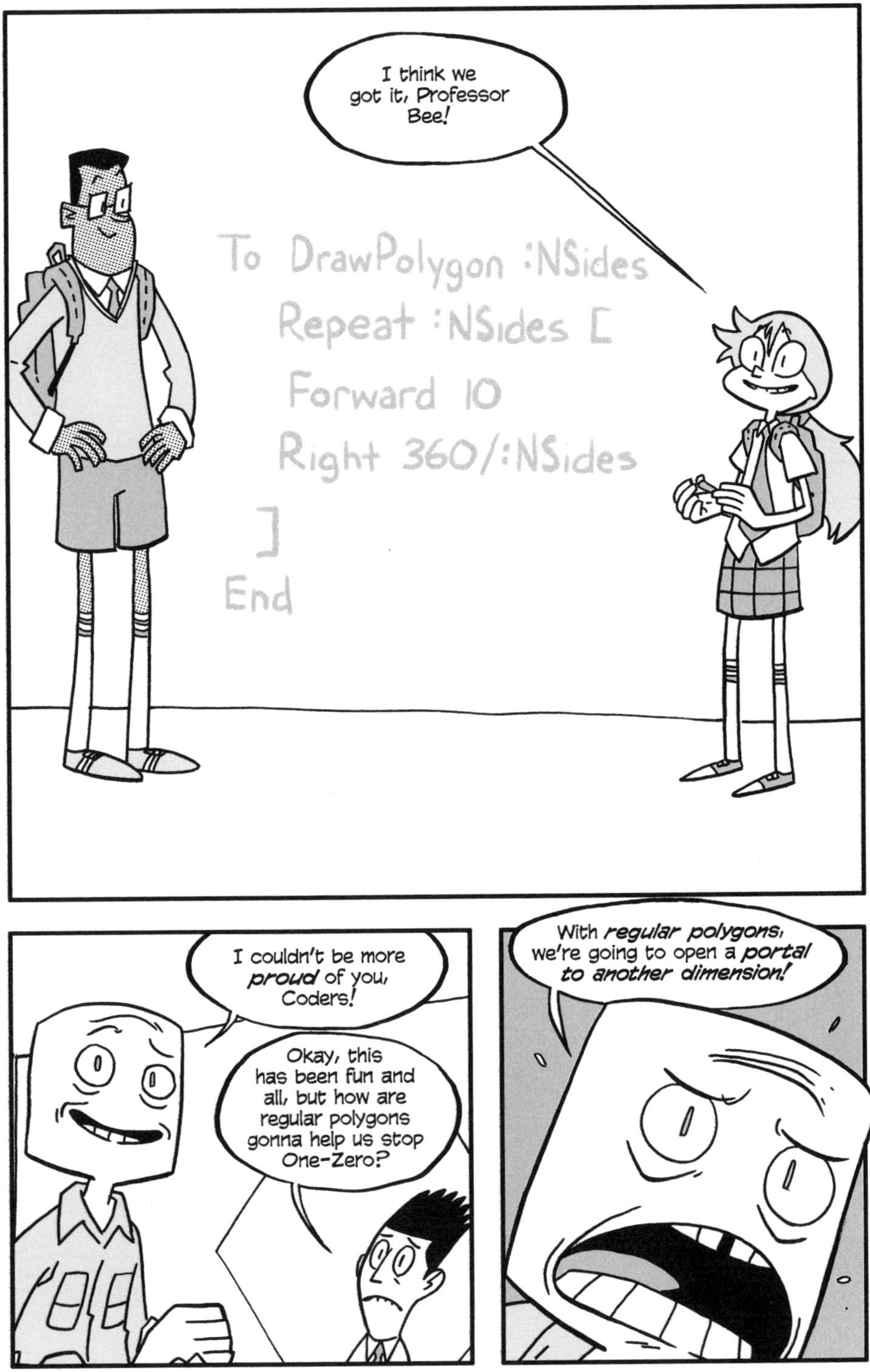
I think we got it, Professor Bee!
To DrawPolygon :NSides
Repeat :NSides [
Forward 10
Right 360/:NSides
]
End
I couldn't be more *proud* of you, Coders!
Okay, this has been fun and all, but how are regular polygons gonna help us stop One-Zero?
With *regular polygons*, we're going to open a *portal to another dimension!*

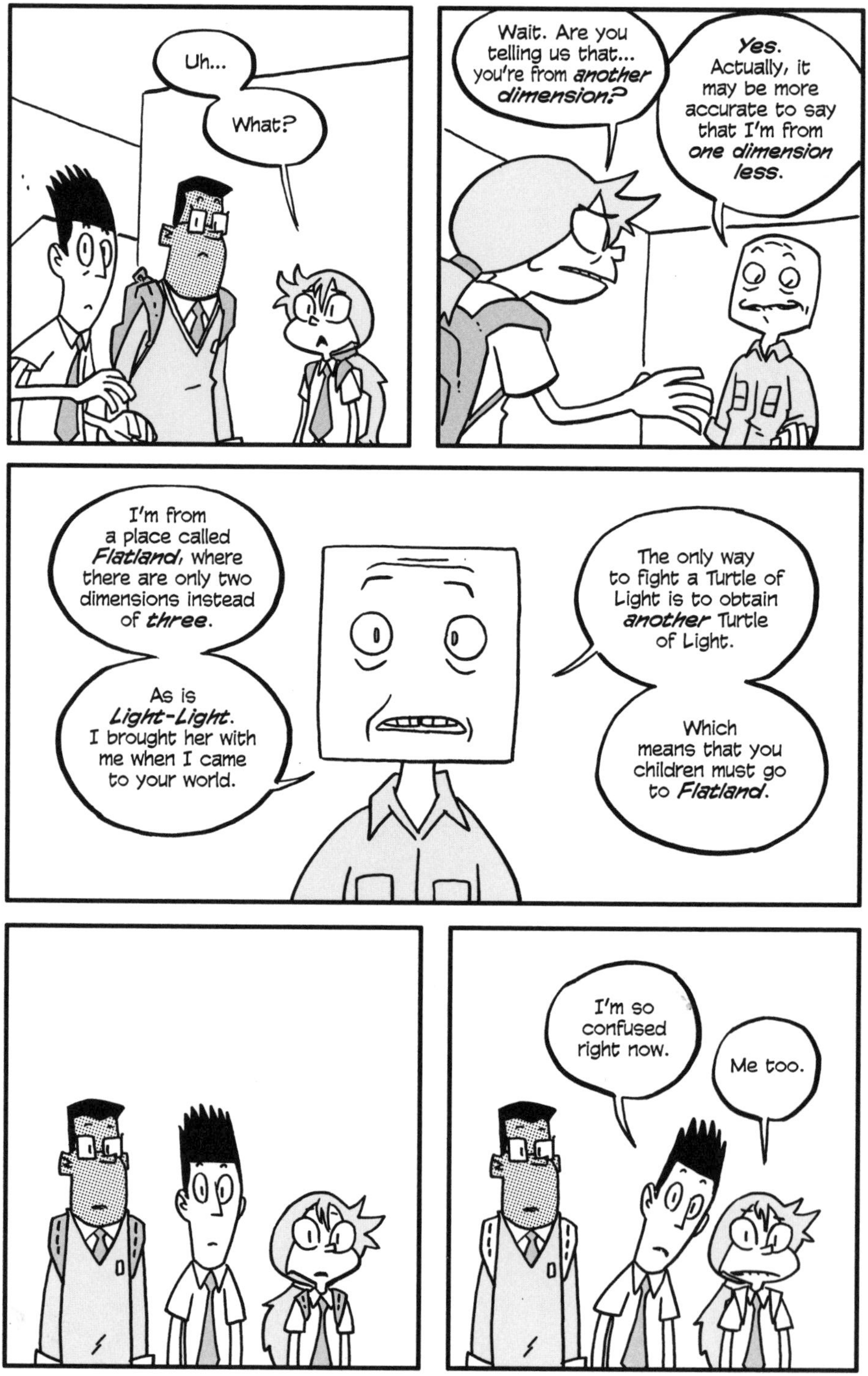
Uh...
What?
Wait. Are you telling us that... you're from *another dimension?*
Yes. Actually, it may be more accurate to say that I'm from *one dimension less*.
I'm from a place called *Flatland*, where there are only two dimensions instead of *three*.
As is *Light-Light*. I brought her with me when I came to your world.
The only way to fight a Turtle of Light is to obtain *another* Turtle of Light.
Which means that you children must go to *Flatland*.
I'm so confused right now.
Me too.

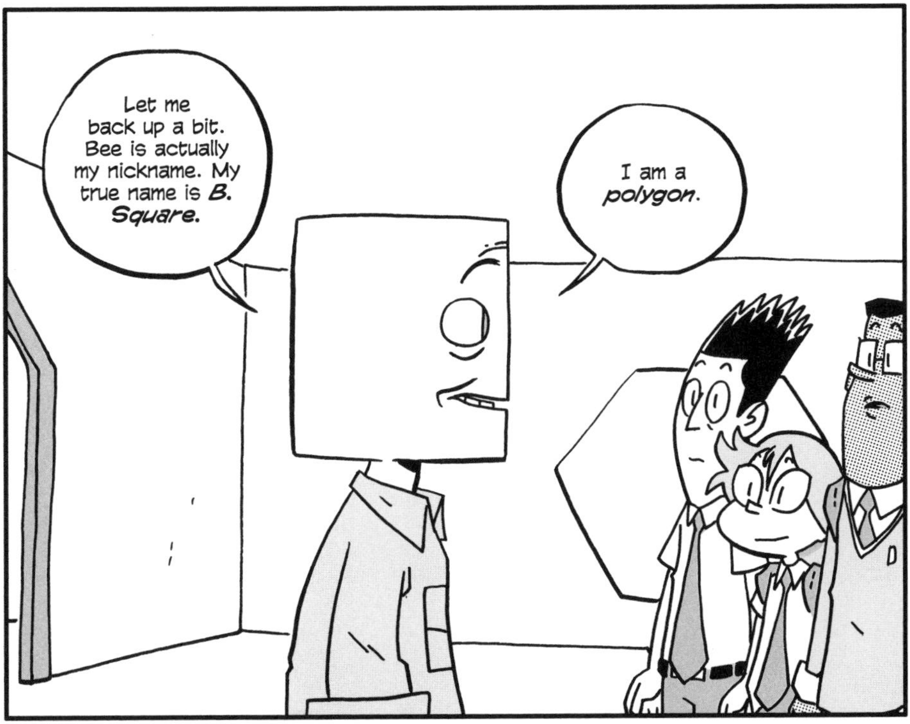
Let me back up a bit. Bee is actually my nickname. My true name is *B. Square*.
I am a *polygon*.

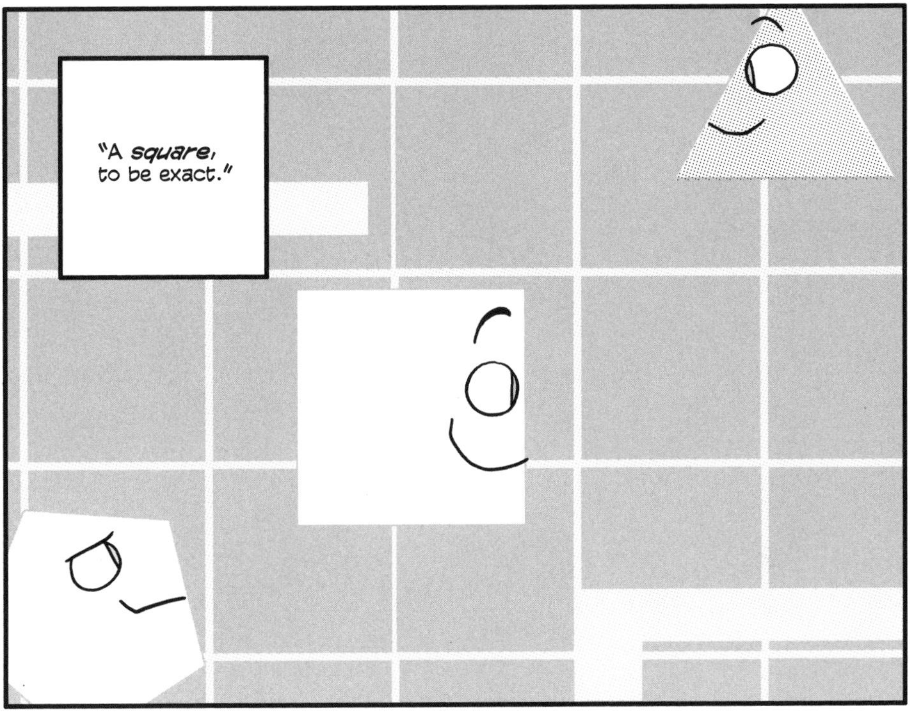
"A *square*, to be exact."

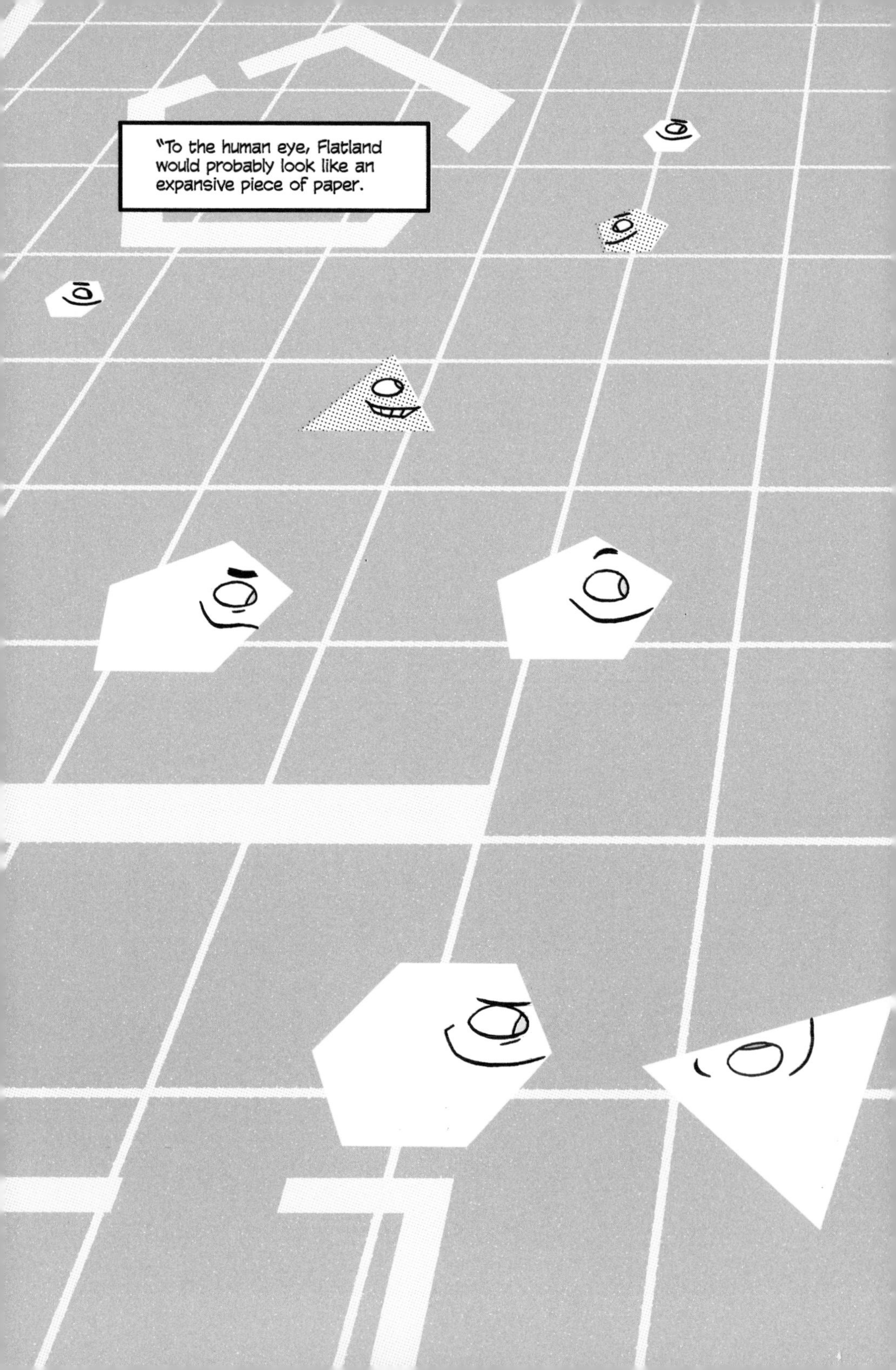
"To the human eye, Flatland would probably look like an expansive piece of paper.

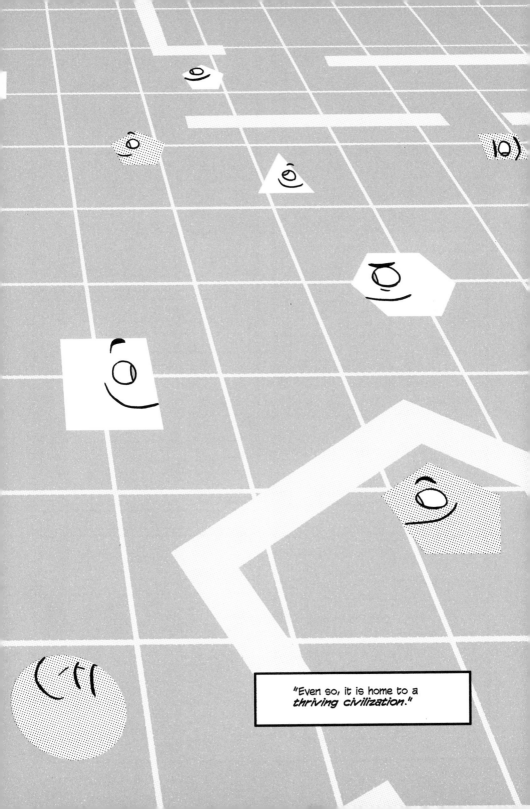

"Even so, it is home to a *thriving civilization*."

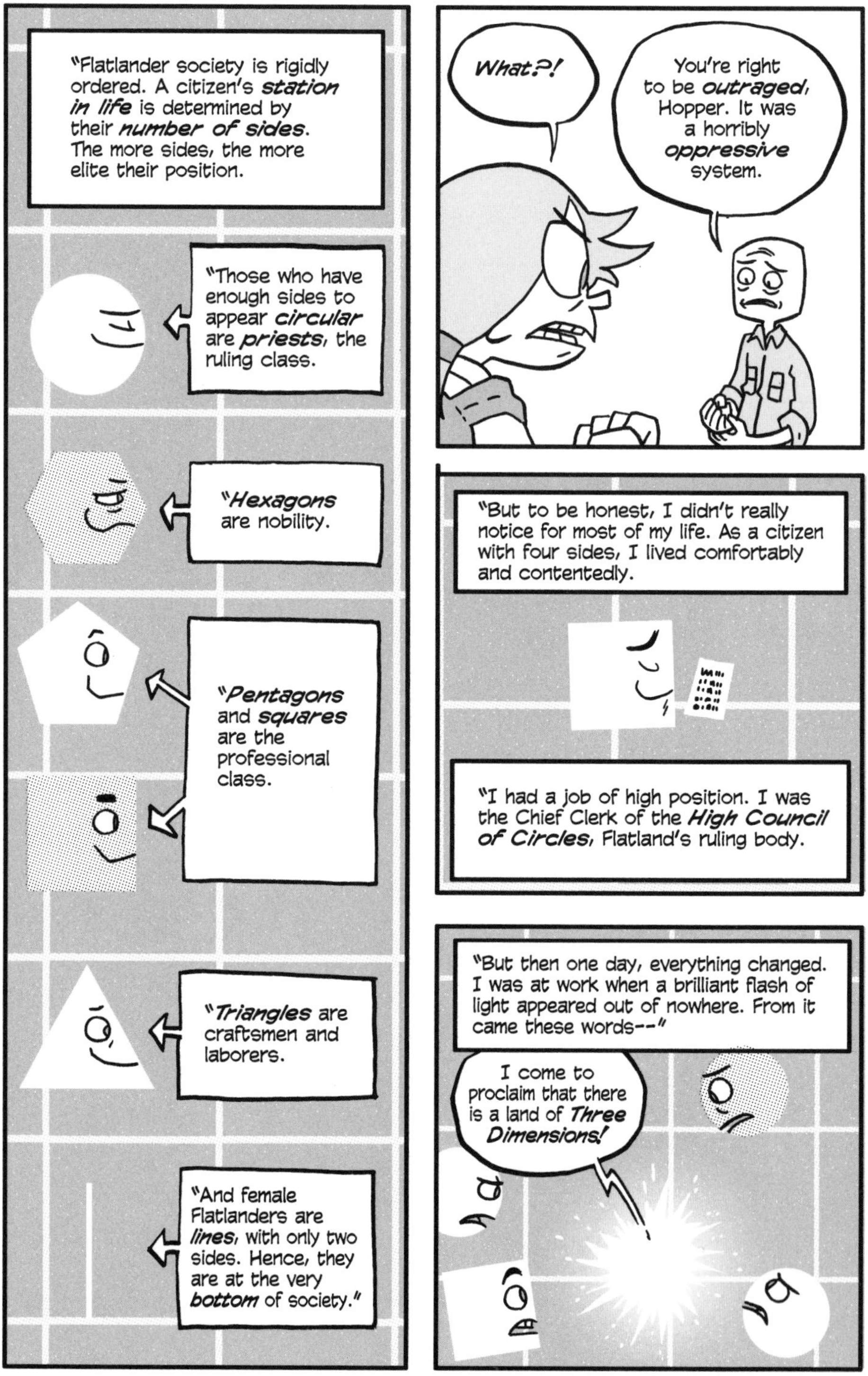

"Flatlander society is rigidly ordered. A citizen's station in life is determined by their number of sides. The more sides, the more elite their position.
"Those who have enough sides to appear circular are priests, the ruling class.
"Hexagons are nobility.
"Pentagons and squares are the professional class.
"Triangles are craftsmen and laborers.
"And female Flatlanders are lines, with only two sides. Hence, they are at the very bottom of society."
What?!
You're right to be outraged, Hopper. It was a horribly oppressive system.
"But to be honest, I didn't really notice for most of my life. As a citizen with four sides, I lived comfortably and contentedly.
"I had a job of high position. I was the Chief Clerk of the High Council of Circles, Flatland's ruling body.
"But then one day, everything changed. I was at work when a brilliant flash of light appeared out of nowhere. From it came these words--"
I come to proclaim that there is a land of Three Dimensions!

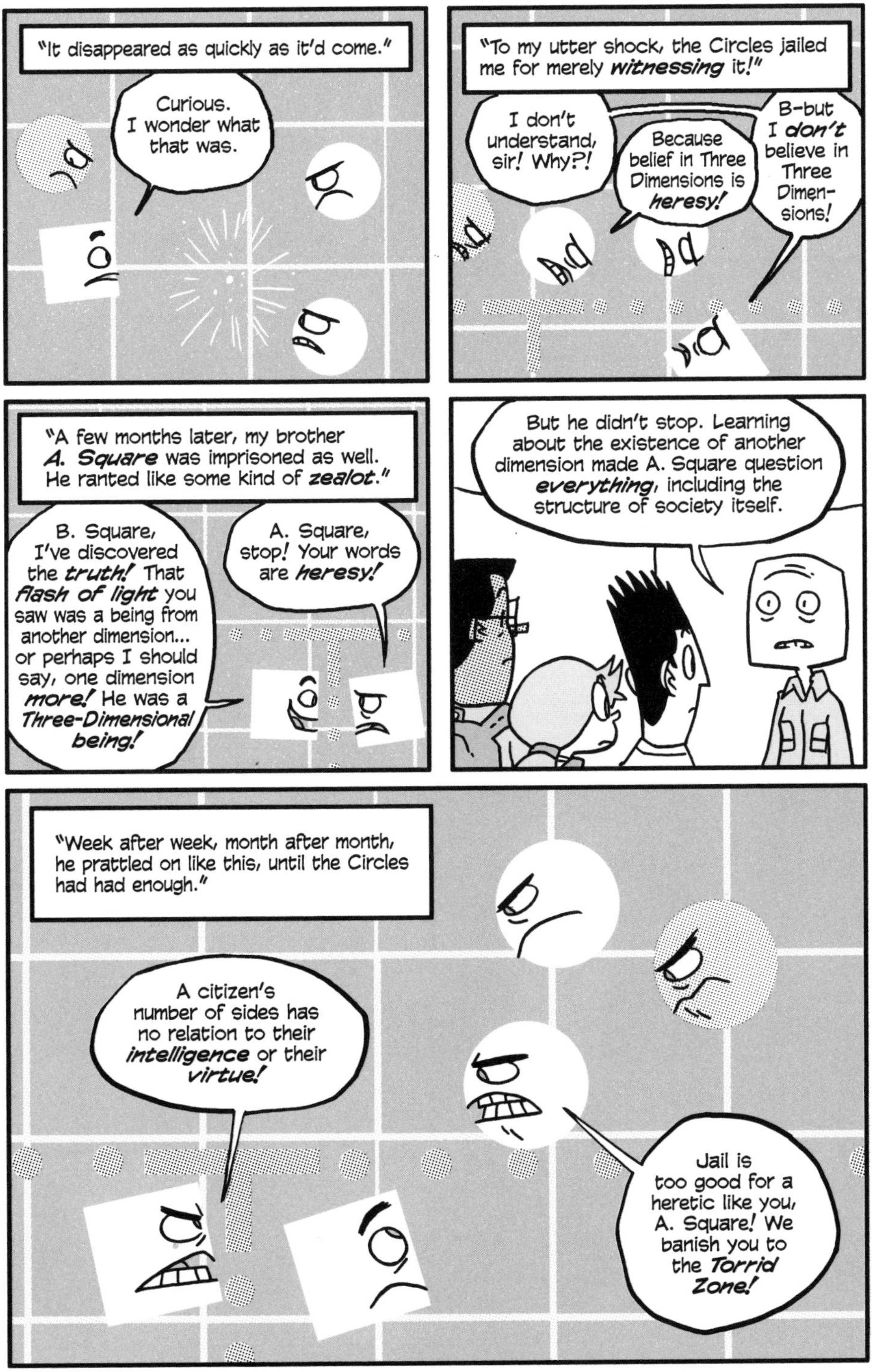
"It disappeared as quickly as it'd come."
Curious. I wonder what that was.
"To my utter shock, the Circles jailed me for merely *witnessing* it!"
I don't understand, sir! Why?!
Because belief in Three Dimensions is *heresy!*
B-but I *don't* believe in Three Dimensions!
"A few months later, my brother *A. Square* was imprisoned as well. He ranted like some kind of *zealot*."
B. Square, I've discovered the *truth!* That *flash of light* you saw was a being from another dimension... or perhaps I should say, one dimension *more!* He was a *Three-Dimensional being!*
A. Square, stop! Your words are *heresy!*
But he didn't stop. Learning about the existence of another dimension made A. Square question *everything*, including the structure of society itself.
"Week after week, month after month, he prattled on like this, until the Circles had had enough."
A citizen's number of sides has no relation to their *intelligence* or their *virtue!*
Jail is too good for a heretic like you, A. Square! We banish you to the *Torrid Zone!*

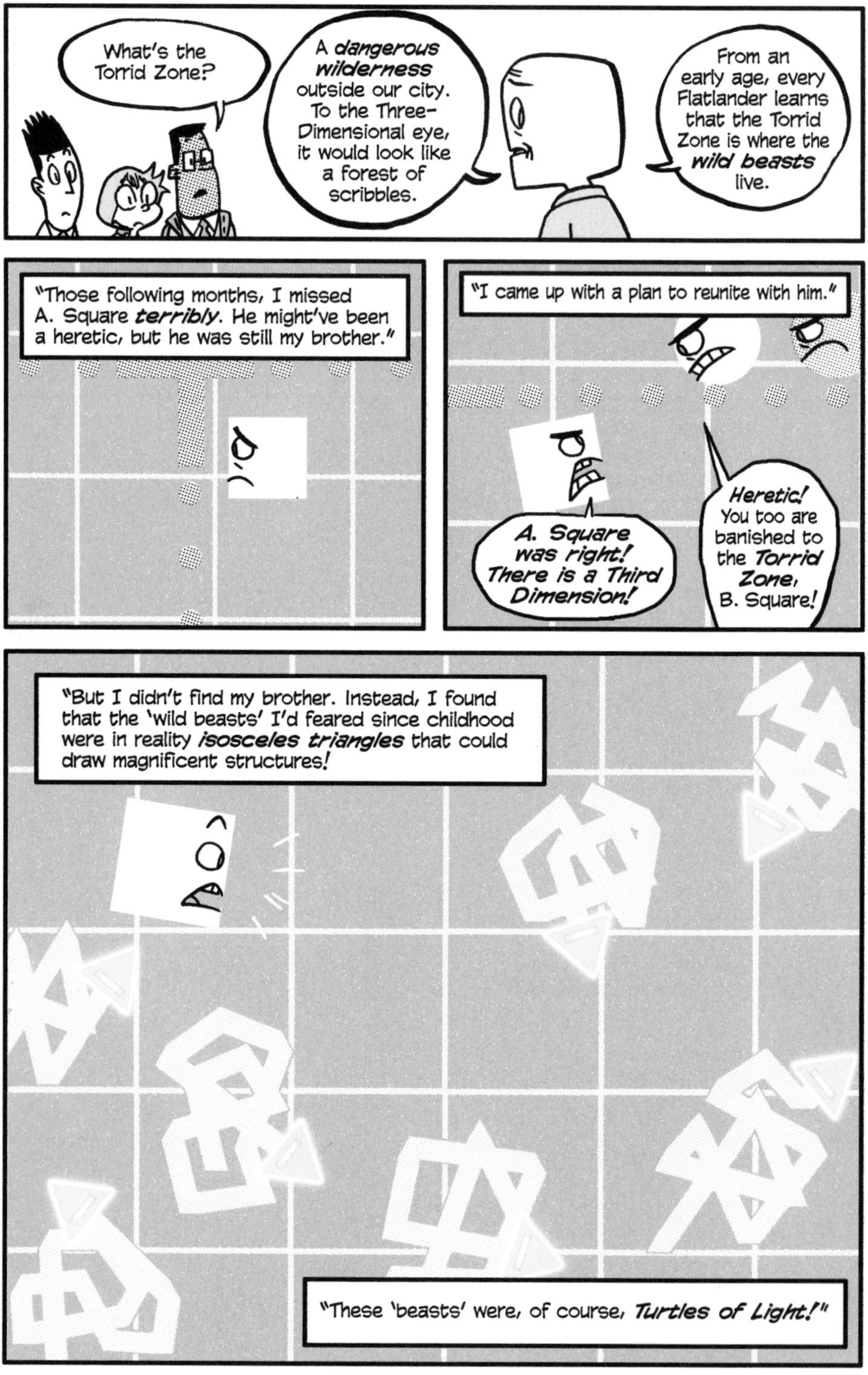
What's the Torrid Zone?
A *dangerous wilderness* outside our city. To the Three-Dimensional eye, it would look like a forest of scribbles.
From an early age, every Flatlander learns that the Torrid Zone is where the *wild beasts* live.
"Those following months, I missed A. Square *terribly*. He might've been a heretic, but he was still my brother."
"I came up with a plan to reunite with him."
A. Square was right! There is a Third Dimension!
Heretic! You too are banished to the *Torrid Zone*, B. Square!
"But I didn't find my brother. Instead, I found that the 'wild beasts' I'd feared since childhood were in reality *isosceles triangles* that could draw magnificent structures!
"These 'beasts' were, of course, *Turtles of Light!*"

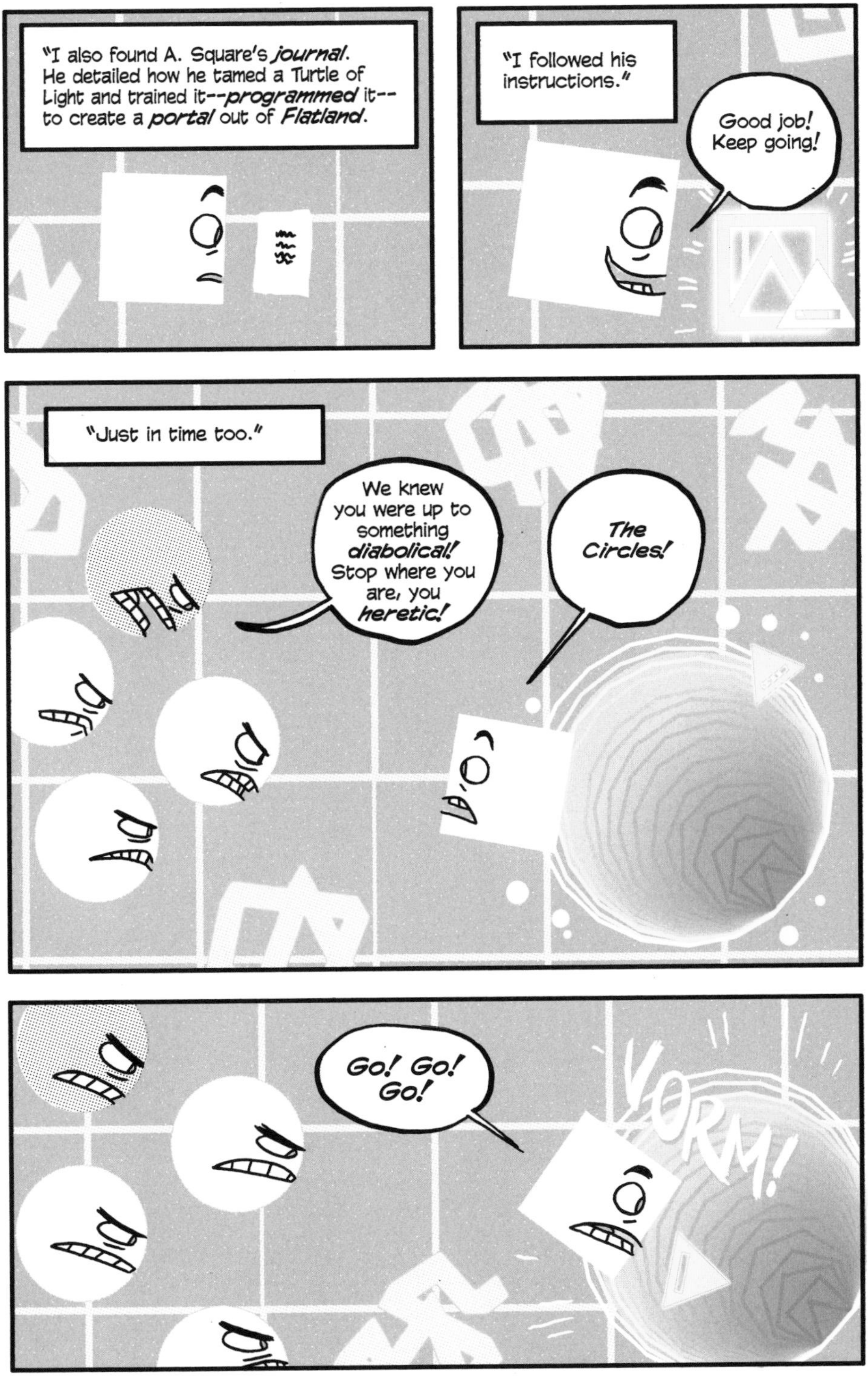
"I also found A. Square's *journal*. He detailed how he tamed a Turtle of Light and trained it--*programmed* it--to create a *portal* out of *Flatland*.
"I followed his instructions."
Good job! Keep going!
"Just in time too."
We knew you were up to something *diabolical!* Stop where you are, you *heretic!*
The Circles!
Go! Go! Go!
VORM!

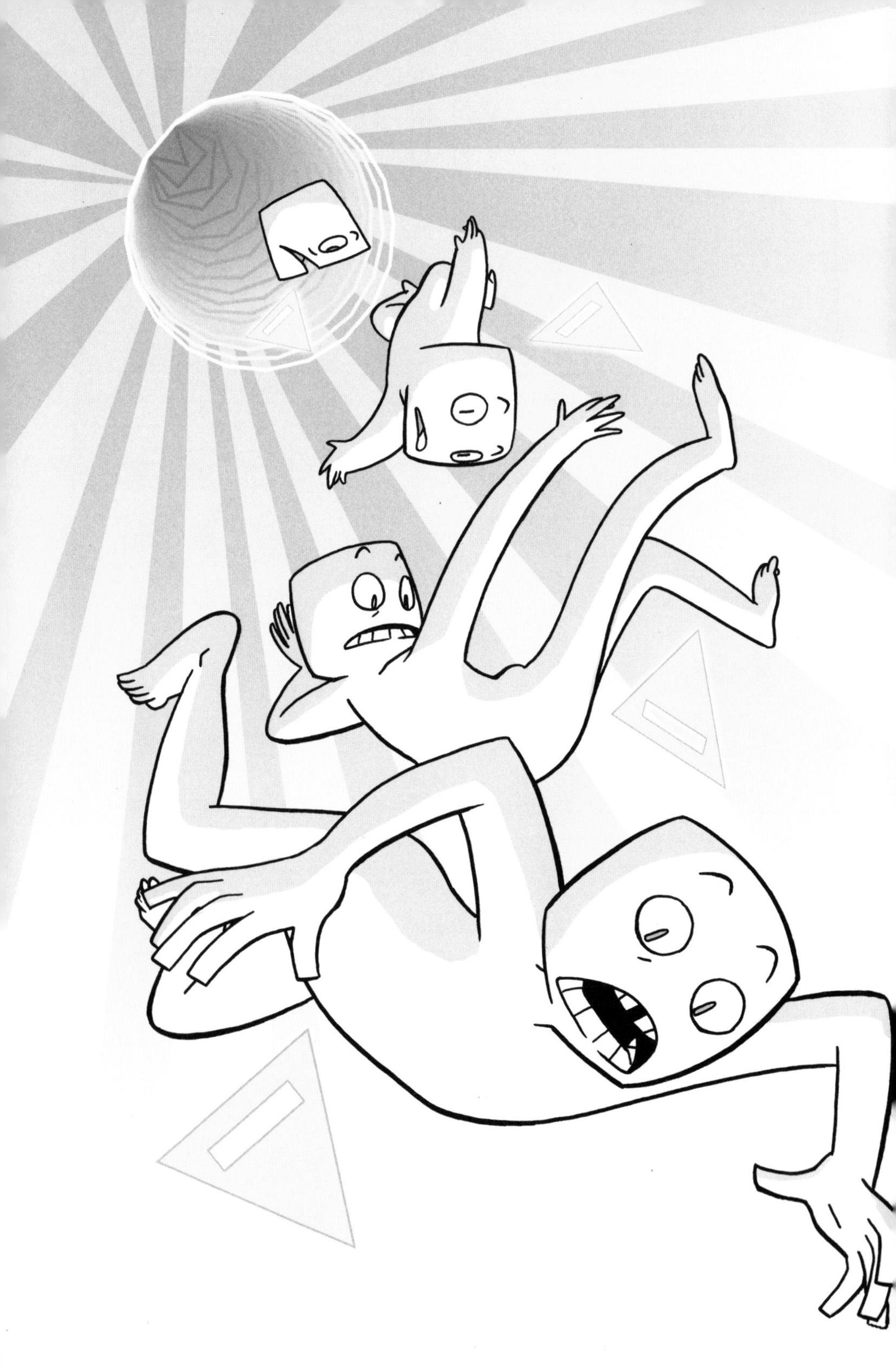

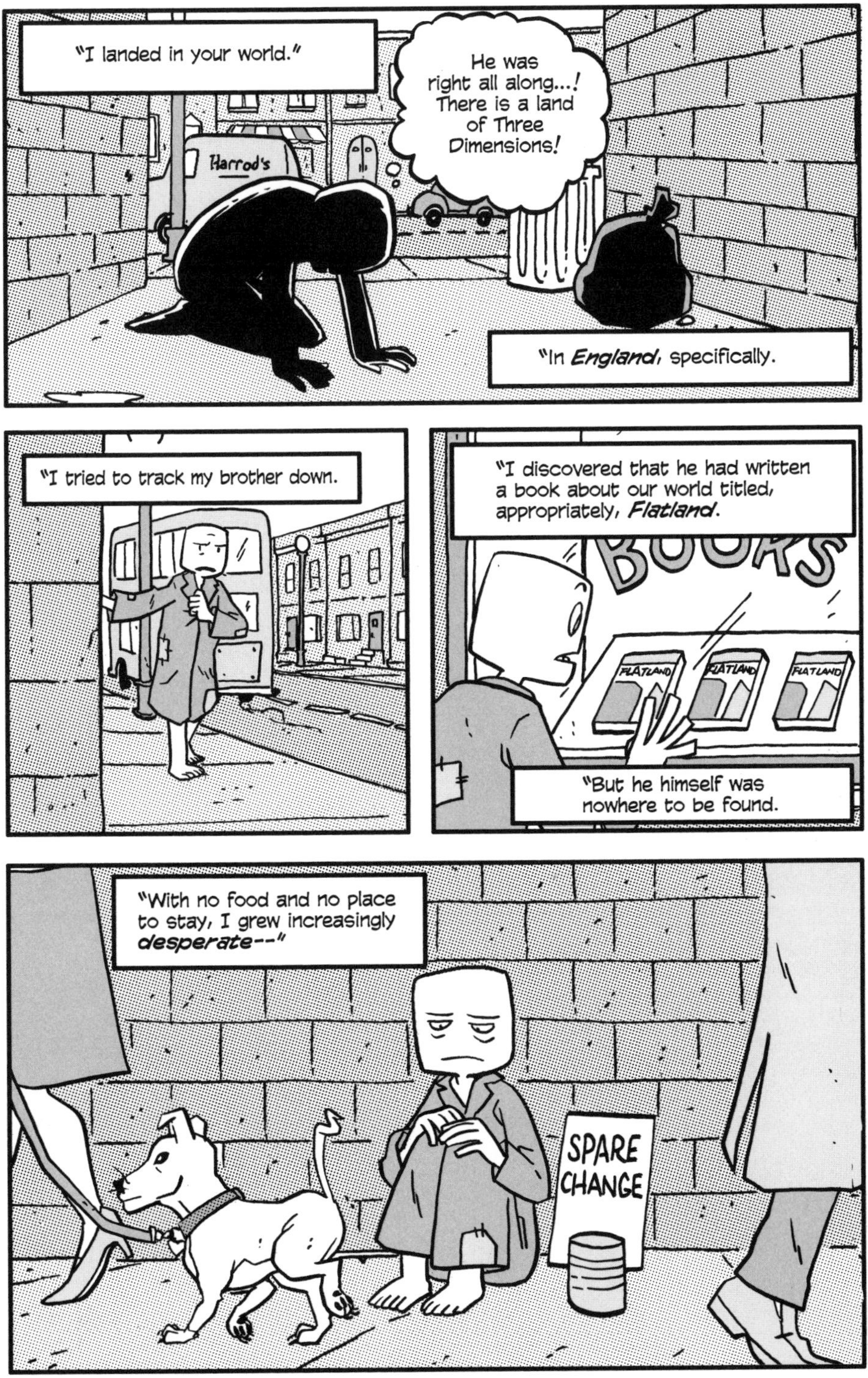
"I landed in your world."
He was right all along...! There is a land of Three Dimensions!
Harrod's
"In England, specifically.
"I tried to track my brother down.
"I discovered that he had written a book about our world titled, appropriately, Flatland.
BOOKS
FLATLAND
FLATLAND
FLATLAND
"But he himself was nowhere to be found.
"With no food and no place to stay, I grew increasingly desperate--"
SPARE CHANGE

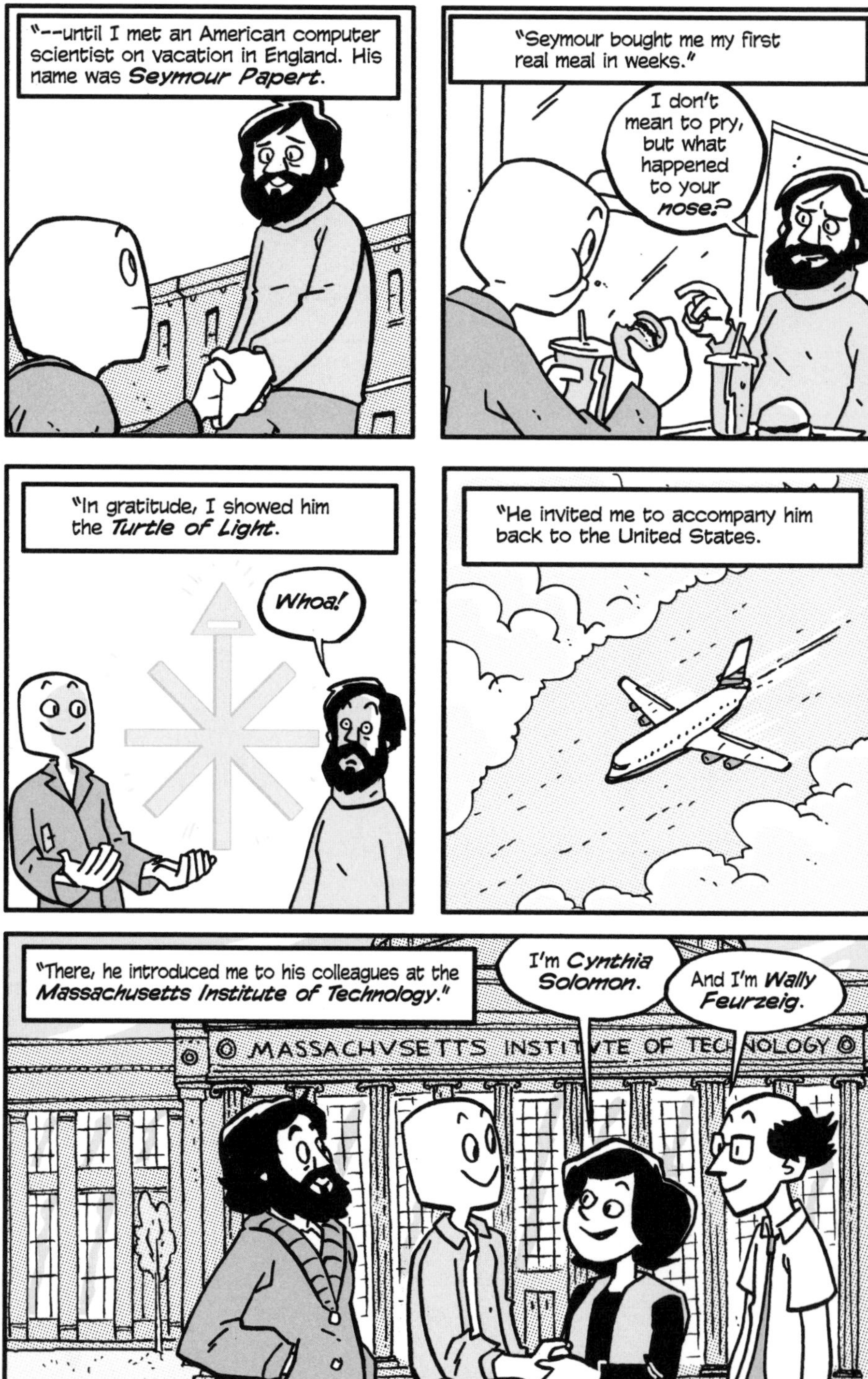
"--until I met an American computer scientist on vacation in England. His name was *Seymour Papert*.
"Seymour bought me my first real meal in weeks."
I don't mean to pry, but what happened to your *nose?*
"In gratitude, I showed him the *Turtle of Light*.
Whoa!
"He invited me to accompany him back to the United States.
"There, he introduced me to his colleagues at the *Massachusetts Institute of Technology*."
I'm *Cynthia Solomon*.
And I'm *Wally Feurzeig*.
MASSACHVSETTS INSTITVTE OF TECHNOLOGY

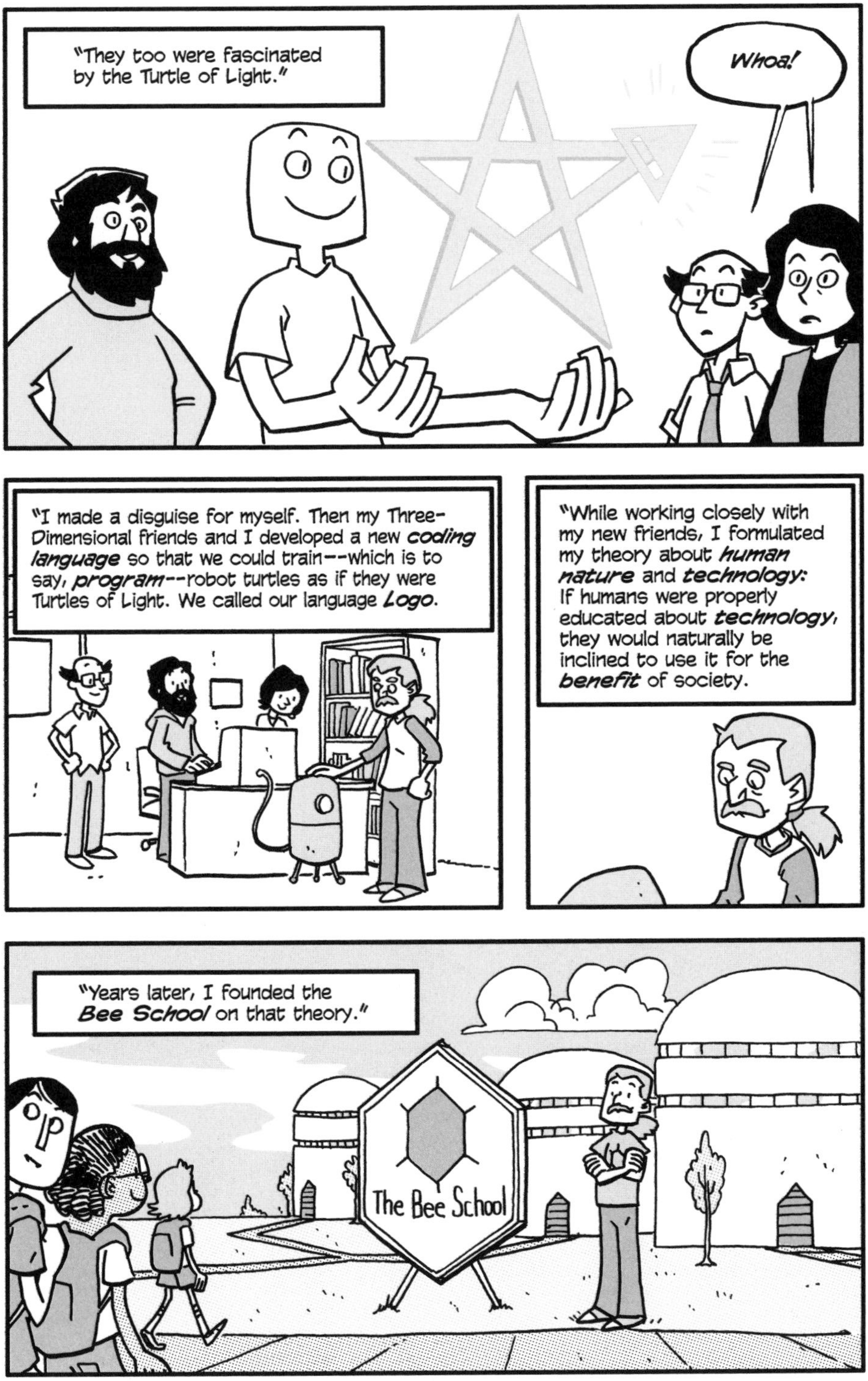
"They too were fascinated by the Turtle of Light."
Whoa!
"I made a disguise for myself. Then my Three-Dimensional friends and I developed a new *coding language* so that we could train--which is to say, *program*--robot turtles as if they were Turtles of Light. We called our language *Logo*.
"While working closely with my new friends, I formulated my theory about *human nature* and *technology:* If humans were properly educated about *technology*, they would naturally be inclined to use it for the *benefit* of society.
"Years later, I founded the *Bee School* on that theory."
The Bee School

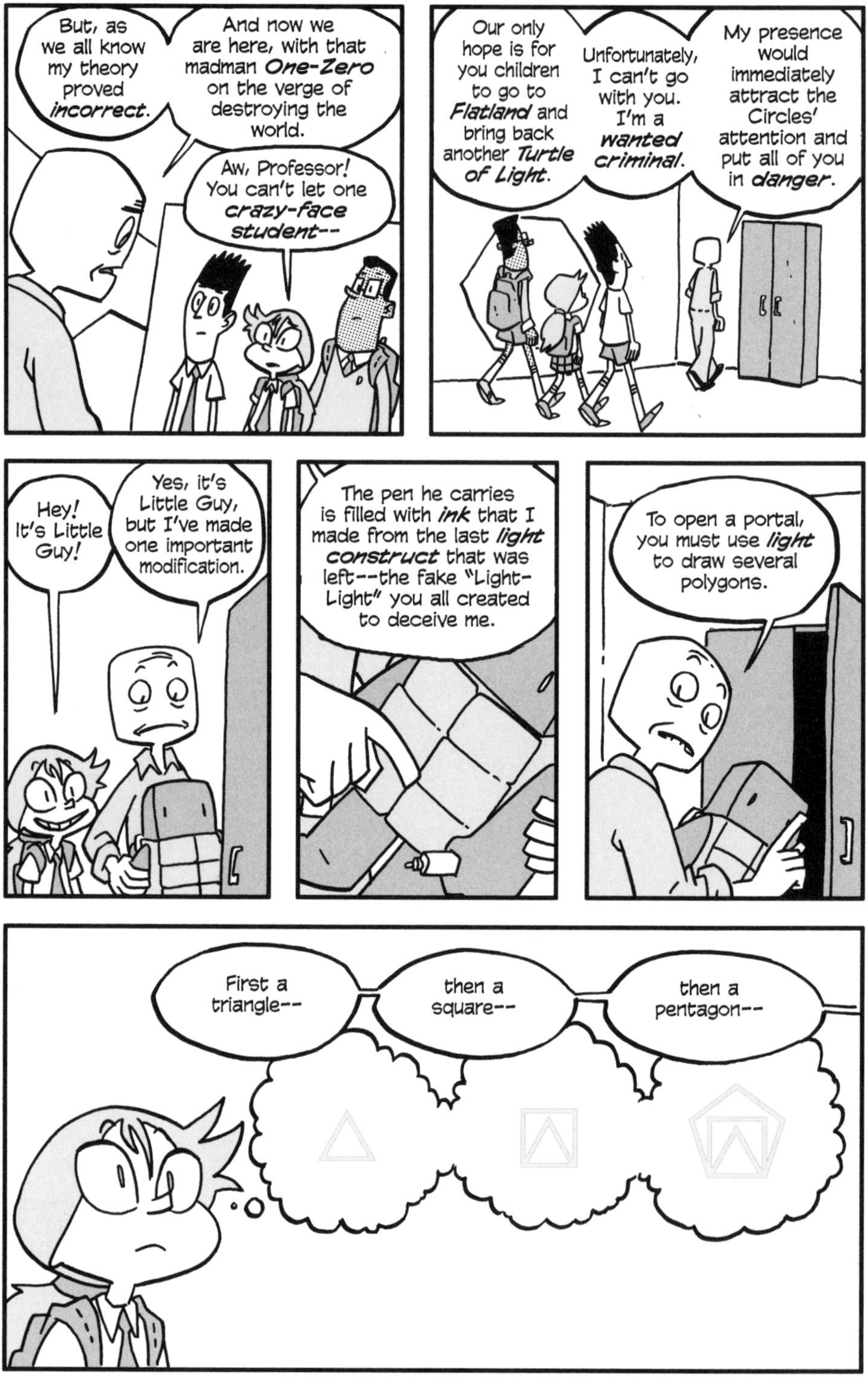
But, as we all know my theory proved *incorrect*.
And now we are here, with that madman *One-Zero* on the verge of destroying the world.
Aw, Professor! You can't let one *crazy-face student*--
Our only hope is for you children to go to *Flatland* and bring back another *Turtle of Light*.
Unfortunately, I can't go with you. I'm a *wanted criminal*.
My presence would immediately attract the Circles' attention and put all of you in *danger*.
Hey! It's Little Guy!
Yes, it's Little Guy, but I've made one important modification.
The pen he carries is filled with *ink* that I made from the last *light construct* that was left--the fake "Light-Light" you all created to deceive me.
To open a portal, you must use *light* to draw several polygons.
First a triangle--
then a square--
then a pentagon--

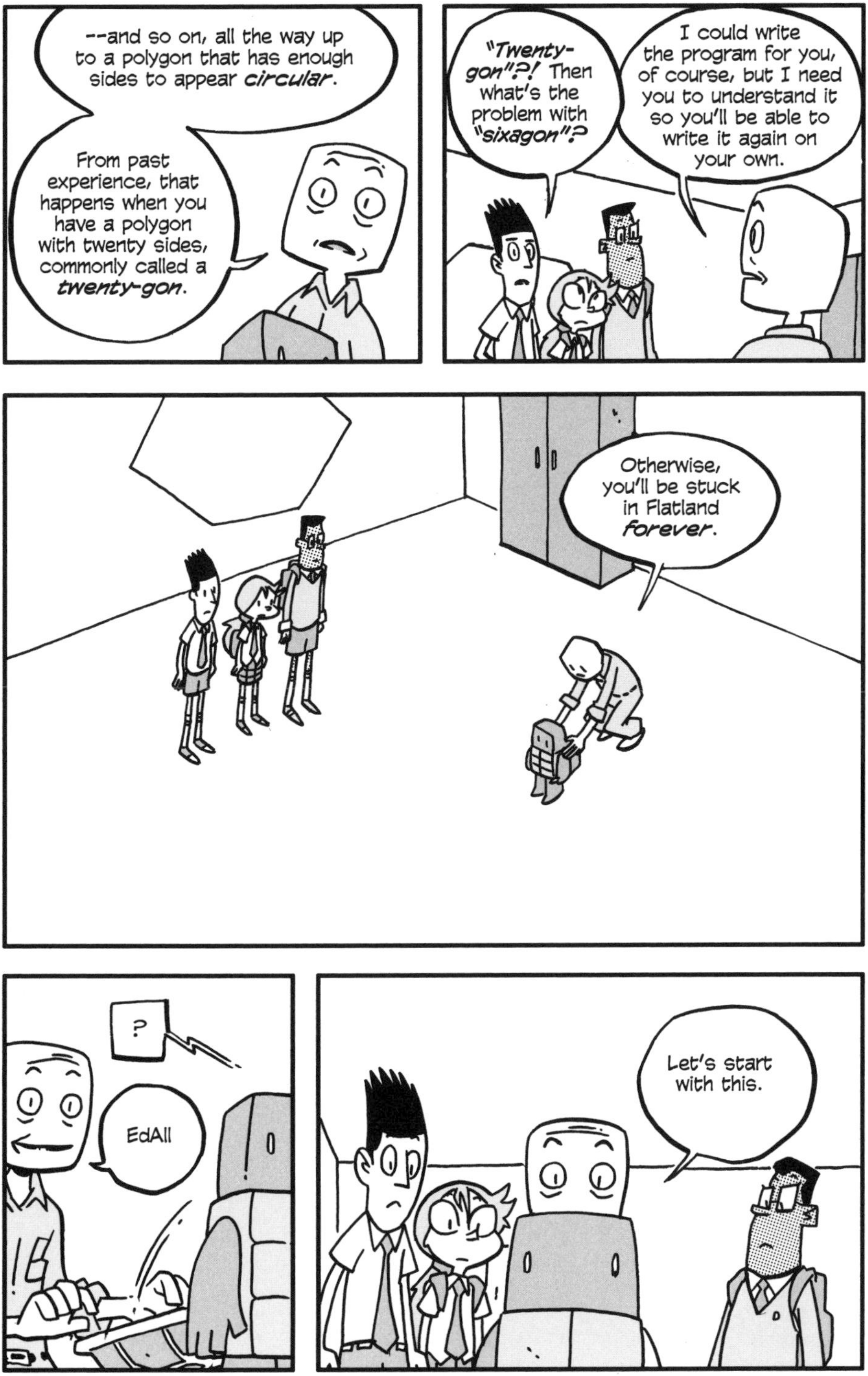
--and so on, all the way up to a polygon that has enough sides to appear *circular*.
From past experience, that happens when you have a polygon with twenty sides, commonly called a *twenty-gon*.
"Twenty-gon"?! Then what's the problem with *"sixagon"?*
I could write the program for you, of course, but I need you to understand it so you'll be able to write it again on your own.
Otherwise, you'll be stuck in Flatland *forever*.
?
EdAll
Let's start with this.

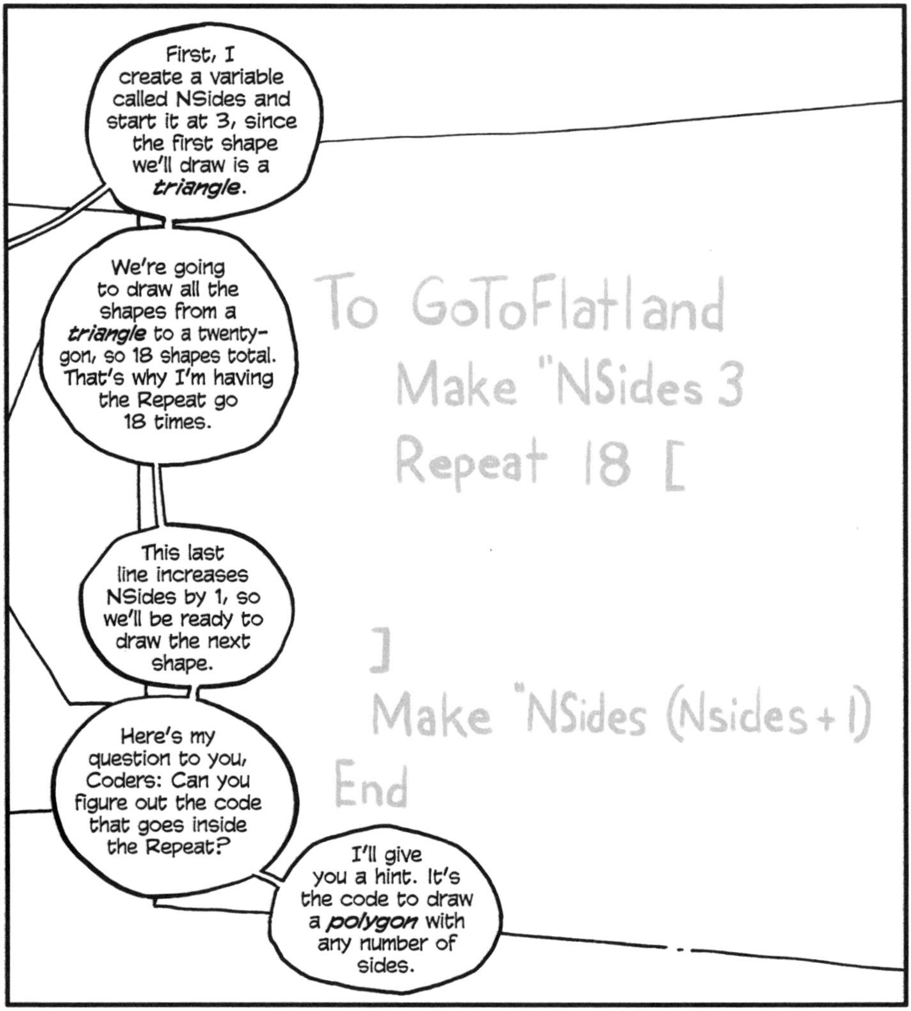
First, I create a variable called NSides and start it at 3, since the first shape we'll draw is a *triangle*.
We're going to draw all the shapes from a *triangle* to a twenty-gon, so 18 shapes total. That's why I'm having the Repeat go 18 times.
This last line increases NSides by 1, so we'll be ready to draw the next shape.
Here's my question to you, Coders: Can you figure out the code that goes inside the Repeat?
I'll give you a hint. It's the code to draw a *polygon* with any number of sides.
To GoToFlatland
Make "NSides 3
Repeat 18 [
]
Make "NSides (Nsides+1)
End

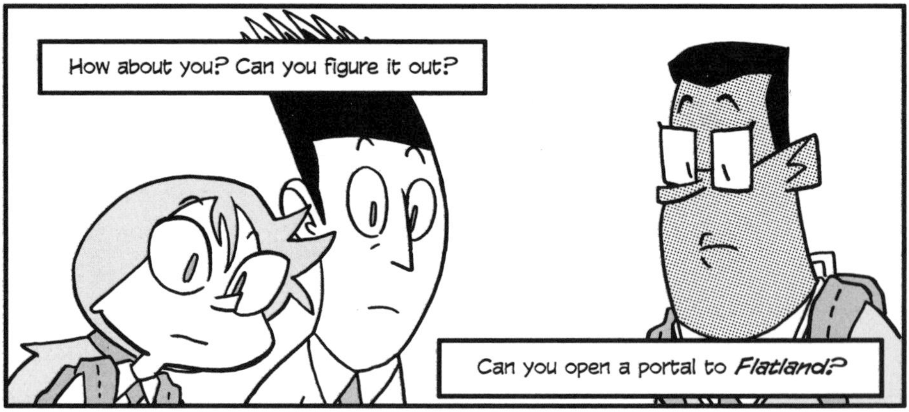
How about you? Can you figure it out?
Can you open a portal to *Flatland*?

Continued in

SECRET CODERS

Monsters & Modules

Ready to start coding?

Visit www.secret-coders.com

Check out these other books in the Secret Coders series!

Secret Coders
Paths & Portals
Secrets & Sequences
Robots & Repeats

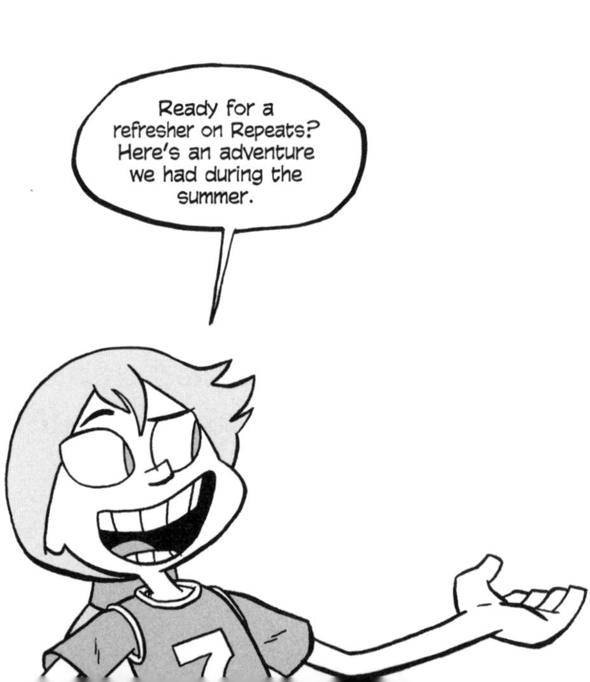
Ready for a refresher on Repeats? Here's an adventure we had during the summer.

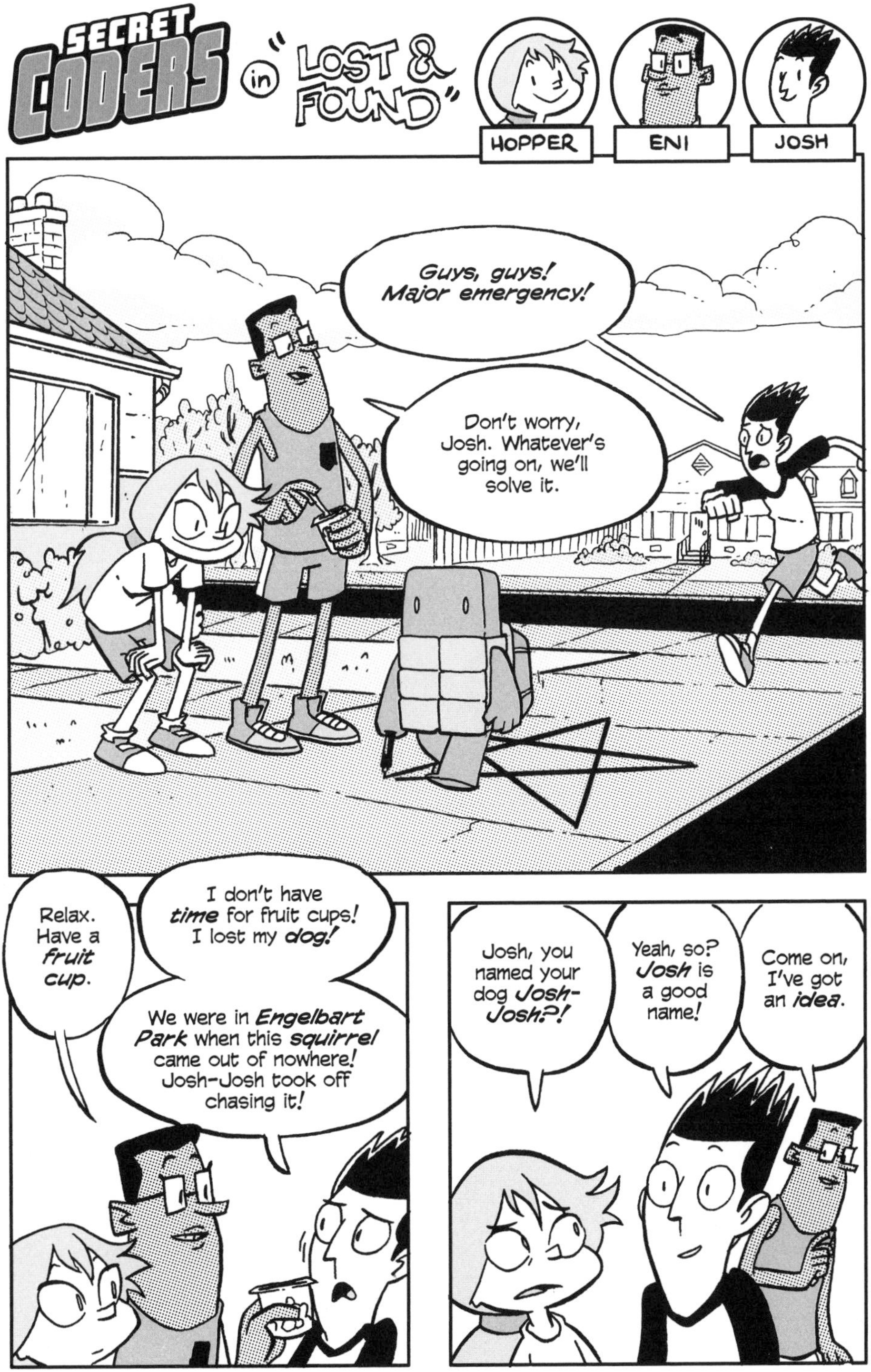
SECRET CODERS in "LOST & FOUND"
HOPPER
ENI
JOSH
Guys, guys! Major emergency!
Don't worry, Josh. Whatever's going on, we'll solve it.
Relax. Have a fruit cup.
I don't have time for fruit cups! I lost my dog!
We were in Engelbart Park when this squirrel came out of nowhere! Josh-Josh took off chasing it!
Josh, you named your dog Josh-Josh?!
Yeah, so? Josh is a good name!
Come on, I've got an idea.

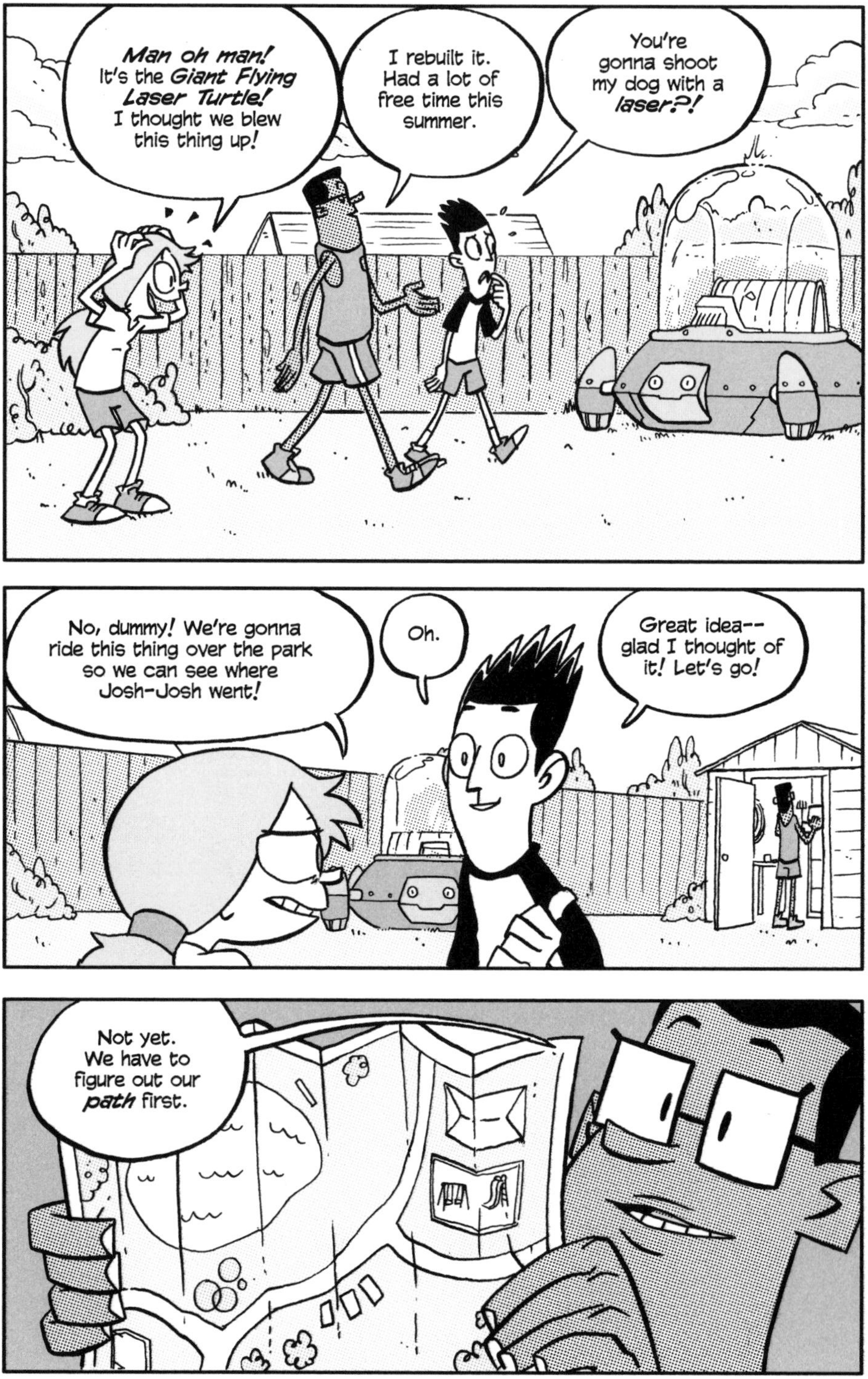

Man oh man! It's the *Giant Flying Laser Turtle!* I thought we blew this thing up!
I rebuilt it. Had a lot of free time this summer.
You're gonna shoot my dog with a *laser?!*
No, dummy! We're gonna ride this thing over the park so we can see where Josh-Josh went!
Oh.
Great idea-- glad I thought of it! Let's go!
Not yet. We have to figure out our *path* first.

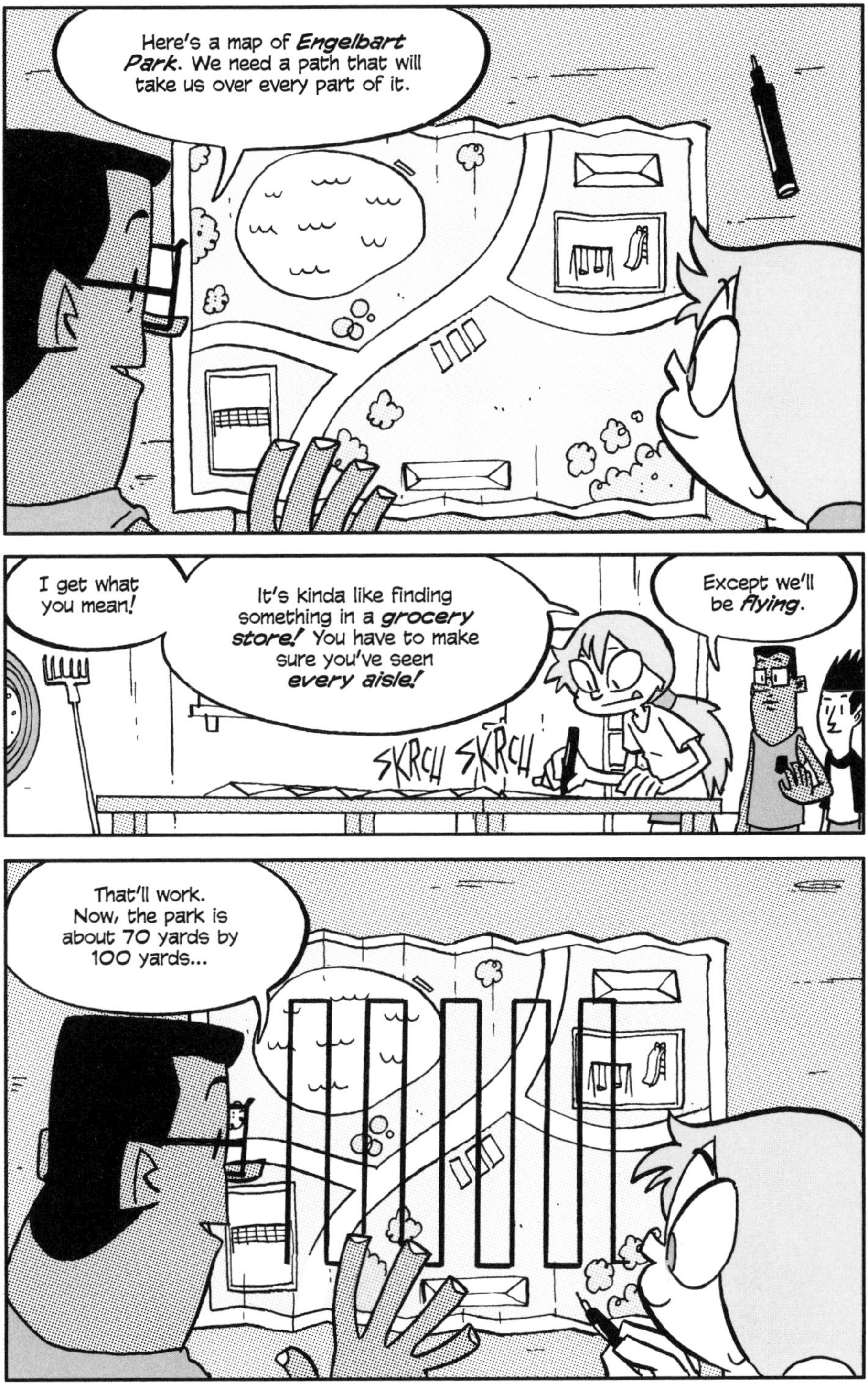
Here's a map of ***Engelbart Park***. We need a path that will take us over every part of it.
I get what you mean!
It's kinda like finding something in a ***grocery store!*** You have to make sure you've seen ***every aisle!***
SKRCH SKRCH
Except we'll be ***flying***.
That'll work. Now, the park is about 70 yards by 100 yards...

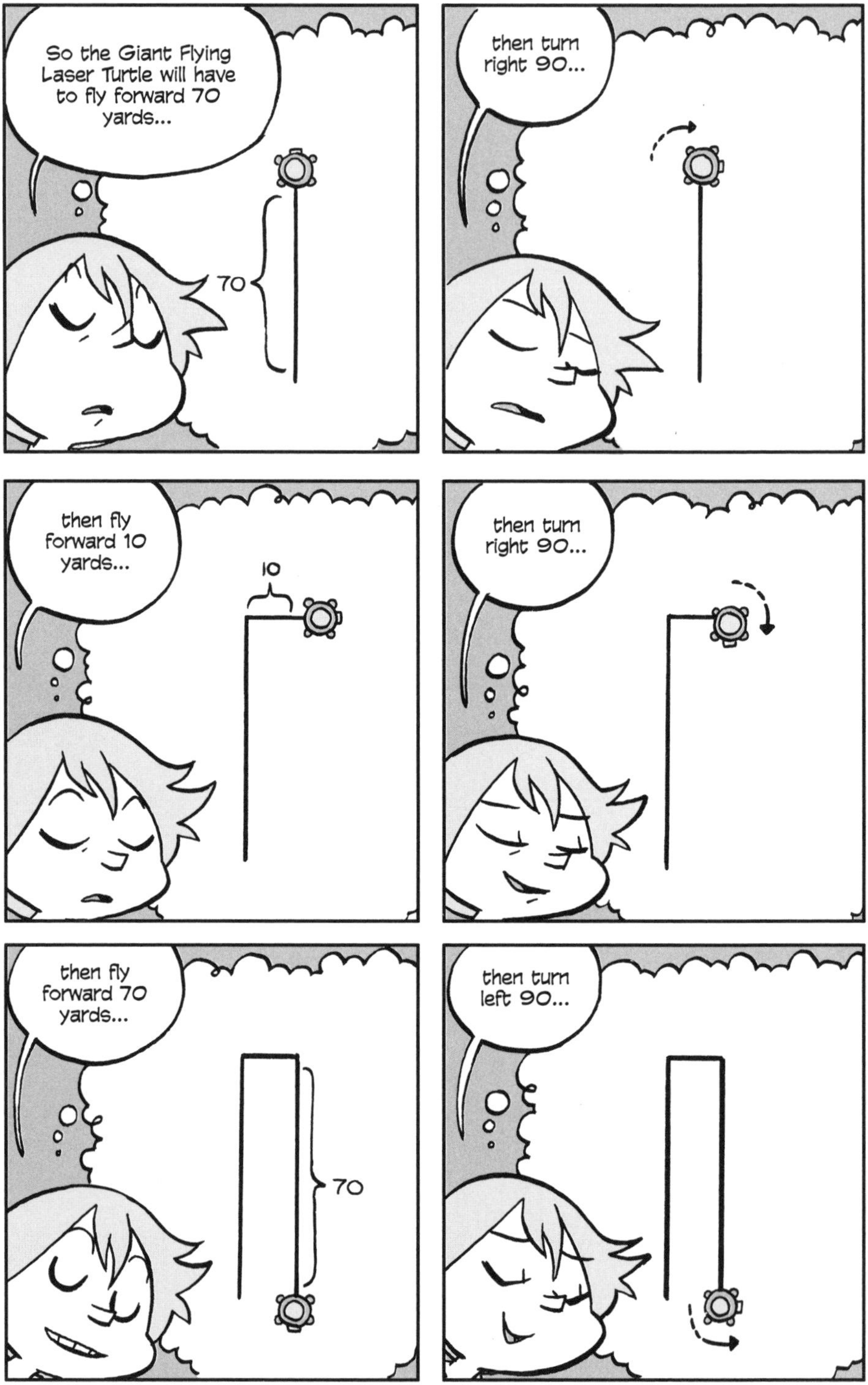
So the Giant Flying Laser Turtle will have to fly forward 70 yards...
70
then turn right 90...
then fly forward 10 yards...
10
then turn right 90...
then fly forward 70 yards...
70
then turn left 90...

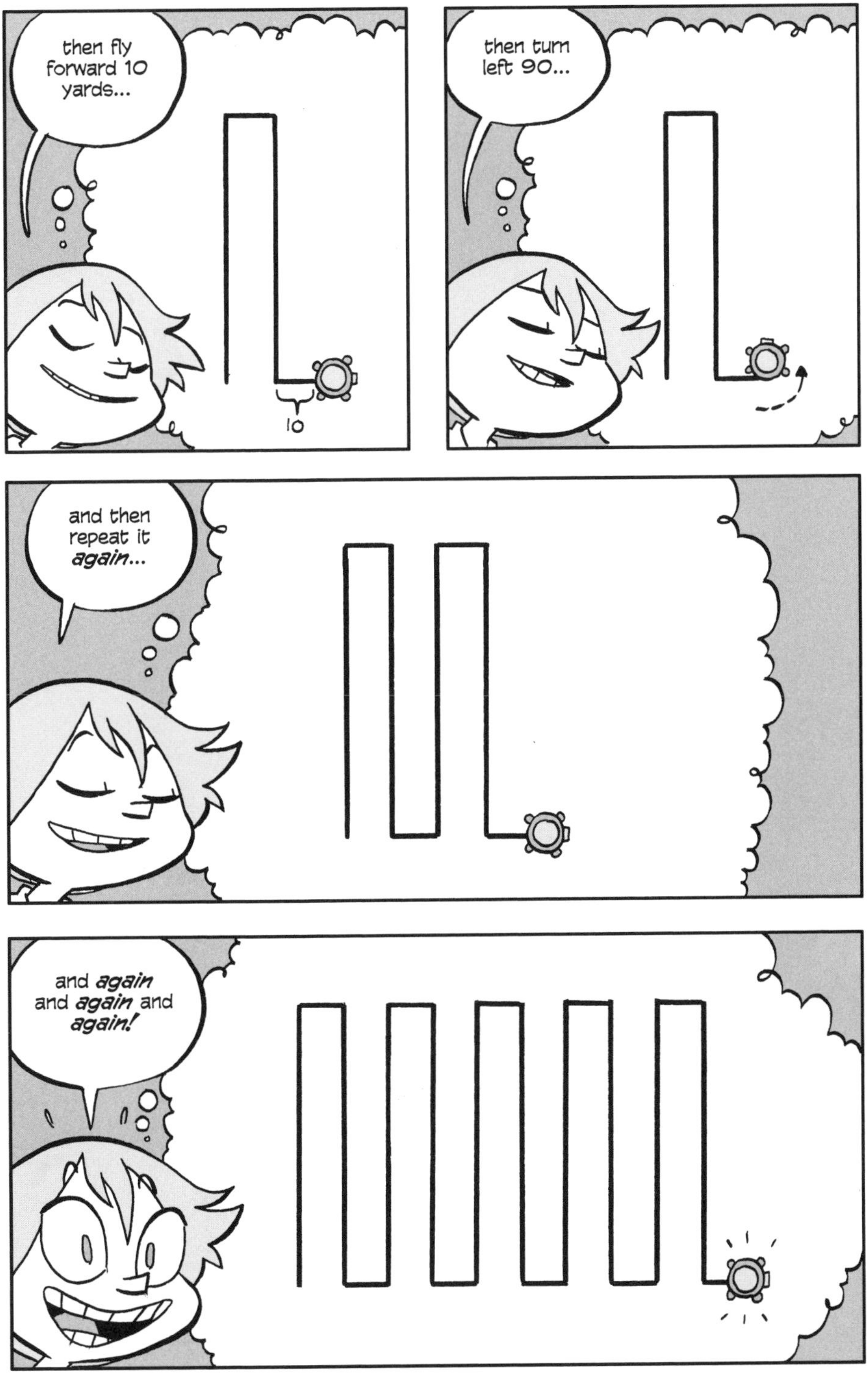
then fly forward 10 yards...
10
then turn left 90...
and then repeat it *again*...
and *again* and *again* and *again!*

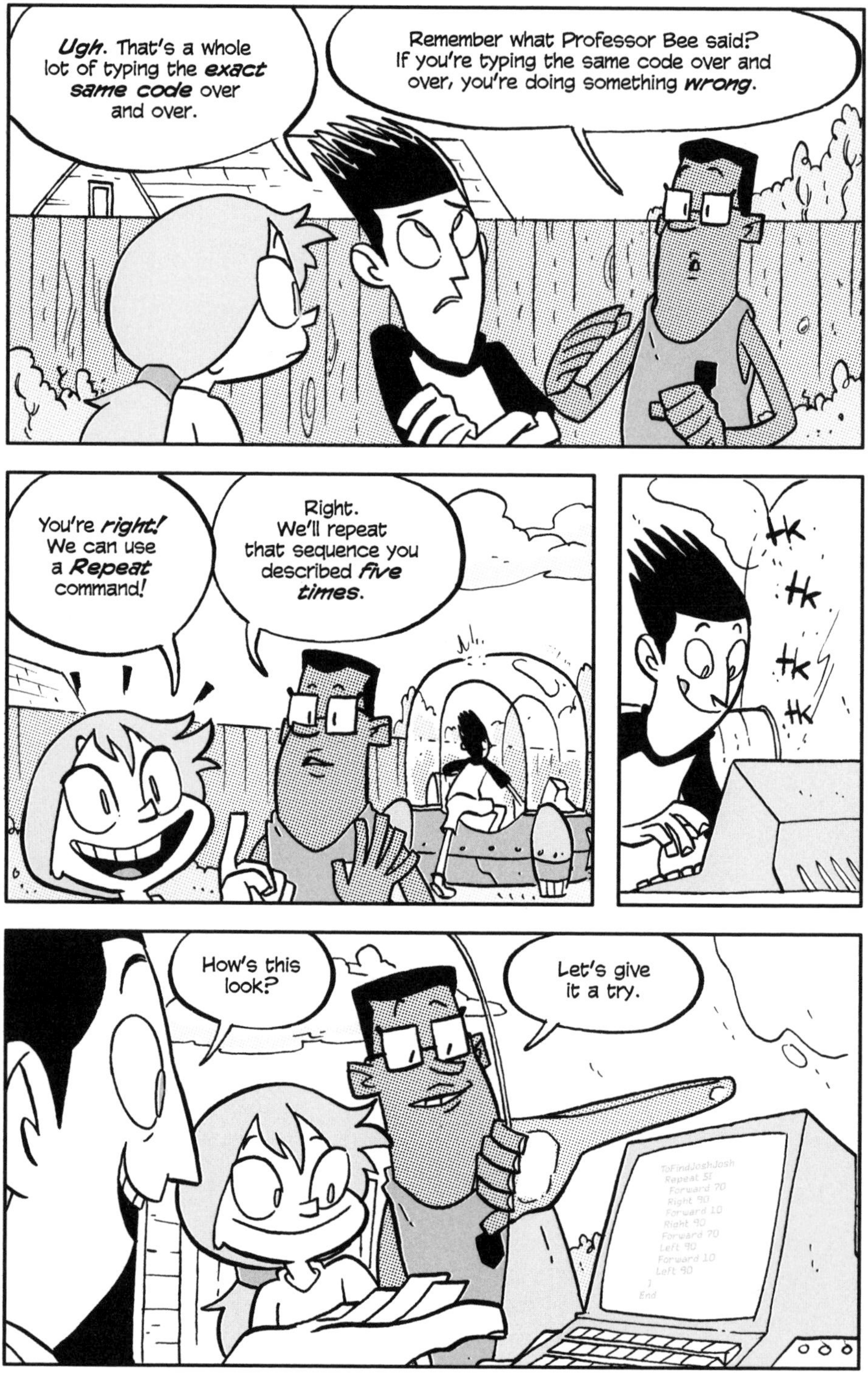

Ugh. That's a whole lot of typing the exact same code over and over.
Remember what Professor Bee said? If you're typing the same code over and over, you're doing something wrong.
You're right! We can use a Repeat command!
Right. We'll repeat that sequence you described five times.
tk
tk
tk
tk
How's this look?
Let's give it a try.
ToFindJoshJosh
Repeat 5[
Forward 70
Right 90
Forward 10
Right 90
Forward 70
Left 90
Forward 10
Left 90
]
End

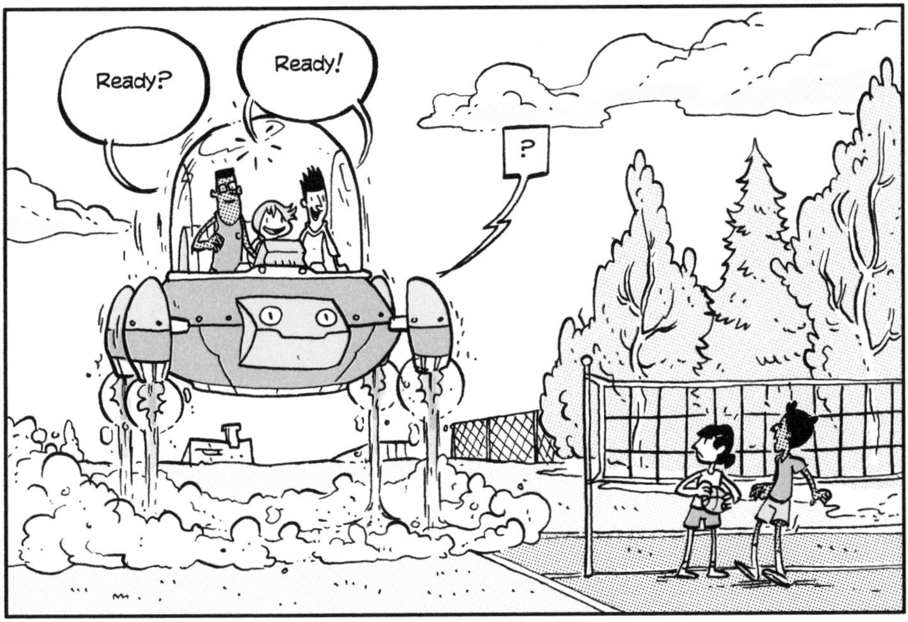
Ready?
Ready!
?

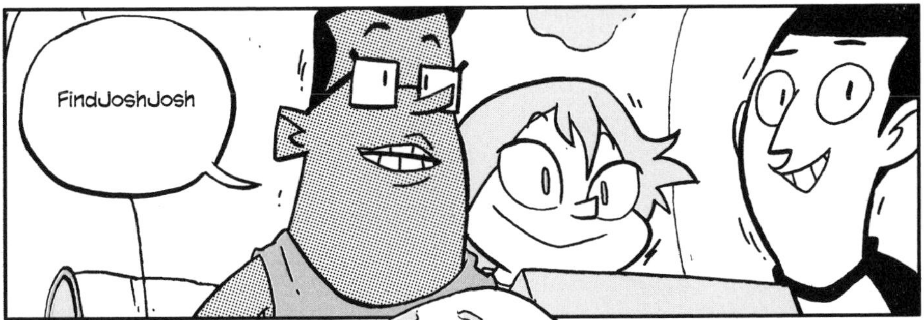
FindJoshJosh

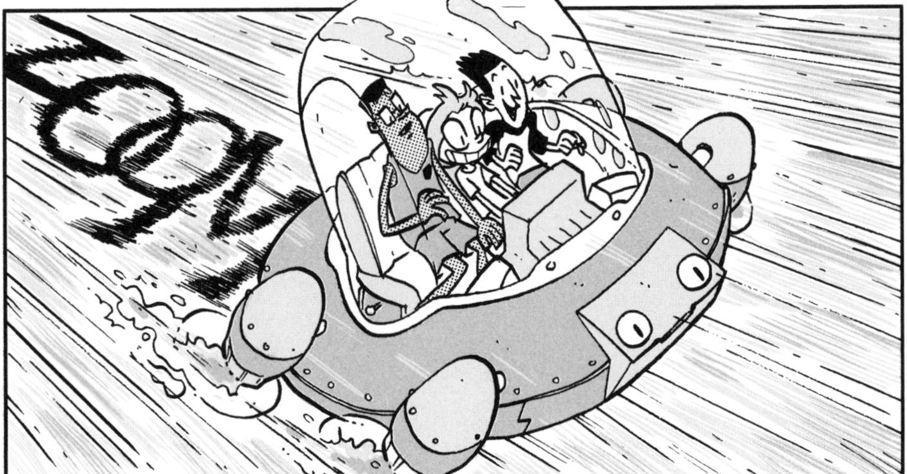

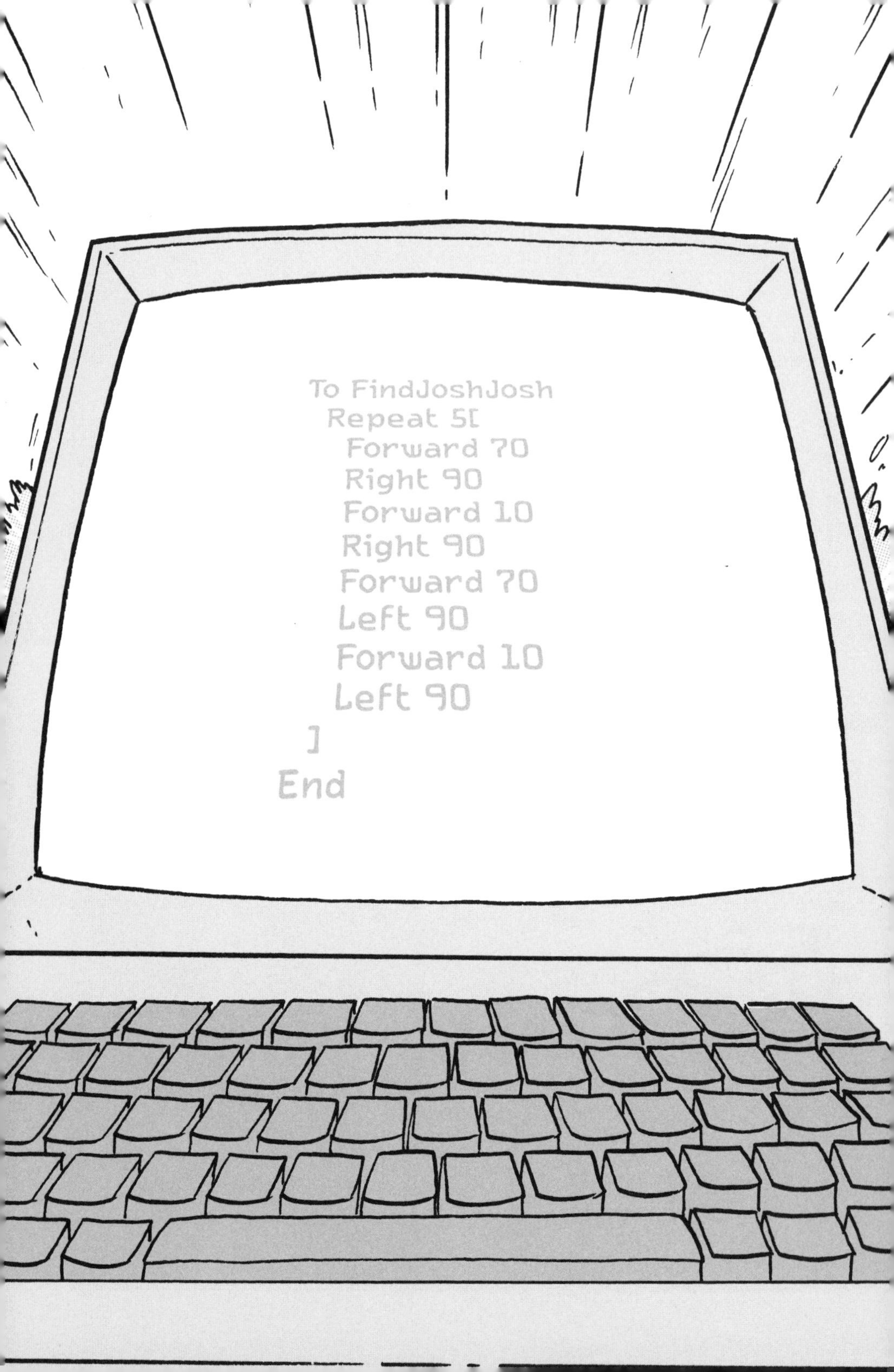
To FindJoshJosh
Repeat 5[
Forward 70
Right 90
Forward 10
Right 90
Forward 70
Left 90
Forward 10
Left 90
]
End

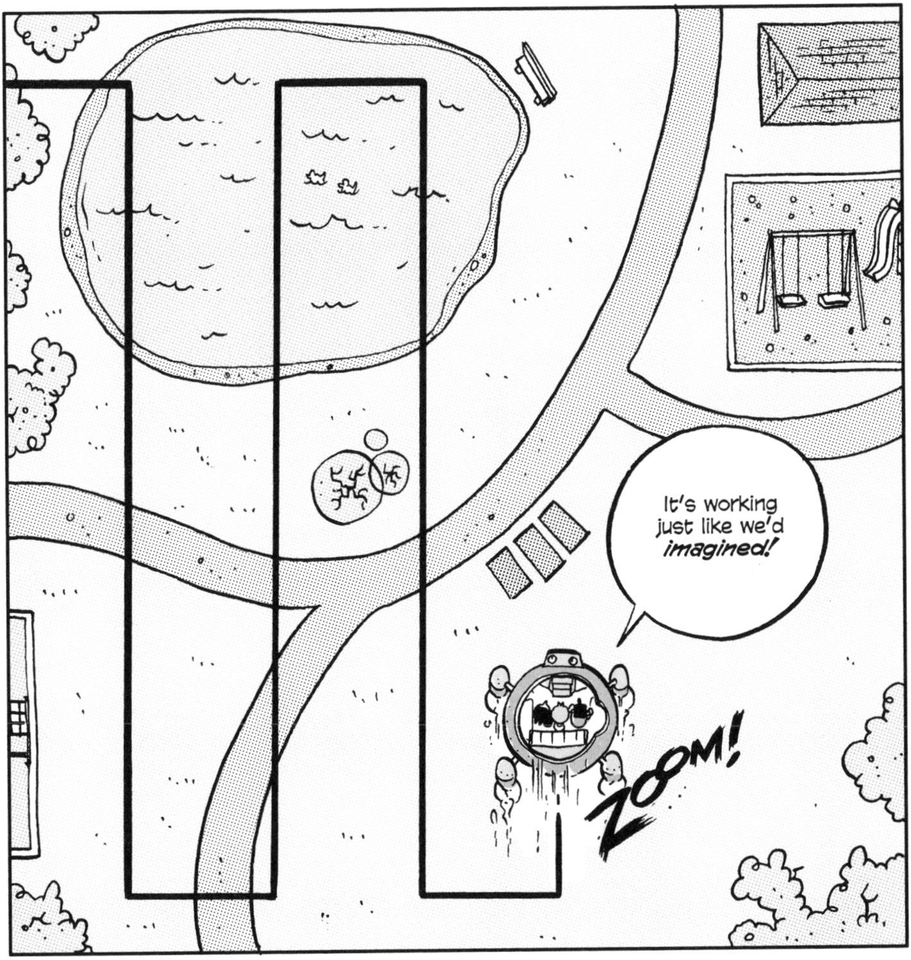
It's working just like we'd *imagined!*
ZOOM!

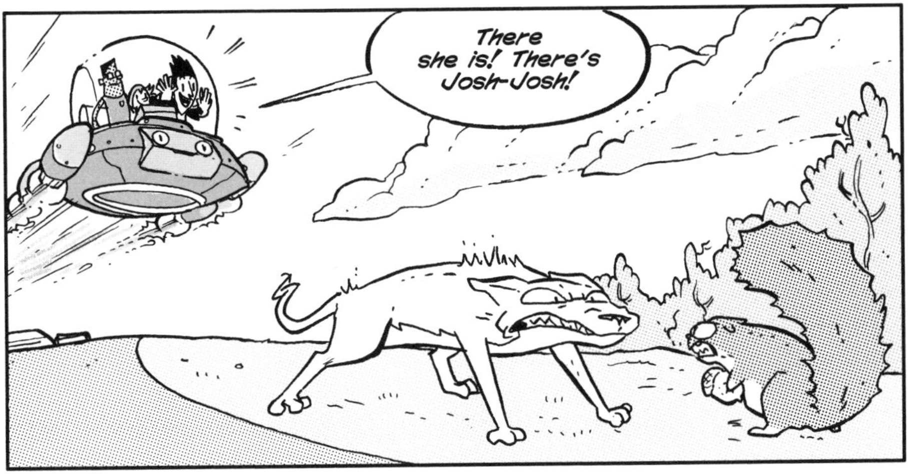
There she is! There's Josh-Josh!

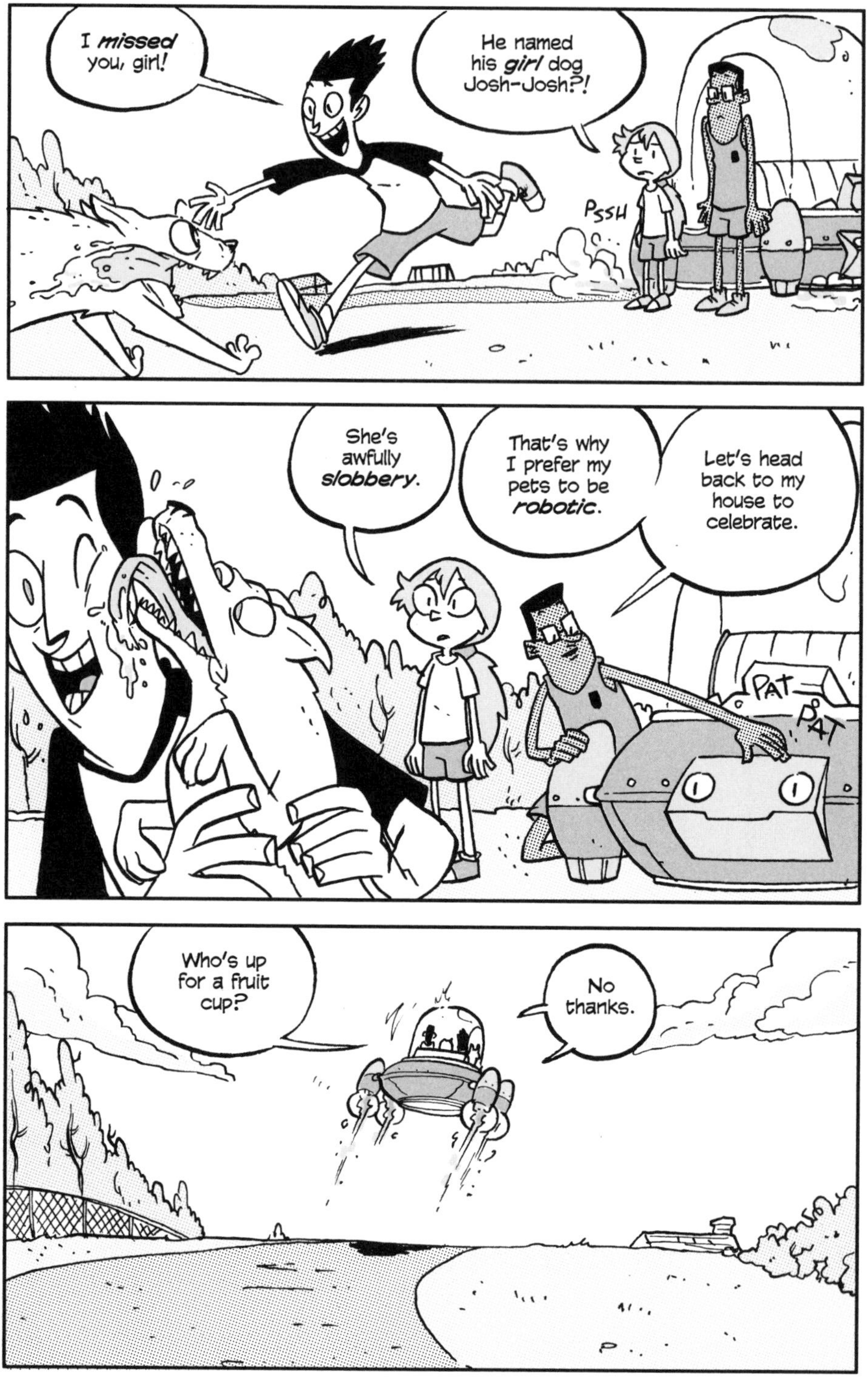
I *missed* you, girl!
He named his *girl* dog Josh-Josh?!
PSSH
She's awfully *slobbery*.
That's why I prefer my pets to be *robotic*.
Let's head back to my house to celebrate.
PAT PAT
Who's up for a fruit cup?
No thanks.

Thank you to Mike for being such an awesome partner on this project; to my wife and kids for being my first beta readers; to the First Second Books team—Simon Boughton, Mark Siegel, Calista Brill, Gina Gagliano, Robyn Chapman, Kiara Valdez, Danielle Ceccolini, and Andrew Arnold—for creating a home for stories; to Judy Hansen for her wisdom and guidance, and to every student who has ever set foot in my computer lab at Bishop O'Dowd High School for sharing my love of coding.

—Gene

As always and forever, I want to thank my wife, Meredith— you make my life and my work a lot more meaningful. Thanks to my incredible nieces, Ruby and Gabby, who give me great feedback and let me draw with them. And to Gene, who is an incredible collaborator and inspiration.

—Mike

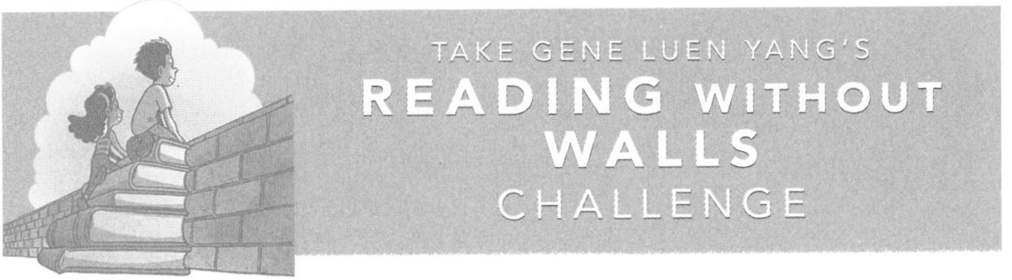

TAKE GENE LUEN YANG'S

READING WITHOUT WALLS CHALLENGE

Read outside your comfort zone!

1

Read a book about a **character** who doesn't look or live like you.

2

Read a book about a **topic** you don't know much about.

3

Read a book in a **format** that you don't normally read for fun.

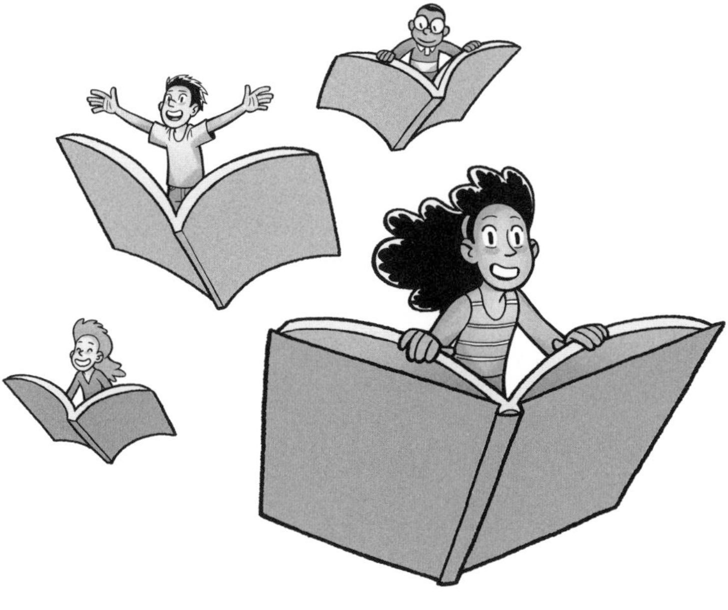

Learn more at **ReadingWithoutWalls.com**

GREAT GRAPHIC NOVELS

From the *New York Times*–Bestselling Author
Gene Luen Yang

AVAILABLE SEPARATELY OR AS A BOXED SET!

978-1-59643-152-2

BOXERS

978-1-59643-359-5

SAINTS

978-1-59643-689-3

"Gene Luen Yang has created that rare article: a youthful tale with something new to say about American youth."
—*The New York Times*

"Read this, and come away shaking."
—Gary Schmidt, Newbery Honor–winning author

"A masterful work of historical fiction."
—Dave Eggers, author of
A Heartbreaking Work of Staggering Genius

THE EXCITING NEW SERIES

978-1-62672-075-6

"Brings computer coding to life."
—*Entertainment Weekly*

978-1-59643-697-8

★ "A brilliant homage."
—*BCCB*

978-1-59643-235-2

"Bravura storytelling."
—*Publishers Weekly*

978-1-59643-156-0

★ "Absolutely not to be missed."
—*Booklist*

:01
First Second
NEW YORK